THE GUERNSEY LITERARY AND POTATO PEEL PIE SOCIETY

Mary Ann Shaffer

BLOOMSBURY

First published in Great Britain 2008

Copyright © 2008 by Mary Ann Shaffer

Map on p. viii © George W. Ward 2008

The moral right of the author has been asserted

Bloomsbury Publishing Plc
36 Soho Square
London W1D 3QY

www.bloomsbury.com
www.guernseyliterary.com

A CIP catalogue record for this book is available from the British Library

ISBN 978 0 7475 9064 4
10 9 8 7 6 5 4 3 2 1

Typeset by Hewer Text UK Ltd, Edinburgh
Printed in Great Britain by Clays Ltd, St Ives plc

Bloomsbury Publishing, London, New York and Berlin

The paper this book is printed on is certified by the © 1996 Forest
Stewardship Council A.C. (FSC). It is ancient-forest friendly.
The printer holds FSC chain of custody SGS-COC-2061

FSC

Mixed Sources
Product group from well-managed
forests and other controlled sources

Cert no. SGS-COC-2061
www.fsc.org
© 1996 Forest Stewardship Council

Lovingly dedicated to my mother,
Edna Fiery Morgan, and to my
dear friend, Julia Poppy

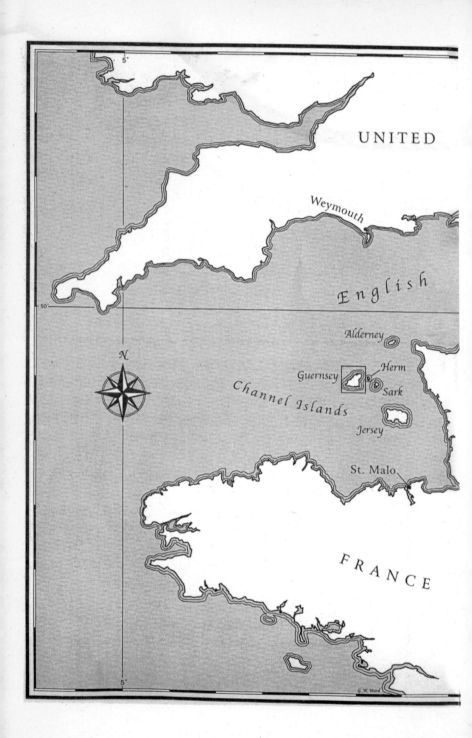

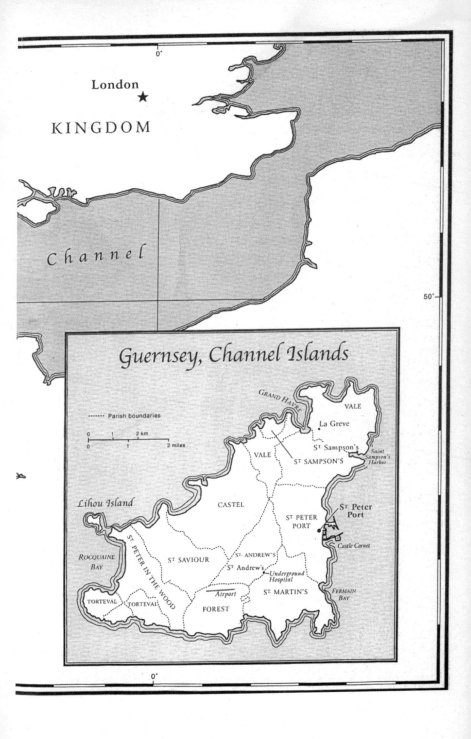

PART ONE

Mr Sidney Stark, Publisher
Stephens & Stark Ltd
21 St James's Place
London SW1

8th January 1946

Dear Sidney,

Susan Scott is a wonder. We sold over forty copies of the book, which was very pleasant, but much more thrilling from my standpoint was the food. Susan managed to get hold of ration coupons for icing sugar and *real eggs* for the meringue. If all her literary luncheons are going to achieve these heights, I won't mind touring the country. Do you suppose that a lavish bonus could spur her on to butter? Let's try it – you may deduct the money from my royalties.

Now for my grim news. You asked me how work on my new book is progressing. Sidney, it isn't. *English Foibles* seemed so promising at first. After all, one should be able to write reams about the Society to Protest Against the Glorification of the English Bunny. I unearthed a photograph of the Vermin Exterminators' Trade Union, marching down an Oxford street with placards screaming 'Down with Beatrix Potter!' But what is there to write about after a caption? Nothing, that's what.

I no longer want to write this book – my head and my heart just aren't in it. Dear as Izzy Bickerstaff is – and was – to me, I don't want to write anything else under that name. I don't want to be considered a light-hearted journalist any more. I do acknowledge that making readers laugh – or at least chuckle – during the war was no mean feat, but I don't want to do it any more. I can't seem to dredge up any sense of proportion or balance these days, and God knows one can't write humour without them.

In the meantime, I am very happy that Stephens & Stark is

making money on *Izzy Bickerstaff Goes to War*. It relieves my conscience over the debacle of my Anne Brontë biography.

My thanks for everything and love,

Juliet

P.S. I am reading the collected correspondence of Mrs Montagu. Do you know what that dismal woman wrote to Jane Carlyle? 'My dear little Jane, everyone is born with a vocation, and yours is to write charming little notes.' I hope Jane spat at her.

From Sidney to Juliet

Miss Juliet Ashton
23 Glebe Place
Chelsea
London SW3

10th January 1946

Dear Juliet,

Congratulations! Susan Scott said you took to the audience at the luncheon like a drunkard to rum – and they to you – so please stop worrying about your tour next week. I have no doubt of your success. Having witnessed your electrifying performance of 'The Shepherd Boy Sings in the Valley of Humiliation' eighteen years ago, I know you will have every listener coiled around your little finger within moments. A hint: perhaps in this case you should refrain from throwing the book at the audience afterwards.

Susan is looking forward to ushering you through bookshops from Bath to Yorkshire. And of course, Sophie is agitating for an extension of the tour into Scotland. I've told her in my most infuriating older-brother manner that It Remains To Be Seen. She misses you terribly, I know, but Stephens & Stark must be impervious to such considerations.

I've just received *Izzy*'s sales figures from London and the Home Counties – they are excellent. Again, congratulations!

Don't fret about *English Foibles*; better that your enthusiasm should die now than after six months spent writing about bunnies. The crass commercial possibilities of the idea were attractive, but I agree that the topic would soon grow horribly fey. Another subject – one you'll like – will occur to you.

Dinner one evening before you go? Say when.

Love,

Sidney

P.S. You write charming little notes.

From Juliet to Sidney

11th January 1946

Dear Sidney,

Yes, lovely – can it be somewhere on the river? I want oysters and champagne and roast beef, if obtainable; if not, a chicken will do. I am very happy that *Izzy*'s sales are good. Are they good enough for me not to have to pack a suitcase and leave London?

As you and S&S have turned me into a moderately successful author, dinner must be my treat.

Love,

Juliet

P.S. I did not throw 'The Shepherd Boy Sings in the Valley of Humiliation' at the audience. I threw it at the elocution mistress. I meant to cast it at her feet, but I missed.

From Juliet to Sophie Strachan

Mrs Alexander Strachan
Feochan Farm
by Oban
Argyll

12th January 1946

Dear Sophie,

Of course I'd adore to see you, but I am a soulless, will-less automaton. I have been ordered by Sidney to Bath, Colchester, Leeds, and several other places I can't remember at the moment, and I can't just slope off to Scotland instead. Sidney's brow would lower – his eyes would narrow – he would stalk. You know how nerve-racking it is when Sidney stalks.

I wish I could sneak away to your farm and be coddled. You'd let me put my feet on the sofa, wouldn't you? And then you'd tuck me up in blankets and bring me tea? Would Alexander mind a permanent presence on his sofa? You've told me he is a patient man, but perhaps he would find it annoying.

Why am I so melancholy? I should be delighted at the prospect of reading *Izzy* to an entranced audience. You know how I love talking about books, and you know how I adore receiving compliments. I should be thrilled. But the truth is that I'm gloomy – gloomier than I ever felt during the war. Everything is so *broken*, Sophie: the roads, the buildings, the people. Especially the people.

It's probably the after-effect of a horrid dinner party I went to last night. The food was ghastly, but that was to be expected. It was the guests who unnerved me – they were the most demoralising collection of individuals I've ever encountered. The talk was of bombs and starvation. Do you remember Sarah Morecroft? She was there, all bones and gooseflesh and bloody lipstick. She used to be pretty, didn't she? Wasn't she mad about that riding chap who went up to Cambridge? He was nowhere to be seen; she's married to a doctor with grey skin who clicks his tongue before he speaks. And he was positively romantic compared to the man sitting next to me, who just happened to be single, presumably the last unmarried man on earth – God, how miserably mean-spirited I sound! I swear, Sophie, I think there's something wrong with me. Every man I meet is intolerable. Perhaps I should set my sights lower – not as low as the grey doctor who clicks, but a bit lower. I can't even blame it on the war – I was never very good at men, was I?

Do you suppose the St Swithin's furnace-man was my one true love? Since I never spoke to him, it seems unlikely, but at least it was a passion unscathed by disappointment. And he had such beautiful black hair. After that, you remember, came the Year of Poets. Sidney scoffs about those poets, though I don't see why, since he introduced me to them. Then poor Adrian. Oh, there's no need to recite the dread rolls to you, but, Sophie – what *is* the matter with me? Am I too choosy? I don't want to be married just for the sake of being married. I can't think of anything lonelier than spending the rest of my life with someone I can't talk to, or worse, someone I can't be silent with.

What a dreadful, complaining letter. You see? I've succeeded in making you feel relieved that I won't be visiting Scotland. But then again, I may – my fate rests with Sidney.

Kiss Dominic for me and tell him I saw a rat the size of a terrier the other day.

Love to Alexander and even more to you,

Juliet

Miss Juliet Ashton
81 Oakley Street
Chelsea
London SW3

12th January 1946

Dear Miss Ashton,

My name is Dawsey Adams, and I live on my farm in St Martin's Parish, Guernsey. I know of you because I have an old book that once belonged to you – *The Selected Essays of Elia*, by an author whose name in real life was Charles Lamb. Your name and address were written inside the front cover.

I will speak plain – I love Charles Lamb. My own book says *Selected*, so I wondered if that meant he had written other things to choose from? These are the pieces I want to read, and though the Germans are gone now, there aren't any bookshops left in Guernsey.

I want to ask a kindness of you. Could you send me the name and address of a bookshop in London? I would like to order more of Charles Lamb's writings by post. I would also like to ask if anyone has ever written his life story, and if they have, could a copy be found for me? For all his bright and turning mind, I think Mr Lamb must have had a great sadness in his life.

Charles Lamb made me laugh during the German Occupation, especially when he wrote about the roast pig. The Guernsey Literary and Potato Peel Pie Society came into being because of a roast pig we had to keep secret from the German soldiers, so I feel a kinship to Mr Lamb.

I am sorry to bother you, but I would be sorrier still not to know about him, as his writings have made me his friend.

Hoping not to trouble you,

Dawsey Adams

P.S. My friend Mrs Maugery bought a pamphlet that once belonged to you, too. It is called *Was There a Burning Bush? A Defence of Moses and the Ten Commandments*. She liked your margin note, 'Word of God or crowd control???' Did you ever decide which?

From Juliet to Dawsey

Mr Dawsey Adams
Les Vaux Lavens
La Bouvée
St Martin's, Guernsey

15th January, 1946

Dear Mr Adams,

I no longer live in Oakley Street, but I'm so glad that your letter found me and that my book found you. It was a sad wrench to part with the *Selected Essays of Elia*. I had two copies and a dire need of shelf-room, but I felt like a traitor selling it. You have soothed my conscience.

I wonder how the book got to Guernsey? Perhaps there is some secret sort of homing instinct in books that brings them to their perfect readers. How delightful if that were true.

Because there is nothing I would rather do than rummage through bookshops. I went at once to Hastings & Sons upon receiving your letter. I have gone to them for years, always finding the one book I wanted – and then three more I hadn't known I wanted. I told Mr Hastings you would like a good, clean copy (and *not* a rare edition) of *More Essays of Elia*. He will send it to you by separate post (invoice enclosed) and was delighted to know you are also a lover of Charles Lamb. He said the best biography of Lamb was by E. V. Lucas, and he would hunt out a copy for you, though it may take a little while.

In the meantime, will you accept this small gift from me? It is his *Selected Letters*. I think it will tell you more about him than any biography ever could. E. V. Lucas sounds too stately to include my favourite passage from Lamb: 'Buz, buz, buz, bum, bum, bum, wheeze, wheeze, wheeze, fen, fen, fen, tinky, tinky, tinky, cr'annch! I shall certainly come to be condemned at last. I have been drinking too much for two days running. I find my moral sense in the last stage of a consumption and my religion getting faint.' You'll find that in the *Letters* (it's on page 244). They were the first Lamb I ever read, and I'm ashamed to say I only bought the book because I'd read elsewhere that a man named Lamb had visited his friend Leigh Hunt, in prison for libelling the Prince of Wales.

While there, Lamb helped Hunt paint the ceiling of his cell sky blue with white clouds. Next they painted a rose trellis on one wall. Then, I further discovered, Lamb offered money to help Hunt's family – though he himself was as poor as a man could be. Lamb also taught Hunt's youngest daughter to say the Lord's Prayer backwards. You naturally want to learn everything you can about a man like that.

That's what I love about reading: one tiny thing will interest you in a book, and that tiny thing will lead you on to another book, and another bit there will lead you on to a third book. It's geometrically progressive – all with no end in sight, and for no other reason than sheer enjoyment.

The red stain on the cover that looks like blood – is blood. I was careless with my paper knife. The enclosed postcard is a reproduction of a painting of Lamb by his friend William Hazlitt.

If you have time to correspond with me, could you answer several questions? Three, in fact. Why did a roast-pig dinner have to be kept a secret? How could a pig cause you to begin a literary society? And, most pressing of all, what is a potato peel pie – and why is it included in your society's name?

I am renting a flat in Chelsea, 23 Glebe Place, London SW3. My Oakley Street flat was bombed in 1945 and I still miss it. Oakley Street was wonderful – I could see the Thames out of three of my windows. I know that I am fortunate to have any place at all to live in London, but I much prefer whining to counting my blessings. I am glad you thought of me to do your *Elia* hunting.

Yours sincerely,

Juliet Ashton

P.S. I never could make up my mind about Moses – it still bothers me.

From Juliet to Sidney

18th January 1946

Dear Sidney,

This isn't a letter: it's an apology. Please forgive my moaning about the teas and luncheons you set up for *Izzy*. Did I call you a tyrant? I take it all back – I love Stephens & Stark for sending me out of London.

Bath is a glorious town: lovely crescents of white, upstanding houses instead of London's black, gloomy buildings or – worse still – piles of rubble that were once buildings. It is bliss to breathe in clean, fresh air with no coal smoke and no dust. The weather is cold, but it isn't London's dank chill. Even the people on the street look different – upstanding, like their houses, not grey and hunched like Londoners.

Susan said the guests at Abbot's book tea enjoyed themselves immensely – and I know I did. I was able to unstick my tongue from the roof of my mouth after the first two minutes and began to have quite a good time.

Susan and I are off tomorrow for bookshops in Colchester, Norwich, King's Lynn, Bradford and Leeds.

Love and thanks,

Juliet

From Juliet to Sidney

21st January 1946

Dear Sidney,

Night-time train travel is wonderful again! No standing in the corridors for hours, no being shunted off for a troop train to pass, and above all, no black-out curtains. All the windows we passed were lighted, and I could snoop once more. I missed it so terribly during the war. I felt we had all turned into moles scuttling along in our separate tunnels. I don't consider myself a real peeper – they go in for bedrooms, but it's families in sitting rooms or kitchens that thrill me. I can imagine their whole lives from a glimpse of bookshelves, or desks, or burning candles, or bright cushions.

There was a nasty, condescending man in Tillman's bookshop today. After my talk about *Izzy*, I asked if there were any questions. He leapt from his seat and pressed his nose to mine – how was it, he demanded, that I, a mere woman, dared to bastardise the name of Isaac Bickerstaff? 'The true Isaac Bickerstaff, noted journalist, nay the sacred heart and soul of eighteenth-century literature; dead now and his name desecrated by you.'

Before I could muster a word, a woman in the back row jumped to her feet. 'Oh, sit down! You can't desecrate a person who never was! He's not dead because he was never alive! Isaac Bickerstaff was a pseudonym for Joseph Addison's *Spectator* columns! Miss Ashton can take up any pretend name she wants to – so shut up!' What a valiant defender – he left the shop in a hurry.

Sidney, do you know a man called Markham V. Reynolds, Jr.? If you don't, will you look him up for me – *Who's Who*, the Domesday Book, Scotland Yard? Or he may simply be in the telephone directory. He sent a beautiful bunch of mixed spring flowers to me at the hotel in Bath, a dozen white roses to my train, and heaps of red roses to Norwich – all with no message, only his card.

Come to that, how does he know where Susan and I are staying? What trains we are taking? All his flowers have been awaiting me on my arrival. I don't know whether to feel flattered or hunted.

Love,

Juliet

From Juliet to Sidney

23rd January, 1946

Dear Sidney,

Susan's just given me the sales figures for *Izzy* – I can scarcely believe them. I honestly thought everyone would be so weary of the war that no one would want a remembrance of it – and certainly not in a book. Happily, and once again, you were right and I was wrong (it half-kills me to admit this).

Travelling, talking in front of a captive audience, signing books and meeting strangers *is* exhilarating. The women I've met have told me such wartime stories of their own, I almost wish I had my column back. Yesterday, I had a lovely, gossipy chat with a Norwich lady. She has four daughters, and only last week, the eldest was invited to a tea with the regiment. In her finest frock and spotless white gloves, the girl made her way to the school, stepped over the threshold, took one look at the sea of shining young faces before her – and fainted away! The poor child had never seen so many men in one place in her life. Think of it – a whole generation grown up without dances or teas or flirting.

I love seeing the bookshops and meeting the booksellers – booksellers really are a special breed. No one in their right mind would take up work in a bookshop for the wages, and no one in their right mind would want to own one – the margin of profit is too small. So, it has to be a love of readers and reading that makes them do it – along with first goes at the new books.

Do you remember the first job your sister and I had in London? In crabby Mr Hawke's second-hand bookshop? How I loved him – he'd simply unpack a box of books, hand one or two to us and say, 'No cigarette ash, clean hands – and for God's sake, Juliet, none of your margin notes! Sophie, dear, don't let her drink coffee while she's reading.' And off we'd go with new books to read.

It was amazing to me then, and still is, that so many people who wander into bookshops don't really know what they're after – they only want to look round in the hope of seeing a book that will take their fancy. And then, being bright enough not to trust the publisher's blurb, they will ask the assistant the three questions: (1) What is it about? (2) Have you read it? (3) Was it any good?

Real dyed-in-the-wool readers – like Sophie and me – can't lie. Our faces always give us away. A raised brow or a curled lip means that it's a poor excuse for a book, and the clever customers ask for a recommendation instead, whereupon we frog-march them over to a particular volume and command them to read it. If they read it and despise it, they'll never come back. But if they like it, they're customers for life. Are you taking notes? You should – a publisher should send not just one reader's copy to a bookshop, but several, so that all the staff can read it, too.

Mr Seton told me today that *Izzy Bickerstaff* makes an ideal present for both someone you like and someone you don't like but have to give a present to anyway. He also claimed that 30 per cent of all books bought are bought as gifts. Thirty per cent??? Did he lie?

Has Susan told you what else she has managed apart from our tour? Me. I hadn't known her half an hour before she told me that my make-up, my clothes, my hair and my shoes were drab, all drab. The war was over, hadn't I heard?

She took me to Madame Helena's for a haircut; it is now short and curly instead of long and lank. I had a light rinse, too – Susan and Madame said it would bring out the golden highlights in my 'beautiful chestnut curls'. But I know better; it's meant to cover any grey hairs (four, by my count) that have begun to creep in. I also bought a jar of face cream, a lovely scented hand lotion, a new lipstick and an eyelash curler – which makes my eyes cross whenever I use it.

Then Susan suggested a new dress. I reminded her that the Queen was very happy to wear her 1939 wardrobe, so why shouldn't I be? She said the Queen doesn't need to impress strangers – but I do. I felt like a traitor to my country: no decent woman has new clothes – but I forgot that the moment I saw myself in the mirror. My first new dress for four years, and what a dress! It is exactly the colour of a ripe peach and falls in lovely folds when I move. The shop assistant said it had 'Gallic chic' and I would too, if I bought it. So I did. New shoes are going to have to wait, since I spent almost a year's worth of clothing coupons on the dress.

Between Susan, my hair, my face and my dress, I no longer look a listless, bedraggled thirty-two-year-old. I look a lively, dashing, haute-coutured (if this isn't a French verb, it should be) thirty.

Apropos my new dress and no new shoes – doesn't it seem shocking to have more stringent rationing after the war than during the war? I realise that hundreds of thousands of people all over Europe must be fed, housed and clothed, but privately I resent it that so many of them are Germans.

I am still without any ideas for a book I want to write. It is beginning to depress me. Do you have any suggestions?

Since I am in what I consider to be the North I'm going to telephone Sophie in Scotland tonight. Any messages for your sister? Your brother-in-law? Your nephew?

This is the longest letter I've ever written – you needn't reply in kind.

Love,

Juliet

From Susan Scott to Sidney

25th January 1946

Dear Sidney,

Don't believe the newspaper reports. Juliet was not arrested and taken away in handcuffs. She was merely reproved by one of Bradford's constables, and he could barely keep a straight face.

She did throw a teapot at Gilly Gilbert's head, but don't believe his claim that she scalded him; the tea was cold. Besides, it was more of a glancing blow than a direct hit. Even the hotel manager refused to let us compensate him for the teapot – it was only dented. He was, however, forced by Gilly's screams to call in the constabulary.

Herewith the story, and I take full responsibility for it. I should have refused Gilly's request for an interview with Juliet. I knew what a loathsome person he was, one of those unctuous little worms who work for *The London Hue and Cry*. I also knew that Gilly and the *LH&C* were horribly jealous of the *Spectator*'s success with the Izzy Bickerstaff columns – and of Juliet.

We had just returned to the hotel from the Brady's Booksmith party for Juliet. We were both tired – and full of ourselves – when up popped Gilly from a chair in the lounge. He begged us to have tea with him. He begged for a short interview with 'our own wonderful Miss Ashton – or should I say England's very own Izzy Bickerstaff?' His smarm alone should have alerted me, but it didn't – I wanted to sit down, gloat over Juliet's success and have a cream tea.

So we did. The talk was going smoothly enough, and my mind was wandering when I heard Gilly say, '. . . You were a war widow yourself, weren't you? Or rather – *almost* a war widow – as good as. You were to marry a Lieutenant Rob Dartry, weren't you? Had made arrangements for the ceremony, hadn't you?'

Juliet said, 'I beg your pardon, Mr Gilbert.' You know how polite she is.

'I haven't got it wrong, have I? You and Lieutenant Dartry *did* apply for a marriage licence. You *did* make an appointment to be married at the Chelsea registry office on the 13th of December 1942, at 11 a.m. You *did* book a table for luncheon at the Ritz – only you didn't turn up for any of it. It's perfectly obvious that you jilted Lieutenant Dartry at the altar – poor fellow – and sent him off alone and humiliated, back to his ship, to carry his broken heart to Burma, where he was killed not three months later.'

I sat up, my mouth gaping open. I just looked on helplessly as Juliet attempted to be civil: 'I didn't jilt him at the altar – it was the day before. And he wasn't humiliated – he was relieved. I simply told him that I didn't want to be married after all. Believe me, Mr Gilbert, he left a happy man – delighted to be rid of me. He didn't slink back to his ship, alone and betrayed – he went straight to the CCB Club and danced all night with Belinda Twining.'

Well, Sidney, surprised as Gilly was, he was not daunted. Little rodents like Gilly never are, are they? He quickly guessed that he was on to an even juicier story for his paper. 'OH-HO!' he smirked. 'What was it, then? Drink? Other women? A touch of the old Oscar Wilde?'

That was when Juliet threw the teapot. You can imagine the hubbub that ensued – the lounge was full of other people having tea – hence, I am sure, the newspapers learning of it.

I thought his headline *IZZY BICKERSTAFF GOES TO WAR – AGAIN! Reporter Wounded in Hotel Bun-Fight*, was a bit harsh, but not too bad. But *JULIET'S FAILED ROMEO – A FALLEN HERO IN BURMA* was sickening, even for Gilly Gilbert and the *Hue and Cry*.

Juliet is worried that she may have embarrassed Stephens & Stark, but Rob Dartry's name being slung around in this fashion is making her ill. All I could get her to say to me was that Rob Dartry was a good man, a very good man – none of it was his fault – and he did not deserve this! Did you know Rob Dartry? Of course the drink, the Oscar Wilde business is pure rot, but why did Juliet call off the wedding? Do you know why? And would you tell me if you did? Of course you wouldn't; I don't know why I'm even asking.

The gossip will die down, of course, but does Juliet have to be in London for the thick of it? Should we extend our tour to Scotland? I admit I'm in two minds about this; the sales there have been spectacular, but Juliet has worked so hard at these teas and luncheons – it isn't easy to get up in front of a roomful of strangers and praise yourself and your book. She's not used to this hoopla like I am and is, I think, very tired.

Sunday we'll be in Leeds, so let me know then about Scotland.

Of course, Gilly Gilbert is despicable and vile and I hope he comes to a bad end, but he has pushed *Izzy Bickerstaff Goes to War* on to the best-seller list. I'm tempted to write him a thank-you note.

Yours in haste,

Susan

P.S. Have you found out who Markham V. Reynolds is yet? He sent Juliet a forest of camellias today.

Telegram from Juliet to Sidney

Am terribly sorry to have embarrassed you and Stephens & Stark STOP Love Juliet

From Sidney to Juliet

Miss Juliet Ashton
The Queens Hotel
City Square
Leeds

26th January 1946

Dear Juliet,

Don't worry about Gilly – you did not embarrass S&S; I'm only sorry that the tea wasn't hotter and you didn't aim lower. The press is hounding me for a statement regarding Gilly's latest muckraking, and I am going to give them one. Don't worry; it's going to be about journalism in these degenerate times – not about you or Rob Dartry.

I've just spoken to Susan about going on to Scotland and have – though I know Sophie will never forgive me – decided against it. *Izzy's* sales figures are going up – right up – and I think you should come home.

The Times wants you to write a long piece for the supplement – one part of a three-part series they plan to publish in successive issues. I'll let them surprise you with the subject, but I can promise you three things now: they want it written by Juliet Ashton, *not by Izzy Bickerstaff*; the subject is a serious one; and the sum mentioned means you can fill your flat with fresh flowers every day for a year, buy a satin quilt (Lord Woolton says you no longer need to have been bombed out to buy new bed-covers), and purchase a pair of real leather shoes – if you can find them. You can have my coupons.

The Times doesn't want the article until late spring, so we will have more time to think up a new book idea for you. All good reasons to hurry back, but the biggest one is that I miss you.

Now, about Markham V. Reynolds, Junior. I do know who he is, and the Domesday Book won't help – he's an American. He is the son and heir of Markham V. Reynolds, Senior, who used to have a monopoly on paper mills in America and now just owns most of them. Reynolds, Junior, being of an artistic bent, does not dirty his hands making paper – he prints on it instead. He's a publisher. The *New York Journal, The Word, View,* – those are all his, and there are several smaller magazines as well. I knew he was in London. Officially, he's here to open the London office of *View,* but rumour has it that he's decided to begin publishing books, and he's here to beguile England's finest authors with visions of plenty and prosperity in America. I didn't know his technique included roses and camellias, but I'm not surprised. He's always had more than his fair share of what we call cheek and Americans call can-do spirit. Just wait till you see him – he's been the undoing of stronger women than you, including my secretary. I'm sorry to say she's the one who gave him your itinerary *and* your address. The silly woman thought he looked so romantic, 'such a lovely suit and handmade shoes'. Dear God! She couldn't seem to grasp the concept of breach of confidentiality, so I had to dismiss her.

He's after you, Juliet, no doubt about it. Shall I challenge him to a duel? He would undoubtedly kill me, so I'd rather not. My dear, I can't promise you plenty or prosperity or even butter, but you do know that you're Stephens & Stark's – especially Stark's – most beloved author, don't you?

Dinner the first evening you are home?

Love,

Sidney

28th January 1946

Dear Sidney,

Yes, dinner with pleasure. I'll wear my new dress and eat like a pig.

I am so glad I didn't embarrass S&S about Gilly and the teapot – I was worried. Susan suggested I make a 'dignified statement' to the press too, about Rob Dartry and why we didn't marry. I couldn't possibly do that. I honestly don't think I'd mind looking a fool, if it didn't make Rob look a worse one. But it would – and of course, he wasn't a fool at all. But he'd *sound like it.* I'd much prefer to say nothing and look like a feckless, flighty, cold-hearted bitch.

But I'd like you to know why – I'd have told you before, but you were in the Navy in 1942, and you never met Rob. Even Sophie never met him – she was up at Bedford that autumn and I swore her to secrecy afterwards. The longer I put off saying anything, the less important it became for you to know, especially in the light of how it made me look – witless and foolish for getting engaged in the first place.

I thought I was in love (*that*'s the pathetic part – my idea of being in love). In preparation for sharing my home with a husband, I made room for him so he wouldn't feel like a visiting aunt. I cleared out half my drawers, half my cupboard, half my bathroom cabinet, half my desk. I gave away my padded hangers and brought in those heavy wooden ones. I took my golliwog off the bed and put her in the attic. Now my flat was meant for two, instead of one.

On the afternoon before our wedding, Rob was moving in the last of his clothes and belongings while I delivered my Izzy article to the *Spectator*. Then I tore home, flew up the stairs and threw open the door to find Rob sitting on the low stool in front of my bookcase, surrounded by cardboard boxes. He was sealing the last one up with tape and string. There were eight boxes – *eight boxes* of my books bound up and ready for the basement!

He looked up and said, 'Hello, darling. Don't mind the mess, the caretaker said he'd help me carry these down to the basement.' He nodded towards my bookshelves and said, 'Don't they look wonderful?'

Well, there were no words! I was too appalled to speak. Sidney, every single shelf – where my books had stood – was filled with athletic trophies: silver cups, gold cups, blue rosettes, red ribbons. There were awards for every game that could possibly be played with a wooden object: cricket bats, squash racquets, tennis racquets, oars, golf clubs, ping-pong bats, bows and arrows, snooker cues, lacrosse sticks, hockey sticks and polo mallets. There were statues for everything a man could jump over, either by himself or on a horse. Next came the framed certificates – for shooting the most birds on such and such a date, for First Place in running races, for Last Man Standing in some filthy tug of war against Scotland.

All I could do was scream, 'How dare you! What have you DONE?! Put my books back!'

Well, that's how it started. Eventually, I said something to the effect that I could never marry a man whose idea of bliss was to strike out at little balls and little birds. Rob countered with remarks about damned bluestockings and shrews. And it all degenerated from there – the only thought we probably had in common was, What the hell have we talked about for the last four months? What, indeed? He huffed and puffed and snorted – and left. And I unpacked my books.

Remember the night last year when you met my train to tell me my home had been bombed flat? You thought I was laughing in hysteria? I wasn't – it was in irony – if I'd let Rob store all my books in the basement, I'd still have them, every one.

Sidney, as a token of our long friendship, you do not need to comment on this story – not ever. In fact, I'd far prefer it if you didn't.

Thank you for tracing Markham V. Reynolds, Junior, to his source. So far, his blandishments are entirely floral, and I remain true to you and the Empire. However, I do have a pang of sympathy for your secretary – I hope he sent her some roses for her trouble – as I'm not certain that my scruples could withstand the sight of hand-made shoes. If I ever do meet him, I'll be careful not to look at his feet – or I'll lash myself to a flagpole first and then peek, like Odysseus.

Bless you for telling me to come home. Am looking forward to *The Times* proposal for a series. Do you promise on Sophie's head it will not be a frivolous subject? They aren't going to ask me to write gossip about the Duchess of Windsor, are they?

Love,

Juliet

From Juliet to Sophie Strachan

31st January 1946

Dear Sophie,

Thank you for your flying visit to Leeds – there are no words to express how much I needed to see a friendly face just then. I honestly was on the verge of stealing away to the Shetlands to take up the life of a hermit. It was beautiful of you to come.

The *London Hue and Cry*'s sketch of me taken away in chains was exaggerated – I wasn't even arrested. I know Dominic would much prefer a godmother in prison, but he will have to settle for something less dramatic this time. I told Sidney the only thing I could do about Gilly's callous, lying accusations was to maintain a dignified silence. He said I could do that if I wanted to, but Stephens & Stark could not!

He called a press conference to defend the honour of *Izzy Bickerstaff*, Juliet Ashton and journalism itself against such rubbish as Gilly Gilbert. Did it make the papers in Scotland? If not – here are the highlights. He called Gilly Gilbert a twisted weasel (well, perhaps not in exactly those words, but his meaning was clear), who lied because he was too lazy to learn the facts and too stupid to understand the damage his lies inflicted upon the noble traditions of journalism. It was lovely.

Sophie, could two girls (now women) ever have had a better champion than your brother? I don't think so. He gave a marvellous speech, though I must admit to a few qualms. Gilly Gilbert is such a snake-in-the-grass, I can't believe he'll just slither away without a hiss. Susan said that, on the other hand, Gilly is also such a frightful little coward, he would not dare retaliate. I hope she's right.

Love to you all,

Juliet

P.S. That man has sent me another bale of orchids. I'm getting a nervous twitch, waiting for him to come out of hiding and make himself known. Do you suppose this is his strategy?

From Dawsey to Juliet

31st January 1946

Dear Miss Ashton,

Your book came yesterday! You are a nice lady and I thank you with all my heart.

I have a job at St Peter Port harbour – unloading ships, so I can read during tea breaks. It is a blessing to have real tea and bread with butter, and now – your book. I like it too because the cover is soft and I can put it in my pocket everywhere I go, though I am careful not to use it up too quickly. And I value having a picture of Charles Lamb – he had a fine head, didn't he?

I would like to keep up our correspondence. I will answer your questions as well as I can. Though there are many who can tell a story better than I, I will tell you about our roast-pig dinner.

I have a cottage and a farm, left to me by my father. Before the war, I kept pigs and grew vegetables for the St Peter Port markets and flowers for Covent Garden. I also worked as a carpenter and roofer.

The pigs are gone now. The Germans took them away to feed their soldiers on the Continent, and ordered me to grow potatoes. We were to grow what they told us and nothing else. At first, before I knew the Germans as I came to later, I thought I could keep a few pigs hidden – for myself. But the Agricultural Officer nosed them out and carried them off. Well, that was a blow, but I thought I'd manage all right, for potatoes and turnips were plentiful, and there was still flour then. But it is strange how the mind turns to food. After six months of turnips and a lump of gristle now and then, I was hard put to think about anything but a fine, full meal.

One afternoon, my neighbour, Mrs Maugery, sent me a note. Come quickly, it said. And bring a butcher's knife. I tried not to get my hopes up – but I set out for the manor house at a great pace. And it was true! She had a pig, a hidden pig, and she invited me to join in the feast with her and her friends!

I didn't talk much while I was growing up – I stuttered badly – and I was not used to dinner parties. To tell the truth, Mrs Maugery's was the first one I was ever invited to. I said yes, because I was thinking of the roast pig, but I wished I could take my piece home and eat it there.

It was my good luck that my wish didn't come true, because that was the first meeting of the Guernsey Literary and Potato Peel Pie Society, even though we didn't know it then. The dinner was a rare treat, but the company was better. Talking and eating, we forgot about clocks and curfews until Amelia (Mrs Maugery) heard the chimes ring nine o'clock – we were an hour late. Well, the good food had strengthened our hearts, and when Elizabeth McKenna said we should strike out for our own homes instead of skulking in Amelia's house all night, we agreed. But breaking curfew was a crime – I'd heard of people being sent to prison camp for it – and keeping a pig was a worse one, so we whispered and picked our way through the fields as quietly as we could.

We would have come out all right if not for John Booker. He'd drunk more than he'd eaten at dinner, and when we got to the road, he forgot himself and broke into song! I grabbed hold of him, but it was too late: six German patrol officers suddenly rose out of the trees with their Lugers drawn and began to shout – Why were we out after curfew? Where had we been? Where were we going? I couldn't think what to do. If I ran, they'd shoot me. I knew that much. My mouth was as dry as chalk and my mind was blank, so I just held on to Booker and hoped.

Then Elizabeth drew in her breath and stepped forward. Elizabeth isn't tall, so those pistols were pointing at her eyes, but she didn't blink. She acted as if she didn't see any pistols at all. She walked up to the officer in charge and started talking. You've never heard such lies. How sorry she was that we had broken curfew. How we had been attending a meeting of the Guernsey Literary Society, and the evening's discussion of *Elizabeth and Her German Garden* had been so delightful that we had all lost track of time. Such a wonderful book – had he read it?

None of us had the presence of mind to back her up, but the patrol officer couldn't help himself – he had to smile back at her. Elizabeth is like that. He took our names and ordered us very politely to report to the Commandant the next morning. Then he bowed and wished us a good evening. Elizabeth nodded, gracious as could be, while the rest of us edged away, trying not to run like rabbits. Even lugging Booker, I got home in no time.

That is the story of our roast-pig dinner.

I'd like to ask you a question of my own. Ships are coming in to St Peter Port harbour every day to bring us things Guernsey still

26

needs: food, clothes, seed, ploughs, animal feed, tools, medicine – and most important, now that we have food to eat, shoes. I don't believe that there was a decent pair left on the island by the end of the war.

Some of the things being sent to us are wrapped up in old newspaper and magazine pages. My friend Clovis and I smooth them out and take them home to read – then we give them to neighbours who, like us, are eager for any news of the outside world in the past five years. Not just any news or pictures: Mrs Saussey wants to see recipes; Madame LePell wants fashion pictures (she is a dressmaker); Mr Brouard reads obituaries (he has his hopes, but won't say who); Claudia Rainey is looking for pictures of Ronald Colman; Mr Tourtelle wants to see beauty queens in bathing costumes; and my friend Isola likes to read about weddings.

There was so much we wanted to know during the war, but we weren't allowed letters or papers from England – or anywhere. In 1942, the Germans called in all the wireless sets – of course, there were hidden ones, listened to in secret, but if you were caught listening, you could be sent to the camps. That's why we don't understand so many things we can read about now.

I enjoy the wartime cartoons, but there is one that bewilders me. It was in a 1944 *Punch* and shows about ten people walking down a London street. The chief figures are two men in bowler hats, holding briefcases and umbrellas, and one man is saying to the other, 'It is ridiculous to say these Doodlebugs have affected people in any way.' It took me several seconds to realise that every person in the cartoon had one normal ear and one *very large* ear on the other side of his head. Perhaps you could explain it to me.

Yours sincerely,

Dawsey Adams

From Juliet to Dawsey

3rd February 1946

Dear Mr Adams,

I am so glad you are enjoying Lamb's letters and the copy of his portrait. He did fit the face I had imagined for him, so I'm glad you agree.

Thank you very much for telling me about the roast pig, but don't think I didn't notice that you only answered one of my questions. I'm hankering to know more about the Guernsey Literary and Potato Peel Pie Society, and not merely to satisfy my idle curiosity – I now have a professional duty to pry.

Did I tell you I am a writer? I wrote a weekly column for the *Spectator* during the war, and Stephens & Stark collected them together into a single volume and published them under the title *Izzy Bickerstaff Goes to War*. Izzy was the nom-de-plume the *Spectator* chose for me, and now, thank heavens, the poor thing has been laid to rest, and I can write under my own name again. I would like to write a book, but I am having trouble thinking of a subject I could live happily with for several years.

In the meantime, *The Times* has asked me to write an article for the literary supplement. They want to address the practical, moral, and philosophical value of reading – spread out over three issues and by three different authors. I am to cover the philosophical side of the debate and so far my only thought is that reading keeps you from going gaga. You can see I need help.

Do you think your literary society would mind being included in such an article? I know that the story of the society's founding would fascinate *Times* readers, and I'd love to learn more about your meetings. But if you'd rather not, please don't worry – I will understand either way, and either way, would like to hear from you again.

I remember the *Punch* cartoon you described very well and think it was the word *Doodlebug* that confused you. That was the name coined by the Ministry of Information; it was meant to sound less terrifying than 'Hitler's V-1 rockets' or 'pilotless bombs'.

We were all used to bombing raids at night and the sights that followed, but these were unlike any bombs we had seen before. They came in the daytime, and they came so fast there was no time for an air-raid siren or to take cover. You could see them; they looked like slim, black, slanted pencils and made a dull, strangled sound above you – like a motor-car running out of petrol. As long as you could hear them coughing and put-putting, you were safe. You could think, Thank God, it's going past me.

But when their noise stopped, it meant there was only thirty seconds before the thing plummeted. So, you listened for them. Listened hard for the sound of their motors cutting out. I did see a Doodlebug fall once. I was quite some distance away when it hit, so I threw myself down in the gutter and hugged the kerb. Some women, in the top storey of a tall office building down the street, had gone to an open window to watch. They were sucked out by the force of the blast.

It seems impossible now that someone could have drawn a cartoon about Doodlebugs, and that everyone, including me, could have laughed at it. But we did. The old adage – humour is the best way to make the unbearable bearable – may be true.

Has Mr Hastings found the Lucas biography for you yet?

Yours sincerely,

Juliet Ashton

From Juliet to Markham Reynolds

Mr Markham Reynolds
63 Halkin Street
London SW1

4th February 1946

Dear Mr Reynolds,

I captured your delivery boy in the act of depositing a clutch
of pink carnations on to my doorstep. I seized him and threatened him until he confessed your address – you see, Mr
Reynolds, you are not the only one who can inveigle innocent
employees. I hope you don't sack him; he seems a nice boy, and
he really had no alternative – I menaced him with *Remembrance of
Things Past.*

Now I can thank you for the dozens of flowers you've sent
me – it's been years since I've seen such roses, such camellias,
such orchids, and you can have no idea how they lift my heart
in this shivering winter. Why I deserve to live in a bower,
when everyone else has to be satisfied with bedraggled leafless
trees and slush, I don't know, but I'm perfectly delighted to do
so.

Yours sincerely,

Juliet Ashton

From Markham Reynolds to Juliet

5th February 1946

Dear Miss Ashton,

I didn't fire the delivery boy – I promoted him. He got me what I couldn't manage to get for myself: an introduction to you. The way I see it, your note is a figurative handshake and the preliminaries are now over. I hope you're of the same opinion, as it will save me the trouble of wangling an invitation to Lady Bascomb's next dinner party on the off-chance you might be there. Your friends are a suspicious lot, especially that fellow Stark, who said it wasn't his job to reverse the direction of the Lend Lease and refused to bring you to the cocktail party I threw at the *View* office.

God knows, my intentions are pure, or at least, non-mercenary. The simple truth of it is that you're the only female writer who makes me laugh. Your Izzy Bickerstaff columns were the wittiest work to come out of the war, and I want to meet the woman who wrote them.

If I swear that I won't kidnap you, will you do me the honour of dining with me next week? You pick the evening – I'm entirely at your disposal.

Yours,

Markham Reynolds

From Juliet to Markham Reynolds

6th February 1946

Dear Mr Reynolds,

I am no proof against compliments, especially compliments about my writing. I'll be delighted to dine with you. Thursday next?
Yours sincerely,

Juliet Ashton

From Markham Reynolds to Juliet

7th February 1946

Dear Juliet,

Thursday's too far away. Monday? Claridge's? Seven?
Yours,

Mark

P.S. I don't suppose you have a telephone, do you?

From Juliet to Markham Reynolds

7th February 1946

Dear Mr Reynolds,

All right – Monday, Claridge's, seven.

I do have a telephone. It's in Oakley Street under a pile of rubble that used to be my flat. I'm only renting here, and my landlady, Mrs Olive Burns, possesses the sole telephone on the premises. If you would like to chat with her, I can give you her number.

Yours sincerely,

Juliet Ashton

From Dawsey to Juliet

7th February 1946

Dear Miss Ashton,

I'm certain the Guernsey Literary Society would like to be included in your article for *The Times*. I have asked Mrs Maugery to write to you about our meetings, as she is an educated lady and her words will sound more at home in an article than mine. I don't think we are much like literary societies in London.

Mr Hastings hasn't found a copy of the Lucas biography yet, but I had a postcard from him saying, 'Hard on the trail. Don't give up.' He is a kind man, isn't he?

I'm heaving slates for the Crown Hotel's new roof. The owners are hoping that tourists may want to come back this summer. I am glad of the work but will be happy to be working on my land soon.

It is nice to come home in the evening and find a letter from you.
I wish you good fortune in finding a subject you would care to
write a book about.

Yours sincerely,

Dawsey Adams

From Amelia Maugery to Juliet

8th February 1946

Dear Miss Ashton,

Dawsey Adams has just been to visit. I have never seen him as
pleased with anything as he is with your gift and letter. He was so
busy convincing me to write to you by the next post that he forgot
to be shy. I don't believe he is aware of it, but Dawsey has a rare gift
for persuasion – he never asks for anything for himself, so everyone
is eager to do what he asks for others.

He told me of your proposed article and asked if I would write to
you about the literary society we formed during – and because of –
the German Occupation. I will be happy to do so, but with a caveat.

A friend from England sent me a copy of *Izzy Bickerstaff Goes to
War*. We had no news from the outside world for five years, so you
can imagine how satisfying it was to learn how England endured
those years herself. Your book was as informative as it was
entertaining and amusing – but it is the amusing tone I must
quibble with.

I realise that our name, the Guernsey Literary and Potato Peel
Pie Society, is an unusual one and could easily be subjected to
ridicule. Would you assure me you will not be tempted to do so?
The Society members are very dear to me, and I do not wish them
to be perceived as objects of fun by your readers.

Would you be willing to tell me of your intentions for the article and also something of yourself? If you can appreciate the import of my questions, I should be glad to tell you about the Society. I hope I shall hear from you soon.

Yours sincerely,

Amelia Maugery

From Juliet to Amelia

Mrs Amelia Maugery
Windcross Manor
La Bouvée
St Martin's, Guernsey

10th February 1946

Dear Mrs Maugery,

Thank you for your letter. I am very glad to answer your questions.

I did make fun of many wartime situations; the *Spectator* felt a light approach to the bad news would serve as an antidote and that humour would help to raise London's low morale. I am very glad *Izzy* served that purpose, but the need to be humorous against the odds is – thank goodness – over. I would never make fun of anyone who loved reading. Nor of Mr Adams – I was glad to learn one of my books fell into such hands as his.

Since you should know something about me, I have asked the Reverend Simon Simpless, of St Hilda's Church near Bury St Edmunds, Suffolk, to write to you. He has known me since I was a child and is fond of me. I have asked Lady Bella Taunton to provide a reference for me too. We were fire wardens together during the

35

Blitz and she wholeheartedly dislikes me. Between the two of them, you may get a fair picture of my character.

I am enclosing a copy of a biography I wrote of Anne Brontë, so you can see that I am capable of a different kind of work. It didn't sell very well – in fact, not at all, but I am much prouder of it than I am of *Izzy Bickerstaff Goes to War.*

If there is anything else I can do to assure you of my good will, I will be glad to do so.

Yours sincerely,

Juliet Ashton

From Juliet to Sophie

12th February 1946

Dearest Sophie,

Markham V. Reynolds, he of the camellias, has finally materialised. Introduced himself, paid me compliments, and invited me out to dinner – Claridge's, no less. I accepted regally – Claridge's, oh yes, I *have* heard of Claridge's – and then spent the next three days fretting about my hair. It's lucky I have my lovely new dress, so I didn't have to waste precious fretting time on what to wear. As Madame Helena said, 'The hairs, they are a disaster.' I tried a French roll; it fell down. A bun; it fell down. I was on the verge of tying an enormous red velvet bow on the top of my head when my neighbour Evangeline Smythe came to the rescue, bless her. She's a genius with my hair. In two minutes, I was a picture of elegance – she caught up all the curls and swirled them round at the back – and I could even move my head. Off I went, feeling perfectly adorable. Not even Claridge's marble lobby could intimidate *me.*

Then Markham V. Reynolds stepped forward, and the bubble

popped. He's dazzling. Honestly, Sophie, I've never seen anything like him. Not even the furnace-man can compare. Tanned, with blazing blue eyes. Ravishing leather shoes, elegant wool suit, blinding white handkerchief in breast pocket. Of course, being American, he's tall, and he has one of those alarming American smiles, all gleaming teeth and good humour, but he's not a genial American. He's quite impressive, and he's used to ordering people about – though he does it so easily, they don't notice. He's got that way of believing his opinion is the truth, but he's not disagreeable about it. He's too sure he's right to bother about being disagreeable.

Once we were seated – in our own velvet-draped alcove – and all the waiters and stewards and maîtres d'hôtel had finished fluttering about, I asked him point-blank why he had sent me all those flowers without including any note.

He laughed. 'To make you interested. If I had written to you directly, asking you to meet me, how would you have replied?' I admitted I would have declined. He raised one pointed eyebrow at me. Was it his fault he could outwit me so easily?

I was awfully insulted to be so transparent, but he just laughed at me again. And then he began to talk about the war and Victorian literature – he knows I wrote a biography of Anne Brontë – and New York and rationing, and before I knew it, I was basking in his attention, utterly charmed.

Do you remember that afternoon in Leeds when we speculated on the possible reasons why Markham V. Reynolds, Junior, was obliged to remain a man of mystery? It's very disappointing, but we were completely wrong. He's not married. He's certainly not bashful. He doesn't have a disfiguring scar that causes him to shun the daylight. He doesn't seem to be a werewolf (no fur on his knuckles, anyway). And he's not a Nazi on the run (he'd have an accent).

Now that I think about it, maybe he *is* a werewolf. I can picture him lunging over the moors in hot pursuit of his prey, and I'm certain that he wouldn't think twice about eating an innocent bystander. I'll watch him closely at the next full moon. He's asked me to go dancing tomorrow – perhaps I should wear a high collar. Oh, that's vampires, isn't it?

I think I am a little giddy.

Love,

Juliet

From Lady Bella Taunton to Amelia

12th February 1946

Dear Mrs Maugery,

Juliet Ashton has written to me, and I am astonished. Am I to understand she wishes me to provide a character reference for her? Well, so be it! I cannot impugn her character – only her common sense. She hasn't any.

War, as you know, makes strange bedfellows, and Juliet and I were thrown together from the very first when we were fire wardens during the Blitz. Fire wardens spent their nights on various London roof-tops, watching out for incendiary bombs that might fall. When they did, we would rush forth with stirrup pumps and buckets of sand to stifle any small blaze before it could spread. Juliet and I were paired off to work together. We did not chat, as less conscientious wardens would have done. I insisted on total vigilance at all times. Even so, I learnt a few details of her life prior to the war.

Her father was a respectable farmer in Suffolk. Her mother, I surmise, was a typical farmer's wife, milking cows and plucking chickens, when not otherwise engaged in owning a bookshop in Bury St Edmunds. Juliet's parents were both killed in a motor-car accident when she was twelve and she went to live with her great-uncle, a renowned classicist, in St John's Wood. There she disrupted his studies and household by running away – twice.

In despair, he sent her to boarding school. Upon leaving, she shunned a higher education, came to London, and shared a flat with her friend Sophie Stark. She worked by day in bookshops. By night, she wrote a book about one of those wretched Brontë girls – I forget which one. I believe the book was published by Sophie's brother's firm, Stephens & Stark. Though it's biologically impossible, I can only assume that some form of nepotism was responsible for the book's publication.

Anyway, she began to publish feature articles for various magazines and newspapers. Her light, frivolous turn of mind gained her a large following among the less intellectually inclined readers – of whom, I fear, there are many. She spent the very last of her inheritance on a flat in Chelsea. Chelsea, home of artists, models, libertines and socialists – completely irresponsible people all, just as Juliet proved herself to be as a fire warden.

I come now to the specifics of our association.

Juliet and I were two of several wardens assigned to the roof of the Inner Temple Hall of the Inns of Court. Let me say first that, for a warden, quick action and a clear head were imperative – one had to be aware of *everything* going on around one. *Everything.*

One night in May 1941, a high-explosive bomb was dropped through the roof of the Inner Temple Hall Library. The Library roof was some distance away from Juliet's post, but she was so aghast by the destruction of her precious books that she sprinted *towards* the flames – as if she could single-handedly deliver the Library from its fate! Of course, her delusions created nothing but further damage, for the firemen had to waste valuable minutes in rescuing her.

I believe Juliet suffered some minor burns in the debacle, but fifty thousand books were blown to Kingdom Come. Juliet's name was struck off the fire-warden list, and rightly so. I discovered that she then volunteered her services to the Auxiliary Fire Services. On the morning after a bombing raid, the AFS would be on hand to offer tea and comfort to the rescue squads. The AFS also provided assistance to the survivors: reuniting families, securing temporary housing, clothing, food, funds. I believe Juliet to have been adequate to that daytime task – causing no catastrophe among the teacups.

She was free to occupy her nights however she chose. Doubtless it included the writing of more light journalism, for the *Spectator* engaged her to write a weekly column on the state of the nation in wartime – under the name of Izzy Bickerstaff.

I read one of her columns and cancelled my subscription. She attacked the good taste of our dear (though dead) Queen Victoria. Doubtless you know of the huge memorial Victoria had built for her beloved consort, Prince Albert. It is the jewel in the crown of Kensington Gardens – a monument to the Queen's refined taste as well as to the Departed. Juliet applauded the Ministry of Food for having ordered peas to be planted in the grounds surrounding that memorial – commenting that no better scarecrow than Prince Albert existed in all England.

While I question her taste, her judgement, her misplaced priorities, and her inappropriate sense of humour, she does indeed have one fine quality – she is honest. If she says she will honour the good name of your literary society, she will do so. I can say no more.

Sincerely yours,

Bella Taunton

From the Reverend Simon Simpless to Amelia

13th February 1946

Dear Mrs Maugery,

Yes, you may trust Juliet. I am unequivocal on this point. Her parents were my good friends as well as my parishioners at St Hilda's. Indeed, I was a guest at their home on the night she was born.

Juliet was a stubborn but nevertheless a sweet, considerate, joyous child – with an unusual bent for integrity in one so young.

I will tell you of one incident when she was ten years old. Juliet, while singing the fourth verse of 'His Eye Is on the Sparrow', slammed her hymnal shut and refused to sing another note. She told our choir master that the words cast a slur on God's character. We should not be singing it. He (the choir master, not God) didn't know what to do, so he escorted Juliet to my study for me to reason with her.

I did not fare very well. Juliet said, 'Well, he shouldn't have written, "His eye is on the sparrow" – what good was that? Did He stop the bird dying? Did He just say, "Oops"? It makes God sound like He's off bird-watching when real people need Him.'

I felt compelled to agree with Juliet on this matter – why had I never thought about it before? The choir has not sung 'His Eye Is on the Sparrow' since then.

Juliet's parents died when she was twelve and she was sent to live with her great-uncle, Dr Roderick Ashton, in London. Though not an unkind man, he was so mired in his Greco-Roman studies he had no time to take any notice of the girl. He had no imagination, either – fatal for someone bringing up a child.

She ran away twice, the first time making it only as far as King's Cross Station. The police found her waiting, with a packed canvas bag and her father's fishing rod, to catch the train to Bury St Edmunds. She was returned to Dr Ashton – and she ran away again. This time, Dr Ashton telephoned me to ask for my help in finding her.

I knew exactly where to go – to her parents' former farm. I found her opposite the farm's entrance, sitting on a little wooded knoll, impervious to the rain – just sitting there, soaked – looking at her old (now sold) home.

I sent a telegram to her uncle and went back with her on the train to London the following day. I had intended to return to my parish on the next train, but when I discovered her fool of an uncle had sent his cook to fetch her, I insisted on accompanying them. I invaded his study and we had a vigorous talk. He agreed that a boarding school might be best for Juliet – her parents had left ample funds for such an eventuality.

Fortunately, I knew of a very good school – St Swithin's. Academically fine, and with a headmistress not carved from granite. I am happy to tell you Juliet thrived there – she found her lessons stimulating, but I believe the true reason for Juliet's regained spirits was her friendship with Sophie Stark – and the Stark family. She often went to Sophie's home at half-term, and Juliet and Sophie came twice to stay with me and my sister at the Rectory. What jolly times we shared: picnics, bicycle rides, fishing. Sophie's brother, Sidney Stark, joined us once – though ten years older than the girls, and despite an inclination to boss them around, he was a welcome fifth to our happy party.

It was rewarding to watch Juliet grow up – as it is now to know her fully grown. I am very glad that she asked me to write to you of her character.

I have included our small history together so that you will realise I know whereof I speak. If Juliet says she will, she will. If she says she won't, she won't.

Very truly yours,

Simon Simpless

From Susan Scott to Juliet

17th February 1946

Dear Juliet,

Was that possibly *you* I glimpsed in this week's *Tatler*, doing the rumba with Mark Reynolds? You looked gorgeous – almost as gorgeous as he did – but might I suggest that you move to an air-raid shelter before Sidney sees a copy?

You can buy my silence with torrid details, you know.

Yours,

Susan

From Juliet to Susan Scott

18th February 1946

Dear Susan,

I deny everything.
Love,

Juliet

From Amelia to Juliet

18th February 1946

Dear Miss Ashton,

Thank you for taking my caveat so seriously. At the Society meeting last night, I told the members about your article for *The Times* and suggested that those who wished to do so should correspond with you about the books they have read and the joy they have found in reading.

The response was so vociferous that Isola Pribby, our Sergeant-at-Arms, was forced to bang her hammer for order (I admit that

Isola needs little encouragement to bang her hammer). I think you will receive a good many letters from us, and I hope they will be of some help to your article.

Dawsey has told you that the Society was invented as a ruse to stop the Germans arresting my guests: Dawsey, Isola, Eben Ramsey, John Booker, Will Thisbee, and our dear Elizabeth McKenna, who manufactured the story on the spot, bless her quick wits and silver tongue.

I, of course, knew nothing of their predicament at the time. As soon as they left, I made haste down to my cellar to bury the evidence of our meal. The first I heard about our literary society was the next morning at seven, when Elizabeth appeared in my kitchen and asked, 'How many books have you got?'

I had quite a few, but Elizabeth looked at my shelves and shook her head. 'We need more. There's too much gardening here.' She was right, of course – I do like a good garden book. 'I'll tell you what we'll do,' she said. 'After I've finished at the Commandant's Office, we'll go to Fox's Bookshop and buy them out. If we're going to be the Guernsey Literary Society, we have to look literary.'

I was frantic all morning, worrying over what was happening at the Commandant's Office. What if they all ended up in the Guernsey prison? Or, worst of all, in a prison camp on the Continent? The Germans were erratic in dispensing their justice, so one never knew what sentence would be imposed. But nothing of the sort occurred.

Odd as it may sound, the Germans allowed – and even encouraged – artistic and cultural pursuits among the Channel Islanders. Their object was to prove to the British that the German Occupation was a model one. How this message was to be conveyed to the outside world was never explained, as the telephone and telegraph cable between Guernsey and London had been cut the day the Germans landed in June 1940. Whatever their skewed reasoning, the Channel Islands were treated much more leniently than the rest of conquered Europe – at first.

At the Commandant's Office, my friends were ordered to pay a small fine and submit the name and membership list of their society. The Commandant announced that he, too, was a lover of literature – might he, with a few like-minded officers, sometimes attend meetings?

Elizabeth told them they would be most welcome. And then she, Eben, and I flew to Fox's, chose armloads of books for our newfound society, and rushed back to the Manor to put them on my shelves. Then we strolled from house to house – looking as carefree and casual as we could – in order to alert the others to come that evening and choose a book to read. It was agonising to walk slowly, stopping to chat here and there, when we wanted to rush! Timing was vital, because Elizabeth feared the Commandant would appear at the next meeting, barely two weeks away. (He did not. A few German officers did attend over the years but, thankfully, left in some confusion and did not return.)

And so it was that we began. I knew all our members, but I did not know them all well. Dawsey had been my neighbour for over thirty years, and yet I don't believe I had ever spoken to him about anything more than the weather and farming. Isola was a dear friend, and Eben, too, but Will Thisbee was only an acquaintance and John Booker was nearly a stranger, for he had only just arrived when the Germans came. It was Elizabeth we had in common. Without her urging, I would never have thought to invite them to share my pig, and the Guernsey Literary and Potato Peel Pie Society would never have drawn breath.

That evening when they came to my house to make their selections, those who had rarely read anything other than scripture, seed catalogues, and *The Pigman's Gazette* discovered a different kind of reading. It was here Dawsey found his Charles Lamb and Isola fell upon *Wuthering Heights*. For myself, I chose *The Pickwick Papers*, thinking it would lift my spirits – it did.

Then each went home and read. We began to meet – for the sake of the Commandant at first, and then for our own pleasure. None of us had any experience of literary societies, so we made our own rules: we took turns to speak about the books we'd read. At the start, we tried to be calm and objective, but that soon fell away, and the purpose of the speakers was to goad the listeners into wanting to read the book themselves. Once two members had read the same book, they could argue, which was our great delight. We read books, talked books, argued over books, and became dearer and dearer to one another. Other Islanders asked to join us, and our evenings together became bright, lively times – we could almost forget, now and then, the darkness outside. We still meet every fortnight.

Will Thisbee was responsible for the inclusion of Potato Peel Pie in our society's name. Germans or not, he wasn't going to go to any meetings unless there were eats! So refreshments became part of our agenda. Since there was scant butter, less flour and no sugar to spare on Guernsey then, Will concocted a potato peel pie: mashed potatoes for the filling, boiled beetroot for sweetness, and potato peelings for the crust. Will's recipes are usually dubious, but this one became a favourite.

I would love to hear from you again and find out how your article progresses.

Yours most sincerely,

Amelia Maugery

From Isola Pribby to Juliet

19th February 1946

Dear Miss Ashton.

Oh my oh my. You have written a book about Anne Brontë, sister to Charlotte and Emily. Amelia Maugery says she will lend it to me, because she knows I have a fondness for the Brontë girls – poor lambs. To think all five of them had weak chests and died so young! What a sadness.

Their dad was a selfish thing, wasn't he? He paid his girls no attention at all – always sitting in his study, shouting for his shawl. He never got up to wait on hisself, did he? Just sat alone in his room while his daughters died like flies. And their brother Branwell – he wasn't much either. Always drinking and sicking up on the carpet. They were always having to clean up after him. Fine work for lady authoresses! It is my belief that with two such men in the household and no way to meet others, Emily had to make Heathcliff up out of thin air! And what a fine job she did. Men are more interesting in books than they are in real life.

Amelia told us you would like to know about our book society and what we talk about at our meetings. I gave a talk on the Brontë girls once when it was my turn to speak. I'm sorry I can't send you my notes on Charlotte and Emily – I used them to kindle a fire in my stove – there being no other paper in the house. I'd already burnt up my tide tables, the Book of Revelation and the story about Job.

You will want to know why I admired those girls. I like stories of passionate encounters. I myself have never had one, but now I can picture one. I didn't like *Wuthering Heights* at first, but the minute that spectre Cathy scratched her bony fingers on the windowpane – I was grasped by the throat and not let go. With that Emily I could hear Heathcliff's pitiful cries upon the moors. I don't believe that after reading such a fine writer as Emily Brontë I will be happy to read again Miss Amanda Gillyflower's *Ill-Used by Candlelight*. Reading good books ruins you for enjoying bad books.

I will tell you now about myself. I have a cottage and smallholding next to Mrs Maugery's manor house and farm. We are both situated by the sea. I tend my chickens and my goat, Ariel, and grow things. I have a parrot in my keeping too – her name is Zenobia and she does not like men.

I have a stall at the market every week, where I sell my jam, vegetables and elixirs I make to restore manly ardour. Kit McKenna – daughter to my dear friend Elizabeth McKenna – helps me make my potions. She is only four and has to stand on a stool to stir my pot, but she is able to whip up quite a froth.

I do not have a pleasing appearance. My nose is big and was broken when I fell off the hen-house roof. One eyeball skitters up to the top, and my hair is wild and will not stay tamped down. I am tall and built of big bones.

I could write to you again, if you want me to. I could tell you more about reading and how it perked up our spirits while the Germans were here. The only time reading didn't help was after Elizabeth was arrested by the Germans. They caught her hiding one of those poor slave workers from Poland, and they sent her to prison on the Continent. There was no book that could lift my heart then, nor for a long time afterwards. It was all I could do not to slap every German I saw. For Kit's sake, I held myself in. She was only a little sprout then, and she needed us. Elizabeth hasn't come home yet. We are afraid for her, but mind you, I say it's early days yet and she might still come home. I pray so for I miss her sorely.

Your friend,

Isola Pribby

From Juliet to Dawsey

20th February 1946

Dear Mr Adams,

How did you know that I like white lilac above all flowers? I always have, and now here they are, plumed over my desk. They are beautiful, and I love having them – the appearance, the delicious scent and the surprise of them. At first I thought, How on earth did he find these in February, and then I remembered that the Channel Islands are blessed by a warm Gulf Stream.

Mr Dilwyn appeared at my door with your present early this morning. He said he was in London on business for his bank. He assured me it was no trouble at all to deliver the flowers – there wasn't much he wouldn't do for you because of some soap you gave Mrs Dilwyn during the war. She still cries every time she thinks of it. What a nice man he is – I am sorry he didn't have time for coffee.

Due to your kind offices, I have received lovely long letters from Mrs Maugery and Isola Pribby. I hadn't realised that the Germans permitted *no outside news at all*, not even letters, in Guernsey. It surprised me so much. It shouldn't have – I knew the Channel Islands had been occupied, but I never, not once, thought what that might have entailed. Wilful ignorance is all I can call it. So, I am off to the London Library to educate myself. The Library suffered terrible bomb damage, but the floors are safe to walk on again, all the books that could be saved are back on the shelf, and I know they have collected copies of *The Times* from 1900 to – yesterday. I shall mug up on the Occupation.

I want to find some travel or history books about the Channel Islands too. Is it really true that on a clear day, you can see the cars on the French coast roads? So it says in my encyclopedia, but I bought it second-hand for 4s and I don't trust it. There I also learnt that Guernsey is 'roughly 7 miles long and 5 miles wide, with a population of 42,000'. Strictly speaking, very informative, but I want to know more than that.

Miss Pribby told me that your friend Elizabeth McKenna had been sent to a prison camp on the Continent and has not yet returned. It knocked the wind out of me. Ever since your letter about the roast-pig dinner, I had been imagining her there among you. Without even knowing it, I depended upon one day receiving a letter from her too. I am sorry. I will hope for her early return.

Thank you again for my flowers. It was a lovely thing for you to do.
Yours ever,

Juliet Ashton

P.S. You may consider this a rhetorical question if you want to, but why did Mrs Dilwyn weep over a cake of soap?

From Juliet to Sidney

21st February 1946

Dearest Sidney,

I haven't heard from you for ages. Does your icy silence have anything to do with Mark Reynolds?

I have an idea for a new book. It's a novel about a beautiful yet sensitive author whose spirit is crushed by her domineering editor. Do you like it?

Love always,

Juliet

From Juliet to Sidney

23rd February 1946

Dear Sidney,

I was only joking.
Love,

Juliet

From Juliet to Sidney

25th February 1946

Sidney?
    Love,

    Juliet

From Juliet to Sidney

26th February 1946

Dear Sidney,

Did you think I wouldn't notice you'd gone? I did. After three notes went unanswered, I made a personal visit to St James's Place, where I encountered the iron Miss Tilley, who said you were out of town. Very enlightening. Upon pressing, I learnt that you'd gone to Australia! Miss Tilley listened coolly to my exclamations. She would not disclose your exact whereabouts – only that you were scouring the Outback, seeking new authors for Stephens & Stark's list. She would forward any letters to you, at her discretion.

Your Miss Tilley does not fool me. Nor do you – I know exactly where you are and what you are doing. You flew to Australia to find Piers Langley and are holding his hand while he sobers up. At least, I hope that's what you are doing. He is such a dear friend – and such a brilliant writer. I want him to be well again and writing poetry. I'd add forgetting all about Burma and the Japanese, but I know that's not possible.

You could have told me, you know. I can be discreet when I

51

really try (you've never forgiven me for that slip about Mrs Atwater in the pergola, have you? I apologised handsomely at the time).

I liked your other secretary more. And you sacked her for nothing, you know: Markham Reynolds and I have met. All right, we've done more than meet. We've danced the rumba. But don't fuss. He hasn't mentioned *View*, except in passing, and he hasn't once tried to lure me to New York. We talk of higher matters, such as Victorian literature. He's not the shallow dilettante you would have me believe, Sidney. He's an expert on Wilkie Collins, of all things. Did you know that Wilkie Collins maintained two separate households with two separate mistresses and two separate sets of children? The organisational difficulties must have been shocking. No wonder he took laudanum.

I do think you would like Mark if you knew him better, and you may have to. But my heart and my writing hand belong to Stephens & Stark.

The article for *The Times* has turned into a lovely treat for me – now and ongoing. I have made a group of new friends from the Channel Islands – the Guernsey Literary and Potato Peel Pie Society. Don't you adore their name? If Piers needs distracting, I'll write you a nice fat letter about how they came by their name. If not, I'll tell you when you come home (when are you coming home?).

My neighbour Evangeline Smythe is going to have twins in June. She is none too happy about it, so I am going to ask her to give one of them to me.

Love to you and Piers,

Juliet

From Juliet to Sophie

28th February 1946

Dearest Sophie,

I am as surprised as you are. He didn't breathe a word to me. On Tuesday, I realised I hadn't heard from Sidney for days, so I went to Stephens & Stark to demand attention and found he'd flown the coop. That new secretary of his is a fiend. To every one of my questions, she said, 'I really can't divulge information of a personal nature, Miss Ashton.' How I wanted to slap her.

Just as I was on the verge of concluding that Sidney had been approached by MI6 and was on a mission in Siberia, horrible Miss Tilley admitted that he'd gone to Australia. Well, it all came clear then, didn't it? He's gone to get Piers. Teddy Lucas seemed quite certain that Piers was going to drink himself steadily to death in that rest home unless someone came and stopped him. I can hardly blame him, after what he's been through – but Sidney won't allow it, thank God.

You know I adore Sidney with all my heart, but there's something terrifically freeing about Sidney *in Australia*. Mark Reynolds has been what your Aunt Lydia would have called persistent in his attentions for the last three weeks, but, even as I've gobbled lobster and guzzled champagne, I've been looking furtively over my shoulder for Sidney. He's convinced that Mark is trying to steal me away from London in general and Stephens & Stark in particular, and nothing I said could persuade him otherwise. I know he doesn't like Mark – I believe aggressive and unscrupulous were the words he used last time I saw him – but really, he was a bit too King Lear about the whole thing. I am a grown woman – mostly – and I can guzzle champagne with whomever I choose.

When not checking under tablecloths for Sidney, I've been having the most wonderful time. I feel as though I've emerged from a black tunnel and found myself in the middle of a carnival. I don't particularly care for carnivals, but after the tunnel, it's delicious. Mark gads about every night – if we're not going to a party (and we usually are), we're off to the cinema, or the theatre, or a nightclub, or a gin house of ill-repute (he says he's trying to introduce me to democratic ideals). It's very exciting.

Have you noticed there are some people – Americans especially – who seem untouched by the war, or at least unmangled by it? I don't mean to imply that Mark was a shirker – he was in their Air Corps – but he's simply not sunk under. And when I'm with him, I feel untouched by the war, too. It's an illusion, I know it is, and truthfully I'd be ashamed of myself if the war hadn't touched me. But it's forgivable to enjoy myself a little – isn't it?

Is Dominic too old for a jack-in-the-box? I saw a diabolical one in a shop yesterday. It pops out, leering and waving, its oily black moustache curling above pointed white teeth, the very picture of a villain. Dominic would adore it, after he had got over his first shock.

Love,

Juliet

From Juliet to Isola

Miss Isola Pribby
Pribby Homestead
La Bouvée
St Martin's, Guernsey

28th February 1946

Dear Miss Pribby,

Thank you so much for your letter about yourself and Emily Brontë. I laughed when I read that Emily had caught you by the throat the second poor Cathy's ghost knocked at the window. She got me at *exactly the same moment.*

Our teacher had assigned *Wuthering Heights* to be read over the Easter holidays. I went home with my friend Sophie Stark, and we whined for two days over the injustice of it all. Finally her brother Sidney told us to shut up and *get on with it.* I did, still fuming, until I got to Cathy's ghost at the window. I have never felt such dread as I did then. Monsters or vampires have never scared me in books – but ghosts are a different matter.

Sophie and I did nothing for the rest of the holidays but move from bed to hammock to armchair, reading *Jane Eyre, Agnes Grey, Shirley*, and *The Tenant of Wildfell Hall.*

What a family they were – but I chose to write about Anne Brontë because she was the least known of the sisters, and, I think, just as fine a writer as Charlotte. God knows how Anne managed to write any books at all, influenced by such a strain of religion as her Aunt Branwell possessed. Emily and Charlotte had the good sense to ignore their bleak aunt, but not poor Anne. Imagine preaching that God meant women to be Meek, Mild, and Gently Melancholic. So much less trouble around the house – pernicious old bat!

I hope you will write to me again.

Yours,

Juliet Ashton

From Eben Ramsey to Juliet

28th February 1946

Dear Miss Ashton,

I am a Guernsey man and my name is Eben Ramsey. My fathers before me were tombstone cutters and carvers – lambs a speciality.

These are things I like to do of an evening, but for my livelihood, I fish.

Mrs Maugery said you would like to have letters about our reading during the Occupation. I was never going to talk – or think, if I could help it – about those days, but Mrs Maugery said we could trust to your judgement in writing about the Society during the war. If Mrs Maugery says you can be trusted, I believe it. Also, you had the kindness to send my friend Dawsey a book – and he all but unknown to you. So I am writing to you and hope it will be a help to your story.

Best to say we weren't a true literary society at first. Apart from Elizabeth, Mrs Maugery, and perhaps Booker, most of us hadn't had much to do with books since school. We took them from Mrs Maugery's shelves fearful we'd spoil the fine paper. I had no zest for such matters in those days. It was only by fixing my mind on the Commandant and jail that I could make myself lift the cover of the book and begin. It was called *Selections from Shakespeare*. Later, I came to see that Mr Dickens and Mr Wordsworth were thinking of men like me when they wrote their words. But most of all, I believe that William Shakespeare was. Mind you, I cannot always make sense of what he says, but it will come.

It seems to me the less he said, the more beauty he made. Do you know what sentence of his I admire the most? It is, 'The bright day is done, and we are for the dark.' I wish I'd known those words on the day I watched those German troops land, planeload after planeload of them – and come off ships down in the harbour! All I could think of was, *Damn them, damn them*, over and over again. If I could have thought the words, 'The bright day is done, and we are for the dark,' I'd have been consoled somehow and ready to go out and contend with circumstance – instead of my heart sinking to my shoes.

They came here on Sunday the 30th of June 1940, after bombing us two days before. They said they hadn't meant to bomb us; they mistook our tomato lorries on the pier for army trucks. How they came to think that strains the mind. They bombed us, killing some thirty men, women, and children – one among them was my cousin's boy. He had sheltered underneath his lorry when he first saw the planes dropping bombs, and it exploded and caught fire. They killed men in their lifeboats at sea. They strafed the Red Cross ambulances carrying our wounded. When no one shot back at them, they saw the British had left us undefended. They just flew in peaceably two days later and occupied us for five years.

At first, they were as nice as could be. They were that full of themselves for conquering a bit of England, and they were thick enough to think it would just be a hop and a skip till they landed in London. When they found out that wasn't to be, they turned back to their natural meanness.

They had rules for everything – do this, don't do that, but they kept changing their minds; trying to seem friendly, like they were poking a carrot in front of a donkey's nose. But we weren't donkeys. So they'd get harsh again. For instance, they were always changing curfew – eight at night, or nine, or five in the evening if they felt really mean-minded. You couldn't visit your friends or even tend your stock.

We started out hopeful, sure they'd be gone in six months. But it stretched on and on. Food grew hard to come by, and soon there was no firewood left. Days were grey with hard work and evenings were black with boredom. Everyone was sickly from so little nourishment and bleak from wondering if it would ever end. We clung to books and to our friends; they reminded us that we had another part to us. Elizabeth used to say a poem. I don't remember all of it, but it began, 'Is it so small a thing to have enjoyed the sun, to have lived light in the spring, to have loved, to have thought, to have done, to have advanced true friends?' It isn't. I hope, wherever she is, she has that in her mind.

Late in 1944, it didn't matter what time the Germans set the curfew for. Most people went to bed around five o'clock anyway to keep warm. We were rationed to two candles a week and then only one. It was very tedious, lying in bed with no light to read by.

After D-Day, the Germans couldn't send any supply ships from France because of the Allied bombers. So they were finally as hungry as we were – and killing dogs and cats to give themselves something to eat. They would raid our gardens, rooting up potatoes – even eating the black rotten ones. Four soldiers died eating handfuls of hemlock, thinking it was parsley.

The German officers said that any soldier caught stealing food from our gardens would be shot. One poor soldier was caught stealing a potato. He was chased by his own people and climbed up a tree to hide. But they found him and shot him down out of the tree. Still, that did not stop them from stealing food. I am not pointing a finger at those practices, because some of us were doing the same. I think hunger makes you desperate when you wake to it every morning.

My grandson Eli was evacuated to England when he was seven. He is home now – twelve years old, and tall – but I will never forgive the Germans for making me miss his childhood.

I must go and milk my cow now, but I will write to you again if you like.

I wish you good health,

Eben Ramsey

From Miss Adelaide Addison to Juliet

1st March 1946

Dear Miss Ashton,

Forgive the presumption of a letter from a person unknown to you. But a clear duty is imposed upon me. I understand from Dawsey Adams that you are to write a long article for *The Times* on the value of reading and you intend to feature the Guernsey Literary and Potato Peel Pie Society therein.

I laugh.

Perhaps you will reconsider when you learn that their founder,

Elizabeth McKenna, is not even an Islander. Despite her fine airs, she is merely a jumped-up servant from the London home of Sir Ambrose Ivers, RA (Royal Academy). Surely, you know of him. He is a portrait painter of some note, though I've never understood why. His portrait of the Countess of Lambeth as Boadicea, lashing her horses, was unforgivable. In any event, Elizabeth McKenna was the daughter of his housekeeper, if you please.

While Elizabeth's mother dusted, Sir Ambrose let the child potter around in his studio, and he kept her at school long after the normal leaving time for one of her station. Her mother died when Elizabeth was fourteen. Did Sir Ambrose send her to an institution to be properly trained for a suitable occupation? He did not. He kept her with him in his home in Chelsea. He proposed her for a scholarship to the Slade School of Fine Art.

Mind you, I do not say Sir Ambrose sired the girl – we know his proclivities too well to admit of that – but he doted upon her in a way that encouraged her besetting sin: lack of humility. The decay of standards is the cross of our times, and nowhere is this regrettable decline more apparent than in Elizabeth McKenna.

Sir Ambrose owned a home in Guernsey – on the clifftops near La Bouvée. He, his housekeeper and the girl summered here when she was a child. Elizabeth was a wild thing – roaming unkempt about the island, even on Sundays. No household chores, no gloves, no shoes, no stockings. Going out on fishing boats with rude men. Spying on decent people through her telescope. A disgrace.

When it became clear that the war was going to start in earnest, Sir Ambrose sent Elizabeth to close up his house. Elizabeth bore the brunt of his haphazard ways in this case, for, in the midst of her putting up the shutters, the German army landed on her doorstep. However, the choice to remain here was hers, and, as is proven by certain subsequent events (which I will not demean myself to mention), she is not the selfless heroine that some people seem to think.

Furthermore, the so-called Literary Society is a scandal. There are those of true culture and breeding here in Guernsey, and they will take no part in this charade (even if invited). There are only two respectable people in the Society – Eben Ramsey and Amelia Maugery. The other members: a rag-and-bone man, a lapsed Alienist who drinks, a stuttering swine-herd, a footman posing as a lord, and Isola Pribby, a practising witch, who, by her own admission, distils and sells potions. They collected a few others of their ilk along the way, and one can only imagine their 'literary evenings'.

You must not write about these people and their books – God knows what they saw fit to read!

Yours in Christian Consternation and Concern,

Adelaide Addison (Miss)

From Mark to Juliet

2nd March 1946

Dear Juliet,

I've just appropriated my music critic's opera tickets. Covent Garden at eight. Will you?

Yours,

Mark

From Juliet to Mark

Dear Mark,

  Tonight?

  Juliet

From Mark to Juliet

Yes!

  M.

From Juliet to Mark

Wonderful! I feel sorry for your critic, though. Those tickets are scarce as hens' teeth.

  Juliet

From Mark to Juliet

He'll make do with standing room. He can write about the uplifting effect of opera on the poor, etc., etc.
  I'll pick you up at seven.

  M.

From Juliet to Eben

Mr Eben Ramsey
Les Pommiers
Calais Lane
St Martin's, Guernsey

3rd March 1946

Dear Mr Ramsey,

It was so kind of you to write to me about your experiences during the Occupation. At the war's end, I, too, promised myself that I wouldn't talk about it any more. I had talked and lived war for six years, and I was longing to pay attention to something – anything – else. But that is like wishing I were someone else. The war is now the story of our lives, and there's no denying it.

I was glad to hear about your grandson Eli returning to you. Does he live with you or with his parents? Did you receive no news of him at all during the Occupation? Did all the Guernsey children return at once? What a celebration, if they did!

I don't mean to inundate you with questions, but I have a few more, if you're in an answering frame of mind. I know you were at the roast-pig dinner that led to the founding of the Guernsey Literary and Potato Peel Pie Society – but how did Mrs Maugery come to have the pig in the first place? How does one hide a pig?

Elizabeth McKenna was brave that night! She truly has grace under pressure, a quality that fills me with hopeless admiration. I know you and the other members of the Society must worry as the months pass without word, but you mustn't give up hope. Friends tell me that Europe is like a hive broken open, teeming with thousands upon thousands of displaced people, all trying to get home. A dear old friend of mine, who was shot down in Burma in

1943, reappeared in Australia last month – not in the best of shape, but alive and intending to remain so.

Thank you for your letter.

Yours sincerely,

Juliet Ashton

From Clovis Fossey to Juliet

4th March 1946

Dear Miss,

At first, I did not want to go to any book meetings. My farm is a lot of work, and I did not want to spend my time reading about people who never were, doing things they never did.

Then in 1942 I started to court the Widow Hubert. When we'd go for a walk, she'd march a few steps ahead of me on the path and never let me take her arm. She let Ralph Murchey take her arm, so I knew I was failing in my suit. Ralph, he's a bragger when he drinks, and he said to all in the tavern, 'Women like poetry. A soft word in their ears and they melt – a grease spot on the grass.' That's no way to talk about a lady, and I knew right then he didn't want the Widow Hubert for her own self, the way I did. He wanted only her grazing land for his cows. So I thought, If it's rhymes the Widow Hubert wants, I will find me some.

I went to see Mr Fox in his bookshop and asked for some love poetry. He didn't have many books left by that time – people bought them to burn, and when he finally caught on, he closed his shop for good – so he gave me some fellow named Catullus. He was a Roman. Do you know the kind of things he said in verse? I knew I couldn't say those words to a nice lady.

He did hanker after one woman, Lesbia, who spurned him after taking him into her bed. I don't wonder she did so – he did not like it when she petted her downy little sparrow. Jealous of a little bird, he was. He went home and took up his pen to write of his anguish at seeing her cuddle the little birdy to her bosom. He took it hard, and he never liked women after that and wrote mean poems about them.

He was a tight one too. Do you want to see a poem he wrote when a fallen woman charged him for her favours – poor lass. I will copy it out for you.

Is that battered strumpet in her senses, who asks me for a thousand sesterces?
That girl with the nasty nose?
Ye kinsmen to whom the care of the girl belongs,
Call together friends and physicians; the girl is insane.
She thinks she is pretty.

Those are love tokens? I told my friend Eben I never saw such spiteful stuff. He said to me I had just not read the right poets. He took me into his cottage and lent me a little book of his own. It was the poetry of Wilfred Owen. He was an officer in the First World War, and he knew what was what and called it by its right name. I was there, too, at Passchendaele, and I knew what he knew, but I could never put it into words for myself.

Well, after that, I thought there might be something to this poetry after all. I began to go to meetings, and I'm glad I did, else how would I have read the works of William Wordsworth – he would have stayed unknown to me. I learnt many of his poems by heart.

Anyway, I did win the hand of the Widow Hubert – my Nancy. I got her to go for a walk along the cliffs one evening, and I said, 'Lookie there, Nancy. The gentleness of Heaven broods o'er the sea – Listen, the mighty Being is awake.' She let me kiss her. She is now my wife.

Yours truly,

Clovis Fossey

P.S. Mrs Maugery lent me a book last week. It's called *The Oxford Book of Modern Verse, 1892–1935*. They let a man named Yeats make the choosings. They shouldn't have. Who is he – and what does he know about verse?

I hunted all through that book for poems by Wilfred Owen or Siegfried Sassoon. There weren't any – not one. And do you know why not? Because this Mr Yeats said – he said, 'I deliberately chose NOT to include any poems from World War I. I have a distaste for them. Passive suffering is not a theme for poetry.'

Passive Suffering? Passive Suffering! I could have hit him. What ailed the man? Lieutenant Owen, he wrote a line, 'What passing-bells for these who die as cattle? Only the monstrous anger of the guns.' What's passive about that, I'd like to know? That's exactly how they do die. I saw it with my own eyes, and I say to hell with Mr Yeats.

From Eben to Juliet

10th March 1946

Dear Miss Ashton,

Thank you for your letter and your kind questions about my grandson, Eli. He is the child of my daughter, Jane. Jane and her newborn baby died in hospital on the day that the Germans bombed us, the 28th of June, 1940. Eli's father was killed in North Africa in 1942, so I have Eli in my keeping now.

Eli left Guernsey on the 20th of June along with the thousands of babies and schoolchildren who were evacuated to England. We knew the Germans were coming and Jane worried for his safety here. The doctor would not let Jane sail with the children, the baby's birth being so close.

We did not have any news of the children for six months. Then I got a postcard from the Red Cross, saying Eli was well, but not where he was situated – we never knew what towns our children were in, though we prayed not in a big city. An even longer time passed before I could send him a card in return, but I was of two minds about that. I dreaded telling him that his mother and the baby had died. I hated to think of my boy reading those cold words on the back of a postcard. But I had to do it. And then a second time, after I got word about his father.

Eli did not come back until the war was over – and they did send all the children home at once. That was a day! More wonderful even than when the British soldiers came to liberate Guernsey. Eli, he was the first boy down the gangway – he'd grown long legs in five years – and I don't think I could have stopped hugging him, if Isola hadn't pushed me a bit so she could hug him herself.

I bless God that he was boarded with a farming family in Yorkshire. They were very good to him. Eli gave me a letter they had written to me – it was full of all the things I had missed. They told of his schooling, how he helped on the farm, how he tried to be steadfast when he got my postcards.

He fishes with me and helps me tend my cow and garden, but carving wood is what he likes best – Dawsey and I are teaching him how to do it. He fashioned a fine snake from a bit of broken fence last week, though it's my guess that the bit of broken fence was really a rafter from Dawsey's barn. Dawsey just smiled when I asked him about it, but spare wood is hard to find on the island now, as we had to cut down most of the trees – banisters and furniture, too – for firewood when there was no more coal or paraffin left. Eli and I are planting trees on my land now, but it is going to take a long time for them to grow – and we do all miss the leaves and shade.

I will tell you now about our roast pig. The Germans were fussy over farm animals. Pigs and cows were kept strict count of. Guernsey was to feed the German troops stationed here and in France. We ourselves could have what was left, if there was any.

How the Germans did fuss about book-keeping. They kept track of every gallon we milked, weighed the cream, recorded every sack of flour. They left the chickens alone for a while. But when feed and scraps became so scarce they ordered us to kill off the older chickens, so the good layers could have enough feed to keep on laying eggs.

We fishermen had to give them the largest share of our catch. They would meet our boats in the harbour to portion out their share. Early in the Occupation, a good many Islanders escaped to England in fishing boats – some drowned, but some made it. So the Germans made a new rule, any person who had a family member in England would not be allowed in a fishing boat – they were afraid we'd try to escape. Since Eli was somewhere in England, I had to lend out my boat. I went to work in one of Mr Privot's greenhouses, and after a time, I got so I could tend the plants well. But goodness, how I did miss my boat and the sea.

The Germans were especially fretful about meat because they didn't want any to go to the Black Market instead of feeding their own soldiers. If your sow had a litter, the German Agricultural Officer would come to your farm, count the piglets, give you a birth certificate for each one, and mark his record book. If a pig died a natural death, you told the AO and out he'd come again, look at the dead body, and give you a death certificate.

They would make surprise visits to your farm, and your number of living pigs had better tally with their number of living pigs. One pig less and you were fined, one time more and you could be arrested and sent to jail in St Peter Port. If too many pigs went missing, the Germans thought you were selling on the Black Market, and you were sent to a labour camp in Germany. With the Germans you never knew which way they'd blow – they were a moody people. In the beginning, though, it was easy to fool the Agricultural Officer and keep a secret live pig for your own use. This is how Mrs Maugery came to have hers.

Will Thisbee had a sickly pig who died. The AO came out and wrote a certificate saying the pig was truly dead and left Will alone to bury the poor animal. But Will didn't – he raced off through the wood with the little body and gave it to Mrs Maugery. She hid her own healthy pig and called the AO saying, 'Come quickly, my pig has died.'

The AO came out straight away and, seeing the pig with its toes turned up, never knew it was the same pig he'd seen earlier that morning. He inscribed his dead-animal book with one more dead pig.

Mrs Maugery took the same carcass over to another friend, and he pulled the same trick the next day. We could do this till the pig turned rank. The Germans caught on finally and began to tattoo each pig and cow at birth, so there was no more dead-animal swapping. But Mrs Maugery, with a live, hidden, fat and healthy pig, needed only Dawsey to come to kill it quietly. It had to be done quietly because there was a German battery by her farm, and it would not do for the soldiers to hear the pig's death squeal and come running.

Pigs have always been drawn to Dawsey – he could come into a yard, and they would rush up to him and have their backs scratched. They'd make racket for anyone else – squealing and snuffling and plunging about. But Dawsey, he could soothe them and he knew just the right spot under their chins to slip his knife in quick. There wasn't time for the pigs to squeal; they'd just slide quietly on to the ground. I told Dawsey they only looked up once in surprise, but he said no, pigs were bright enough to know betrayal when they met it, and I wasn't to whitewash matters.

Mrs Maugery's pig made us a fine dinner – there were onions and potatoes to fill out the roast. We had almost forgotten what it felt like to have full stomachs, but it came back to us. With the curtains closed against the sight of the German battery, and food and friends at the table, we could make believe that none of it had happened.

You are right to call Elizabeth brave. She is that, and always was. She came from London to Guernsey as a little girl with her mother and Sir Ambrose Ivers. She met my Jane her first summer here, when they were both ten, and they were ever staunch to one another since then.

When Elizabeth came back in the spring of 1940 to close up Sir Ambrose's house, she stayed longer than was safe, because she wanted to stand by Jane. My girl had been feeling poorly since her husband John went to England to sign up – that was in December 1939 – and she had a difficult time holding on to the baby till her time came. Dr Martin ordered her to bed, so Elizabeth stayed on to keep her company and play with Eli. Nothing Eli liked more than to play with Elizabeth. They were a threat to the furniture, but it was good to hear them laugh. I went over once to collect the two of them for supper and when I stepped in, there they were – sprawled on a pile of pillows at the foot of the staircase. They had polished Sir Ambrose's fine oak banister and come sailing down three floors!

It was Elizabeth who did what was needed to get Eli on the evacuation ship. We Islanders were given only one day's notice when the ships were coming from England to take the children away. Elizabeth worked like a whirligig, washing and sewing Eli's clothes and helping him to understand why he could not take his pet rabbit with him. When we set out for the school, Jane had to turn away so as not to show Eli a tearful face at parting, so Elizabeth took him by the hand and said it was good weather for a sea voyage.

Even after that, Elizabeth wouldn't leave Guernsey when every-one else was trying to get away. 'No,' she said. 'I'll wait for Jane's baby to come, and, when she's fattened up enough, then she and Jane and I will go to London. Then we'll find out where Eli is and go and get him.' For all her winning ways, Elizabeth was wilful. She'd stick out that jaw of hers and you could see it wasn't any use arguing with her about leaving. Not even when we could all see the smoke coming from Cherbourg, where the French were burning up their fuel tanks, so the Germans couldn't have them. But, no matter, Elizabeth wouldn't go without Jane and the baby. I think Sir Ambrose had told her he and one of his yachting friends could sail right into St Peter Port and take them off Guernsey before the Germans came. To tell the truth, I was glad she did not leave us. She was with me at the hospital when Jane and her new baby died. She sat by Jane, holding on hard to her hand.

After Jane died, Elizabeth and me, we stood in the hallway, numb and staring out of the window. It was then we saw seven German planes come in low over the harbour. They were just on one of the reconnaissance flights, we thought – but then they began dropping bombs – they tumbled from the sky like sticks. We didn't speak, but I know what we were thinking – thank God Eli was safely away.

Elizabeth stood by Jane and me in the bad time, and afterwards. I was not able to stand by Elizabeth, so I thank God her daughter Kit is safe and with us, and I pray for Elizabeth to come home soon.

I was glad to hear of your friend who was found in Australia. I hope you will correspond with me and Dawsey again, as he enjoys hearing from you as much as I do myself.

Yours sincerely,

Eben Ramsey

From Dawsey to Juliet

12th March 1946

Dear Miss Ashton,

I am glad you liked the white lilacs.

I will tell you about Mrs Dilwyn's soap. Around about the middle of the Occupation, soap became scarce; families were only allowed one tablet per person a month. It was made of some kind of French clay and lay like a dead thing in the washtub. It made no lather – you just had to scrub and hope it worked.

Being clean was hard work, and we had all got used to being more or less dirty, along with our clothes. We were allowed a tiny bit of soap powder for dishes and clothes, but it was a laughable amount; no bubbles there either. Some of the ladies felt it keenly, and Mrs Dilwyn was one of those. Before the war, she had bought her dresses in Paris, and those fancy clothes went to ruins faster than the plain kind.

One day, Mr Scope's pig died of milk fever. Because no one dared eat it, Mr Scope offered me the carcass. I remembered my mother making soap from fat, so I thought I could try it. It came out looking like frozen dishwater and smelling worse. So I melted it all down and started again. Booker, who had come over to help, suggested paprika for colour and cinnamon for scent. Mrs Maugery let us have some of each, and we put it in the mix.

When the soap had hardened enough, we cut it into circles with Mrs Maugery's biscuit cutter. I wrapped the soap in cheesecloth, Elizabeth tied bows of red yarn, and we gave it as presents to all the ladies at the Society's next meeting. For a week or two, anyway, we looked like respectable people.

I am working several days a week now at the quarry, as well as at the port. Isola thought I looked tired and mixed up a balm for aching muscles – it's called Angel Fingers. Isola has a cough syrup called Devil's Suck and I pray I'll never need it.

Yesterday, Mrs Maugery and Kit came over for supper, and we took a blanket down to the beach afterwards to watch the moon rise. Kit loves doing that, but she always falls asleep before it is fully risen, and I carry her home. She is certain she'll be able to stay awake all night as soon as she's five.

Do you know much about children? I don't, and although I am learning, I think I am a slow learner. It was much easier before Kit learnt to talk, but it was not so much fun. I try to answer her questions, but I am usually behindhand and she has moved on to a new question before I can answer the first. Also, I don't know enough to please her. I don't know what a mongoose looks like.

I like getting your letters, but I often feel I don't have any news worth telling, so it is good to answer your rhetorical questions.

Yours,

Dawsey Adams

12th March 1946

Dear Miss Ashton,

I see you will not be advised by me. I came upon Isola Pribby at her market stall, scribbling a letter – in response to a letter from you! I tried to resume my errands calmly, but then I came upon Dawsey Adams posting a letter – to you! Who will be next, I ask? This is not to be borne, and I seize my pen to stop you.

I was not completely candid with you in my last letter. In the interests of delicacy, I drew a veil on the true nature of that group and their founder, Elizabeth McKenna. But now, I see that I must reveal all: The Society members have colluded to raise the bastard child of Elizabeth McKenna and her German paramour, Dr/ Captain Christian Hellman. Yes, a German soldier! I don't wonder at your shock.

Now, I am nothing if not just. I do not say that Elizabeth was what the ruder classes called a Jerry-bag, cavorting around Guernsey with *any* German soldier who could give her gifts. I never saw Elizabeth wearing silk stockings or silk dresses (indeed, her clothing was as disreputable as ever), smelling of Parisian scent, guzzling chocolates and wine, or SMOKING CIGARETTES, like other Island hussies.

But the truth is bad enough.

Herewith, the sorry facts: in April 1942, the UNWED Elizabeth McKenna gave birth to a baby girl – in her own cottage. Eben Ramsey and Isola Pribby were present at the birth – he to hold the mother's hand and she to keep the fire going. Amelia Maugery and Dawsey Adams (An unmarried man! For shame!) did the actual work of delivering the child, before Dr Martin could arrive. The putative father? Absent! In fact, he had left the Island a short time before. 'Ordered to duty on the Continent' – SO THEY SAID. The case is perfectly clear – when the evidence of their illicit connection was irrefutable, Captain Hellman abandoned his mistress and left her to her just deserts.

I could have foretold this scandalous outcome. I saw Elizabeth with her lover on several occasions – walking together, deep in talk, gathering nettles for soup, or collecting firewood. And once, I saw him put his hand on her face and follow her cheekbone down with his thumb.

Though I had little hope of success, I knew it was my duty to warn her of the fate that awaited her. I told her she would be cast out of decent society, but she did not heed me. In fact, she laughed. I bore it. Then she told me to get out of her house.

I take no pride in my prescience. It would not be Christian.

Back to the baby – named Christina, called Kit. Barely a year later, Elizabeth, as feckless as ever, committed a criminal act expressly forbidden by the German Occupying Force – she helped shelter and feed an escaped prisoner of the German Army. She was arrested and sentenced to prison on the Continent.

Mrs Maugery, at the time of Elizabeth's arrest, took the baby into her home. And since that night? The Literary Society has raised that child as its own – passing her around from house to house. The principal work of the baby's maintenance was undertaken by Amelia Maugery, with other Society members taking her out – like a library book – for several weeks at a time.

They all cosseted the baby, and now that the child can walk, she goes everywhere with one or another of them – holding hands or riding on their shoulders. Such are their standards! You must not glorify such people in *The Times*!

You won't hear from me again – I have done my best. On your head be it.

Adelaide Addison

Cable from Sidney to Juliet

20th March 1946

Dear Juliet, Trip home delayed. Fell off horse, broke leg. Piers nursing. Love, Sidney

Cable from Juliet to Sidney

21st March 1946

Oh, God, which leg? Am so sorry. Love, Juliet

Cable from Sidney to Juliet

22nd March 1946

It was the other one. Don't worry – little pain. Piers excellent nurse. Love, Sidney

Cable from Juliet to Sidney

22nd March 1946

So happy it wasn't the one I broke. Can I send anything to help your convalescence? Books – recordings – poker chips – my life's blood?

Cable from Sidney to Juliet

23rd March 1946

No blood, no books, no poker chips. Just keep sending long letters to entertain us. Love, Sidney and Piers

From Juliet to Sophie

23rd March 1946

Dear Sophie,

I only got a cable so you know more than I do. But whatever the circumstances, it's absolutely ridiculous for you to consider flying off to Australia. What about Alexander? And Dominic? And your lambs? They'll pine away.

Stop and think for a moment, and you'll realise why you shouldn't fuss. First, Piers will take excellent care of Sidney. Second, better Piers than us – remember what a vile patient Sidney was last time? We should be glad he's thousands of miles away. Third, Sidney has been stretched as tight as a bow-string for years. He needs a rest, and breaking his leg is probably the only way he'll allow himself to take one. Most important of all, Sophie: *he doesn't want us there.*

I'm perfectly certain Sidney would prefer me to write a new book than to appear at his bedside in Australia, so I intend to stay right here in my dreary flat and cast about for a subject. I do have a tiny infant of an idea, much too frail and defenceless to risk describing, even to you. In honour of Sidney's leg, I'm going to nurse it and feed it and see if I can make it grow.

Now, about Markham V. Reynolds (Junior). Your questions regarding that gentleman are very delicate, very subtle, very much like being struck on the head by a mallet. Am I in love with him? What kind of a question is that? It's a tuba among the flutes, and I expect better of you. The first rule of snooping is to come at it sideways – when you began writing me dizzy letters about Alexander, I didn't ask if you were in love with him, I asked what his favourite animal was. And your answer told me everything I needed to know about him – how many men would admit that they loved ducks? (This brings up an important point: I don't know what Mark's favourite animal is. I doubt if it's a duck.)

Would you care for a few suggestions? You could ask me who his favourite author is (Dos Passos! Hemingway!!). Or his favourite colour (blue, not sure what shade, probably royal). Is he a good dancer? (Yes, far better than I, never steps on my toes, but doesn't talk or even hum while dancing. Doesn't hum at all as far as I know.) Does he have brothers or sisters? (Yes, two older sisters, one married to a sugar baron and the other widowed last year. Plus one younger brother, dismissed with a sneer as an ass.)

So – now that I've done all your work for you, perhaps you can answer your own ridiculous question, because I can't. I feel addled when I'm with Mark, which might be love but might not. It certainly isn't restful. I'm rather dreading this evening, for instance. Another dinner party, very brilliant, with men leaning across the table to make a point and women gesturing with their cigarette holders. Oh dear, I want to nuzzle into my sofa, but I have to get up and put on an evening dress. Love aside, Mark is a terrible strain on my wardrobe.

Now, darling, don't fret about Sidney. He'll be stalking around in no time.

Love,

Juliet

25th March 1946

Dear Mr Adams,

I have received a long letter (two, in fact!) from a Miss Adelaide Addison, warning me not to write about the Society in my article. If I do, she will wash her hands of me for ever. I will try to bear that affliction with fortitude. She does work up quite a head of steam about Jerry-bags, doesn't she?

I have also had a wonderful long letter from Clovis Fossey about poetry, and one from Isola Pribby about the Brontë sisters. Apart from delighting me – they gave me brand-new thoughts for my article. Between them, you, Mr Ramsey and Mrs Maugery, Guernsey is virtually writing my article for me. Even Miss Adelaide Addison has done her bit – defying her will be such a pleasure.

I don't know as much about children as I would like to. I am the godmother to a marvellous three-year-old boy named Dominic, the son of my friend Sophie. They live in Scotland, near Oban, and I don't see him very often. I am always astonished, when I do, by his increasing personhood – no sooner had I got used to carrying a warm lump of baby than he stopped being one and started rushing around on his own. I missed six months, and lo and behold, he learnt how to talk! Now he talks to himself, which I find terribly endearing, as I do, too.

A mongoose, you may tell Kit, is a weaselly-looking creature with very sharp teeth and a bad temper. It is the only natural enemy of the cobra and is impervious to snake venom. Failing snakes, it snacks on scorpions. Perhaps you could get her one for a pet.

Yours,

Juliet Ashton

P.S. I had second thoughts about sending this letter – what if Adelaide Addison is a friend of yours? Then I decided no, she couldn't possibly be – so off it goes.

From John Booker to Juliet

27th March 1946

Dear Miss Ashton,

Amelia Maugery has asked me to write to you, because I am a founding member of the Guernsey Literary and Potato Peel Pie Society – though I only read one book over and over again. It was *The Letters of Seneca: Translated from Latin in One Volume, with Appendix.* Seneca and the Society, between them, kept me from the direful life of a drunk.

From 1940 to 1944, I pretended to the German authorities that I was Lord Tobias Penn-Piers – my former employer, who had fled to England in a frenzy when Guernsey was bombed. I was his valet and I stayed. My true name is John Booker, and I was born and bred in London.

With the others, I was caught out after curfew on the night of the pig roast. I can't remember it with any clarity. I expect I was tipsy, because I usually was. I recall soldiers shouting and waving guns about and Dawsey holding me upright. Then came Elizabeth's voice. She was talking about books – I couldn't fathom why. After that, Dawsey was pulling me through a field at great speed, and then I fell into bed. That's all.

But you want to know about the influence of books on my life, and as I've said, there was only one. Seneca. Do you know who he was? He was a Roman philosopher who wrote letters to imaginary friends telling them how to behave for the rest of their lives. Maybe that sounds dull, but the letters aren't –

they're witty. I think you learn more if you're laughing at the same time.

It seems to me that his words travel well – to all men in all times. I will give you an example: the Luftwaffe and their hairdos. During the Blitz, the Luftwaffe took off from Guernsey and joined in with the big bombers on their way to London. They only flew at night so their days were their own, to spend in St Peter Port as they liked. And how did they spend them? In beauty parlours: having their nails buffed, their faces massaged, their eyebrows shaped, their hair waved and coiffed. When I saw them in their hairnets, walking five abreast down the street, elbowing Islanders off the pavement, I thought of Seneca's words about the praetorian guard. He'd written, 'who of those would not rather see Rome disordered than his hair?'

I will tell you how I came to pretend to be my former employer. Lord Tobias wanted to sit out the war in a safe place, so he purchased La Fort manor in Guernsey. He had spent World War I in the Caribbean but had suffered greatly from prickly heat there. In the spring of 1940, he moved to La Fort with most of his possessions, including Lady Tobias. Chausey, his London butler, had locked himself in the pantry and refused to come. So I, his valet, came in Chausey's stead, to supervise the placing of his furniture, the hanging of his curtains, the polishing of his silver, and *the stocking of his wine cellar.* It was there I bedded each bottle, gentle as a baby to its cot, in its little rack.

Just as the last picture was being hung on the wall, the German planes flew over and bombed St Peter Port. Lord Tobias, panicking at all the racket, called the captain of his yacht and ordered him, 'Get ready the ship!' We were to load the boat with his silver, his paintings, his bibelots, and, if enough room, Lady Tobias, and set sail at once for England. I was the last one up the gangway, with Lord Tobias screaming, 'Hurry up, man! Hurry up, the Huns are coming!'

My true destiny struck me at that moment, Miss Ashton. I still had the key to his Lordship's wine cellar. I thought of all those bottles of wine, champagne, brandy, cognac that had been left behind – and pictured myself alone with them. I thought of no more bells, no more livery, no more Lord Tobias. In fact, *no more being in service at all.*

I turned my back on him and quickly walked down the gangway. I ran up the road to La Fort and watched the yacht sail away, Lord Tobias still screaming. Then I went inside, laid a fire, and stepped into the wine cellar. I took down a bottle of claret and drew my first cork. I let the wine breathe. Then I returned to the library, sipped, and began to read *The Wine-Lover's Companion.* I read about grapes, tended the garden, slept in silk pyjamas – and drank wine. And so it went until September when Mrs Maugery and Elizabeth McKenna came to call on me. Elizabeth I knew slightly – she and I had chatted several times at the market – but Mrs Maugery was a stranger to me. Were they going to turn me in to the constable? I wondered.

No. They were there to warn me. The Commandant of Guernsey had ordered all Jews to report to the Grange Lodge Hotel and register. According to the Commandant, our ID cards would merely be marked *Juden* and then we were free to go home. Elizabeth knew my mother was Jewish; I had mentioned it once. They had come to tell me that I must not, under any circumstances, go to the Grange Lodge Hotel.

But that wasn't all. Elizabeth had considered my predicament thoroughly (more thoroughly than I) and made a plan. As all Islanders were to have identity cards anyway, why couldn't I declare myself to be Lord Tobias Penn-Piers himself? I could claim that, as a visitor, all my documents had been left behind in my London bank. Mrs Maugery was sure Mr Dilwyn would be happy to back up my impersonation, and he was. He and Mrs Maugery went with me to the Commandant's Office, and we all swore that I was Lord Tobias Penn-Piers.

It was Elizabeth who came up with the finishing touch. The Germans were taking over all Guernsey's grand houses for their officers to live in, and they wouldn't ignore a residence like La Fort – it was too good to miss. And when they came, I must be ready for them as Lord Tobias Penn-Piers. I must look like a lord of leisure and act at ease. I was terrified.

'Nonsense,' said Elizabeth. 'You have presence, Booker. You're tall, dark, handsome, and all valets know how to look down their noses.'

She decided that she would quickly paint my portrait as a sixteenth-century Penn-Piers. So I posed in a velvet cloak and ruff, seated against a background of dark tapestries and dim shadows, fingering my dagger. I looked Noble, Aggrieved and Treasonous.

It was a masterly stroke, for, not two weeks later, a body of German officers (six in all) appeared in my library – without knocking. I received them there, sipping a Château Margaux 1893 and bearing an uncanny resemblance to the portrait of my 'ancestor' hanging above me over the mantelpiece.

They bowed to me and were all politeness, which did not prevent them from taking over the house and moving me into the gatekeeper's cottage the very next day. Eben and Dawsey slipped over after curfew that night and helped me carry most of the wine down to the cottage, where we cleverly hid it behind the woodpile, down the well, up the chimney, under the haystack and above the rafters. But even so, I still ran out of wine by early 1941. A sad day, but I had friends to help distract me – and then, then I found Seneca.

I came to love our book meetings – they helped to make the Occupation bearable. Some of their books sounded all right, but I stayed true to Seneca. I came to feel that he was talking to me – in his funny, biting way – but talking only to me. His letters helped to keep me alive in what was to come later.

I still go to all our Society meetings. Everyone is sick of Seneca, and they are begging me to read someone else. But I won't do it. I also act in plays that one of our repertory companies puts on – impersonating Lord Tobias gave me a taste for acting, and besides, I am tall, loud and can be heard in the back row.

I am glad the war is over, and I am John Booker again.

Yours truly,

John Booker

From Juliet to Sidney and Piers

Mr Sidney Stark
Monreagle Hotel
Broadmeadows Avenue, 79
Melbourne
Victoria
Australia

31st March 1946

Dear Sidney and Piers,

No life's blood – just sprained thumbs from copying out the enclosed letters from my new friends in Guernsey. I love their letters and could not bear the thought of sending the originals to the bottom of the earth where they would undoubtedly be eaten by wild dogs.

I knew the Germans occupied the Channel Islands, but I barely gave them a thought during the war. I have since scoured *The Times* for articles and anything I can cull from the London Library on the Occupation. I also need to find a good travel book on Guernsey – one with descriptions, not timetables and hotel recommendations – to give me the feel of the island.

Quite apart from my interest *in their interest* in reading, I have fallen in love with two men: Eben Ramsey and Dawsey Adams. Clovis Fossey and John Booker, I like. I want Amelia Maugery to adopt me; and I want to adopt Isola Pribby. I will leave you to discern my feelings for Adelaide Addison (Miss) by reading her letters. The truth is, I am living more in Guernsey than I am in London at the moment – I pretend to work with one ear cocked for the sound of the post dropping in the box, and when I hear it, I scramble down the stairs, breathless for the next piece of the story. This must be how people felt when they gathered around the publisher's door to seize the latest instalment of *David Copperfield* as it came off the printing press.

I know you're going to love the letters, too – but would you be interested in more? To me, these people and their wartime experiences are fascinating and moving. Do you agree? Do you think there could be a book here? Don't be polite – I want your opinion (both of your opinions) unvarnished. And you needn't worry – I'll continue to send you copies of the letters even if you don't want me to write a book about Guernsey. I am (mostly) above petty vengeance.

Since I have sacrificed my thumbs for your amusement, you should send me one of Piers's latest in return. So glad you are writing again, my dear.

My love to you both,

Juliet

From Dawsey to Juliet

2nd April 1946

Dear Miss Ashton,

Having fun is the biggest sin in Adelaide Addison's bible (lack of humility following close on its heels), and I'm not surprised she wrote to you about Jerry-bags. Adelaide lives on her wrath.

There were few eligible men left in Guernsey and certainly no one exciting. Many of us were tired, scruffy, worried, ragged, shoeless and dirty – we were defeated and looked it. We didn't have the energy, time or money for fun. Guernsey men had no glamour – and the German soldiers did. They were, according to a friend of mine, tall, blond, handsome and tanned – like gods. They gave lavish parties, were jolly and zestful company, had cars and money and could dance all night long.

But some of the girls who went out with soldiers gave the cigarettes to their fathers and the bread to their families. They would come home from parties with rolls, pâté, fruit, meat pies and jellies stuffed into their bags, and their families would have a full meal the next day. I don't think some Islanders ever credited the boredom of those years. Boredom is a powerful reason to befriend the enemy, and the prospect of fun is a powerful draw – especially when you are young. There were many people who would have no dealings with the Germans – if you said so much as good morning you were abetting the enemy, according to their way of thinking. But circumstances were such that I could not abide by that with Captain Christian Hellman, a doctor in the Occupation forces and my good friend.

In late 1941 there wasn't any salt on the Island, and none was coming to us from France. Root vegetables and soups are listless without salt, so the Germans got the idea of using seawater to supply it. They carried it up from the bay and poured it into a big tanker set in the middle of St Peter Port. Everyone was to walk to town, fill up their buckets, and carry them home again. Then we were to boil the water away and use the sludge in the bottom of the pan as salt. That plan failed – there wasn't enough wood to waste building up a fire hot enough to boil the pot of water dry. So we decided to cook all our vegetables in the seawater itself.

That worked well enough for flavour, but there were many older people who couldn't manage the walk into town or haul heavy buckets home. No one had much strength left for such chores. I have a slight limp from a badly set leg, and though it kept me from army service, it has never been bad enough to bother me. I was very hale, and so I began to deliver water to some cottages. I exchanged a spare spade and some twine for Madame LePell's old pram, and Mr Soames gave me two small oak wine casks, each with a spigot. I sawed off the barrel tops to make moveable lids and fitted them into my pram – so now I had transport. Several of the beaches weren't mined, and it was easy to climb down the rocks, fill a cask with seawater, and carry it back up.

The November wind is bleak, and one day my hands were numb

after I climbed up from the bay with the first barrel of water. I was standing by my pram, trying to limber up my fingers, when Christian drove by. He stopped his car, backed up and asked if I wanted any help. I said no, but he got out of his car anyway and helped me lift the barrel into my pram. Then, without a word, he went down the cliff with me, to help with the second barrel.

I hadn't noticed that he had a stiff shoulder and arm, but between those, my limp, and the loose scree, we slipped coming back up and fell against the hillside, losing our grip on the barrel. It tumbled down, splintered against the rocks and soaked us. God knows why it struck us both as funny, but it did. We sagged against the cliffside, unable to stop laughing. That was when Elia's essays slipped out of my pocket, and Christian picked the book up, sopping wet. 'Ah, Charles Lamb,' he said, and handed it to me. 'He was not a man to mind a little damp.' My surprise must have shown, because he added, 'I read him often at home. I envy you your portable library.'

We climbed back up to his car. He wanted to know if I could find another barrel. I said I could and explained my water-delivery route. He nodded, and I started out with the pram. But then I turned back and said, 'You can borrow the book, if you like.' You would have thought I was giving him the moon. We exchanged names and shook hands.

After that, he would often help me carry up water, and then he'd offer me a cigarette, and we'd stand in the road and talk – about Guernsey's beauty, about history, about books, about farming, but never about the present – always things far away from the war. Once, as we were standing, Elizabeth rattled up the road on her bicycle. She had been on nursing duty all day and probably most of the night before, and like the rest of us her clothes were more patches than cloth. But Christian broke off in mid-sentence to watch her coming. Elizabeth drew up to us and stopped. Neither said a word, but I saw their faces, and I left as soon as I could. I hadn't realised they knew each other.

Christian had been a field surgeon, until his shoulder wound sent him from Eastern Europe to Guernsey. In early 1942, he was ordered to a hospital in Caen; his ship was sunk by Allied bombers and he was drowned. Dr Lorenz, the head of the German Occupation hospital, knew we were friends and came to tell me of his death. He meant for me to tell Elizabeth, so I did.

The way that Christian and I met may have been unusual, but our friendship was not. I'm sure many Islanders grew to be friends with some of the soldiers. But sometimes I think of Charles Lamb and marvel that a man born in 1775 enabled me to make two such friends as you and Christian.

Yours truly,

Dawsey Adams

From Juliet to Amelia

4th April 1946

Dear Mrs Maugery,

The sun is out for the first time for months, and if I stand on my chair and crane my neck, I can see it sparkling on the river. I'm averting my eyes from the mounds of rubble across the road and pretending London is beautiful again.

I've received a sad letter from Dawsey Adams, telling me about Christian Hellman, his kindness and his death. The war goes on and on, doesn't it? Such a good life – lost. And what a grievous blow it must have been to Elizabeth. I am thankful she had you, Mr Ramsey, Isola Pribby and Mr Adams to help her when she had her baby.

Spring is nearly here. I'm almost warm in my puddle of sunshine. And down the street – I'm not averting my eyes now – a man in a patched jumper is painting the door to his house sky blue. Two small boys, who have been walloping one another with sticks, are begging him to let them help. He is giving them a tiny brush each. So – perhaps there is an end to war.

Yours sincerely,

Juliet Ashton

From Mark to Juliet

5th April 1946

Dear Juliet,

You're being elusive and I don't like it. I don't want to see the play with someone else – I want to go with you. In fact, I don't give a damn about the play. I'm only trying to rout you out of that apartment. Dinner? Tea? Cocktails? Boating? Dancing? You choose, and I'll obey. I'm rarely so docile – don't throw away this opportunity to improve my character.

Yours,

Mark

From Juliet to Mark

Dear Mark,

Do you want to come to the British Museum with me? I've got an appointment in the Reading Room at two o'clock. We can look at the mummies afterwards.

Juliet

From Mark to Juliet

To hell with the Reading Room and the mummies. Come have lunch with me.

Mark

From Juliet to Mark

You consider that docile?

Juliet

From Mark to Juliet

To hell with docile.

M.

From Will Thisbee to Juliet

7th April 1946

Dear Miss Ashton,

I am a member of the Guernsey Literary and Potato Peel Pie Society. I am an antiquarian ironmonger, though it pleases some to call me a rag-and-bone man. I also invent labour-saving devices – my latest being an electric clothes peg that wafts the washing on the breeze, saving the wrists.

Did I find solace in reading? Yes, but not at first. I'd just go and eat my pie quietly in a corner. Then Isola got hold of me and said I had to read a book and talk about it like the others. She gave me a book called *Past and Present* by Thomas Carlyle, and a tedious thing he was – he gave me shooting pains in my head – until I came to a bit on religion.

I was not a religious man, though not for want of trying. Off I'd go, like a bee among blossoms, from church to chapel to church again. But I was never able to get hold of faith – until Mr Carlyle put religion to me in a different way. He was walking among the ruins of the Abbey at Bury St Edmunds, when a thought came to him, and he wrote it down thus:

> Does it ever give thee pause that men used to have a soul – not by hearsay alone, or as a figure of speech; but as a truth that they knew, and acted upon! Verily it was another world then . . . but yet it is a pity we have lost the tidings of our souls . . . we shall have to go in search of them again, or worse in all ways shall befall us.

Isn't that something? To know your own soul by hearsay, instead of its own tidings? Why should I let anyone tell me whether I had one or not? If I could believe I had a soul, all by myself, then I could listen to its tidings all by myself. I gave my talk on Mr Carlyle to the Society, and it stirred up a great argument about the soul. Yes? No? Maybe? Dr Stubbins shouted the loudest, and soon everyone stopped arguing and listened to him.

Thompson Stubbins is a man of long, deep thoughts. He was a psychiatrist in London until he ran amok at the annual dinner of the Friends of Sigmund Freud Society in 1934. He told me the whole tale once. The Friends were great talkers and their speeches went on for hours – while their plates stayed bare. At last, dinner was served, and silence fell upon the hall as the psychiatrists bolted their chops.

Thompson saw his chance: he beat his spoon upon his glass and shouted from the floor to be heard. 'Did any of you ever think that around the time the notion of a SOUL disappeared, Freud popped up with the EGO to take its place? The timing of the man! Did he not pause to reflect? Irresponsible old coot! It is my belief that men must spout this twaddle about egos because they fear they have no souls! Think upon it!'

Thompson was barred from their doors for ever, and he moved to Guernsey to grow vegetables. Sometimes he drives around with me in my cart and we talk about Man and God and all the In-between. I would have missed all this if I had not belonged to the Guernsey Literary and Potato Peel Pie Society.

Tell me, Miss Ashton, what are your views on the matter? Isola thinks you should come to visit Guernsey, and if you do, you could join us in my cart. I'd bring a cushion.

Best wishes for your continued health and happiness,

Will Thisbee

From Mrs Clara Saussey to Juliet

8th April 1946

Dear Miss Ashton,

I've heard about you. I once belonged to that Literary Society, though I'll wager none of them ever told you about me. I didn't read from any book by a dead writer, no. I read from a work I wrote myself – my cookery book of recipes. I venture to say my book caused more tears and sorrow than anything Charles Dickens ever wrote.

I chose to read about the correct way to roast a suckling pig. Butter its little body, I said. Let the juices run down and cause the fire to sizzle. The way I read it, you could smell the pig roasting, hear its flesh crackle. I spoke of my five-layer cakes – using a dozen eggs – my spun-sugar sweets, chocolate-rum balls, sponge cakes with pots of cream. Cakes made with good white flour – not that cracked-grain and bird-seed stuff we were using at the time.

Well, Miss, my audience couldn't stand it. They was pushed over the edge, listening to my tasty recipes. Isola Pribby, that never had a manner to call her own, she cried out I was tormenting her and she was going to hex my saucepans. Will Thisbee said I would burn like my cherries jubilee. Then Thompson Stubbins cursed at me, and it took both Dawsey and Eben to get me away safely.

Eben called the next day to apologise for the Society's bad manners. He asked me to remember that most of them had come to the meeting straight from a supper of turnip soup (with not even a bone in it to give pith), or parboiled potatoes scorched on an iron – there being no cooking fat to fry them in. He asked me to be tolerant and forgive them.

Well, I won't do it – they called me bad names. There wasn't one of them who truly loved literature. Because that's what my cookery book was – sheer poetry in a pot. I believe they was made so bored, what with the curfew and other nasty Nazi laws, they only wanted an excuse to get out of an evening, and reading is what they chose.

I want the truth of them told in your story. They'd never have touched a book, but for the OCCUPATION. I stand by what I say, and you can quote me direct.

My name is Clara S-A-U-S-S-E-Y. Three 's's in all.

Clara Saussey (Mrs)

From Amelia to Juliet

10th April 1946

My dear Juliet,

I, too, have felt that the war goes on and on. When my son Ian died at El Alamein – side by side with Eli's father, John – visitors offering their condolences, meaning to comfort me, said, 'Life goes on.' What nonsense, I thought, of course it doesn't. It's death that goes on; Ian is dead now and will be dead tomorrow and next year and for ever. There's no end to that. But perhaps there will be an end to the sorrow of it. Sorrow has rushed over the world like the waters of the Deluge, and it will take time to recede. But already, there are small islands of – hope? Happiness? Something like that, anyway. I like the picture of you standing on your chair to catch a glimpse of the sun, averting your eyes from the mounds of rubble.

My greatest pleasure has been in resuming my evening walks along the clifftops. The Channel is no longer framed in rolls of barbed wire, the view is unbroken by huge *VERBOTEN* signs. The mines are gone from our beaches, and I can walk when, where, and for as long as I like. If I stand on the cliffs and turn out to face the sea, I don't see the ugly cement bunkers behind me, or the land naked without its trees. Not even the Germans could ruin the sea. This summer, gorse will begin to grow around the fortifications, and by next year, perhaps, vines will creep over them. I hope they are soon covered. For all that I can look away, I will never be able to forget how they were made.

The Todt workers built them. I know you have heard of Germany's slave workers in camps on the Continent, but did you know that Hitler sent over sixteen thousand of them here, to the Channel Islands?

Hitler was fanatical about fortifying these islands – England was never to get them back! His generals called it Island Madness. He ordered large-gun emplacements, anti-tank walls on the beaches, hundreds of bunkers and batteries, arms and bomb depots, miles and miles of underground tunnels, a huge underground hospital, and a railway across the island to carry materials. The coastal fortifications were absurd – the Channel Isles were better fortified than the Atlantic Wall built against an Allied invasion. The installations loomed over every bay. The Third Reich was to last one thousand years – in concrete.

So, of course, he needed the thousands of slave workers; men and boys were conscripted, some were arrested, and some were just picked up in the street – from cinema queues, cafés, and from the country lanes and fields of any German Occupied territory. There were even political prisoners from the Spanish Civil War. The Russian prisoners of war were treated the worst, perhaps because of their victory over the Germans on the Russian Front.

Most of these slave workers came to the Islands in 1942. They were kept in open sheds, dug-out tunnels, some of them in houses. They were marched all over the island to their work sites: thin to the bone, dressed in ragged trousers with bare skin showing through, often no coats to protect them from the cold. No shoes or boots, their feet tied up in bloody rags. Young lads, fifteen and sixteen, were so weary and starved they could hardly put one foot in front of another. Guernsey Islanders would stand by their gates to offer them what little food or warm clothing they could spare. Sometimes the Germans guarding the Todt work columns would let the men break ranks to accept these gifts – other times they would beat them to the ground with rifle butts.

Thousands of those men and boys died here, and I have recently learnt that their inhuman treatment was the deliberate policy of Himmler. He called his plan Death by Exhaustion, and he implemented it. Work them hard, don't waste valuable food on them, and let them die. They could, and would, always be replaced by new slave workers from Europe's occupied countries.

Some of the Todt workers were kept down on the common, behind a wire fence – they were white as ghosts, covered in cement dust; there was only one water standpipe for over a hundred men to wash themselves. Children sometimes went down there. They would poke walnuts and apples, sometimes potatoes, through the wire for the Todt workers. There was one who did not take the food – he came to see the children. He would put his arm through the wire just to hold their faces in his hands, to touch their hair.

The Germans did give the Todt workers one half-day a week off – Sunday. That was the day when the German Sanitary Engineers emptied all the sewage into the sea through a big pipe. Fish would swarm for the waste, and the Todt workers would stand in that faeces and filth up to their chests – trying to catch the fish in their hands, to eat them.

No flowers or vines can cover such memories as these, can they?

I have told you the most hateful story of the war. Juliet, Isola thinks you should come and write a book about the German Occupation. She told me she did not have the skill to write it herself, but, as dear as Isola is to me, I am terrified she might buy a notebook and begin anyway.

Yours ever,

Amelia Maugery

From Juliet to Dawsey

11th April 1946

Dear Mr Adams,

After promising never to write to me again, Adelaide Addison has sent me another letter. It is devoted to all the people and practices she deplores, and you are one of them, along with Charles Lamb.

It seems she called on you to deliver the April issue of the parish magazine – and you were nowhere to be found. Not milking your cow, or hoeing your garden, or cleaning your house, or doing anything a good farmer should be doing. So she went into your yard, and – what did she see? You, lying in your hay-loft, reading a book by Charles Lamb! You were 'so enraptured with that drunkard' that you failed to notice her presence. What a blight that woman is. Do you happen to know why? I suspect a malignant fairy at her christening.

Anyway, the picture of you lolling in the hay reading Charles Lamb pleased me very much. It made me think of my own childhood in Suffolk. My father was a farmer there, and I helped on the farm; though I admit all I did was jump out of our car, open the gate, close it and jump back in, gather eggs, weed our garden and turn the hay when I was in the mood.

I remember lying in our hay-loft reading *The Secret Garden* with a cowbell beside me. I'd read for an hour and then ring the bell for a glass of lemonade to be brought to me. Mrs Hutchins, the cook, eventually grew weary of this arrangement and told my mother, and that was the end of my cowbell, but not my reading in the hay.

Mr Hastings has found the E. V. Lucas biography of Charles Lamb. He has decided not to quote you a price, but just to send the book to you at once. He said, 'A lover of Charles Lamb ought not to have to wait.'

Yours,

Juliet Ashton

From Susan Scott to Sidney

11th April 1946

Dear Sidney,

I'm as tender-hearted as the next girl, but damn it, if you don't get back here soon, Charlie Stephens is going to have a nervous breakdown. He's not cut out for work; he's cut out for handing over large wads of cash and letting you do the work. He actually turned up at the office *before ten o'clock* yesterday, but the effort exhausted him. He was deathly white by eleven, and had a whisky at eleven-thirty. At noon, one of the innocent young things handed him a jacket to approve – his eyes bulged with terror and he began that disgusting trick with his ear – he's going to pull it right off one day.

He went home at one, and I haven't seen him today (it's four in the afternoon).

In other depressing developments, Harriet Munfries has gone completely berserk; she wants to 'colour-coordinate' the entire children's list. Pink and red. I'm not joking. The boy in the postroom (I don't bother learning their names any more) got drunk and threw away all letters addressed to anyone whose name started with an S. Don't ask me why. Miss Tilley was so impossibly rude to Kendrick that he tried to hit her with her telephone. I can't say I blame him, but telephones are hard to come by and we can't afford to lose one. You must sack her the minute you come home.

If you need any further inducement to buy an aeroplane ticket, I can also tell you that I saw Juliet and Mark Reynolds looking very cosy at Café de Paris the other night. Their table was behind the velvet cordon, but from my seat in the slums, I could spy all the telltale signs of romance – he murmuring sweet nothings in her ear, her hand lingering in his beside the cocktail glasses, he touching her shoulder to point out an acquaintance. I considered it my duty (as your devoted employee) to break it up, so I elbowed my way past the cordon to say hello to Juliet. She seemed delighted and invited me to join them, but it was apparent from Mark's smile that he didn't want company, so I retreated. He's not a man to cross, that one, with his thin smile, no matter how beautiful his ties are, and it would break my mother's heart if my lifeless body was found bobbing in the Thames.

In other words, get a wheelchair, get a crutch, get a donkey, but come home *now*.

Yours,

Susan

12th April 1946

Dear Sidney and Piers,

I've been ransacking the libraries of London for background on Guernsey. I even got a ticket to the Reading Room, which shows my devotion to duty – as you know, I'm petrified of the place.

I've found out quite a lot. Do you remember a wretchedly silly series of books in the 1920s called *A-Tramp in Skye* . . . or *A-Tramp in Lindisfarrne* . . . or *in Sheepholm* – or whatever harbour the author happened to sail his yacht into? Well, in 1930 he sailed into St Peter Port, Guernsey, and wrote a book about it (with day trips to Sark, Herm, Alderney and Jersey, where he was mauled by a duck and had to return home).

Tramp's real name was Cee Cee Meredith. He was an idiot who thought he was a poet, and he was rich enough to sail anywhere, then write about it, then have it privately printed, and then give a copy to any friend who would take it. Cee Cee didn't trouble himself with dull fact: he preferred to scamper off to the nearest moor, beach or flowery field, and go into transports with his Muse. But bless him anyhow; his book, *A-Tramp in Guernsey*, was just what I needed to get the feel of the island.

Cee Cee went ashore at St Peter Port, leaving his mother, Dorothea, to bob about the adjacent waters, retching in the wheel-house.

In Guernsey, Cee Cee wrote poems to the freesias and the daffodils. Also to the tomatoes. He was agog with admiration for the Guernsey cows and the pedigree bulls, and he composed a little song in honour of their bells ('Tinkle, tinkle, such a merry sound . . .'). Beneath the cows, in Cee Cee's estimation, were 'the simple folk of the country parishes, who still speak the Norman patois and believe in fairies and witches'. Cee Cee entered into the spirit of the thing and saw a fairy in the gloaming.

After going on about the cottages and hedgerows and the shops, Cee Cee at last reached the sea, or, as he'd have it, '*The SEA!* It is everywhere! The waters: azure, emerald, silver-laced, when they are not as hard and dark as a bag of nails.' Thank God *Tramp* had a co-author, Dorothea, who was made of sterner stuff and loathed Guernsey and everything about it. She was in charge of delivering the history of the island: and she was not one to gild the lily:

As to Guernsey's history – well, least said, soonest mended. The Islands once belonged to the Duchy of Normandy, but when William, Duke of Normandy, became William the Conqueror, he took the Channel Islands and he gave them to England – with special privileges. These privileges were later added to by King John, and added to yet again by Edward III. WHY? What did they do to deserve it? Absolutely nothing! Later, when that weakling Henry VI managed to lose most of France to the French, the Channel Islands elected to stay a Crown Possession of England, as who would not.

The Channel Islands freely owe their allegiance and love to the English Crown, but heed this, dear reader – THE CROWN CANNOT MAKE THEM DO ANYTHING THEY DO NOT WANT TO DO!

Guernsey's ruling body, such as it is, is named the States of Deliberation but called the States for short. The real head of everything is the President of the States, who is elected by the STATES, and called the Bailiff. In fact, everyone is elected, not appointed by the King. Pray, what is a monarch for, if NOT TO APPOINT PEOPLE TO THINGS?

The Crown's only representative in this unholy mélange is the Lieutenant Governor. While he is welcome to attend the meetings of the States, and may talk and advise all he wants, he does NOT HAVE A VOTE. At least he is allowed to live in Government House, the only mansion of any note in Guernsey – if you don't count Sausmarez Manor, which I don't.

The Crown cannot impose taxes on the Islands – or conscription. Honesty forces me to admit the Islanders don't need conscription to make them go to war for dear, dear England. They volunteered and made very respectable, even heroic, soldiers and sailors against Napoleon and the Kaiser. But take note – these selfless acts do not make amends for the fact THAT THE CHANNEL ISLANDS PAY NO INCOME TAX TO ENGLAND. NOT ONE SHILLING. IT MAKES ONE WANT TO SPIT!

Those are her kindest words – I will spare you the rest, but you get her drift.

One of you, or better still both of you, write to me. I want to hear how the patient *and* the nurse are. What does your doctor say about your leg, Sidney – I swear you've had time to grow a new one.

XXXXXX,

Juliet

From Dawsey to Juliet

15th April 1946

Dear Miss Ashton,

I don't know what ails Adelaide Addison. Isola says she is a blight because she likes being a blight – it gives her a sense of destiny. Adelaide did me one good turn though, didn't she? She told you, better than I could, how much I was enjoying Charles Lamb.

The biography came. I read it quickly – too impatient not to. But I'll go back and start again – reading more slowly this time, so I can take everything in. I did like what Mr Lucas said about him – he could make any homely and familiar thing into something fresh and beautiful. Lamb's writings make me feel more at home in his London than I do here and now in St Peter Port.

But what I cannot imagine is Charles, coming home from work and finding his mother stabbed to death, his father bleeding and his sister Mary standing over both with a bloody knife. How did he make himself go into the room and take the knife away from her? After the police had taken her off to the madhouse, how did he persuade the Judge to release her to his care and his care alone? He was only twenty-one years old – how did he talk them into it?

He promised to look after Mary for the rest of her life – and, once he put his foot on that road, he never stepped off it. It is sad he had to stop writing poetry, which he loved, and had to write criticism and essays, which he did not honour much, to make money.

I think of him working as a clerk at the East India Company, so that he could save money for the day, and it always came, when Mary would go mad again, and he would have to place her in a private home.

And even then he did seem to miss her – they were such friends. Picture them: he had to watch her like a hawk for the awful symptoms, and she could tell when the madness was coming on and could do nothing to stop it – that must have been worst of all. I imagine him sitting there, watching her on the sly, and her sitting there, watching him watching her. How they must have hated the way the other was forced to live.

But doesn't it seem to you that when Mary was sane there was no one saner – or better company? Charles certainly thought so, and so did all their friends: Wordsworth, Hazlitt, Leigh Hunt and, above all, Coleridge. On the day Coleridge died they found a note he had scribbled in the book he was reading. It said, 'Charles and Mary Lamb, dear to my heart, yes, as it were, my heart.'

Perhaps I've written over-long about him, but I wanted you and Mr Hastings to know how much the books have given me to think about, and what pleasure I find in them.

I like the story from your childhood – the bell and the hay. I can see it in my mind. Did you like living on a farm – do you ever miss it? You are never really away from the countryside in Guernsey, not even in St Peter Port, so I cannot imagine the difference living in a big city like London would make.

Kit has taken against mongooses, now that she knows they eat snakes. She is hoping to find a boa constrictor under a rock. Isola dropped in this evening and sent her best wishes – she will write to you as soon as she gets her crops in – rosemary, dill, thyme and henbane.

Yours,

Dawsey Adams

From Juliet to Dawsey

18th April 1946

Dear Mr Adams,

I am so glad you want to talk about Charles Lamb. I have always thought Mary's sorrow made Charles into a great writer – even if he had to give up poetry and work for the East India Company because of it. He had a genius for sympathy that not one of his great friends could touch. When Wordsworth chided him for not caring enough about nature, Charles wrote, 'I have no passion for groves and valleys. The rooms where I was born, the furniture which has been before my eyes all my life, a bookcase which has followed me about like a faithful dog wherever I have moved – old chairs, old streets, squares where I have sunned myself, my old school – have I not enough, without your Mountains? I do not envy you. I should pity you, did I not know, that the Mind will make friends of any thing.' A mind that can 'make friends of any thing' – I thought of that often during the war.

By chance, I came upon another story about him today. He often drank too much, far too much, but he was not a sullen drunk. Once, his host's butler had to carry him home, slung over his shoulder in a fireman's hold. The next day Charles wrote his host such a hilarious note of apology, the man bequeathed it to his son in his will. I hope Charles wrote to the butler too.

Have you ever noticed that when your mind is awakened or drawn to someone new, that person's name suddenly pops up everywhere? My friend Sophie calls it coincidence, and Reverend Simpless calls it grace. He thinks that if one cares deeply about someone or something new one throws a kind of energy out into the world, and 'fruitfulness' is drawn in.

Yours ever,

Juliet Ashton

From Isola to Juliet

18th April 1946

Dear Juliet,

Now that we are corresponding friends, I want to ask you some questions – they are highly personal. Dawsey said it would not be polite, but I say that's a difference between men and women, not polite and rude. Dawsey hasn't asked me a personal question in fifteen years. I'd take it kindly if he would, but Dawsey's got quiet ways. I don't expect to change him, nor myself either. You wanted to know about us, so I think you would like us to know about you – only you just didn't happen to think of it first.

I saw a picture of you on the cover of your book about Anne Brontë, so I know you are under forty years of age – how much under? Was the sun in your eyes, or does it happen that you have a squint? Is it permanent? It must have been a windy day because your curls were blowing about. I couldn't quite make out the colour of your hair, though I could tell it wasn't blonde – for which I am glad. I don't like blondes very much.

Do you live by the river? I hope so, because people who live near running water are much nicer than people who don't. I'd be cross as a snake if I lived inland. Do you have a serious suitor? I do not.

Is your flat cosy or grand? Be fulsome, as I want to be able to picture it in my mind. Do you think you would like to visit us in Guernsey? Do you have a pet? What kind?

Your friend,

Isola

From Juliet to Isola

20th April 1946

Dear Isola,

I am glad you want to know more about me and am only sorry I didn't think of it myself, and sooner.

Present-day first: I am thirty-two years old, and you were right – the sun was in my eyes. In a good mood, I call my hair chestnut with gold glints. In a bad mood, I call it mousy brown. It wasn't a windy day; my hair always looks like that. Naturally curly hair is a curse, and don't ever let anyone tell you different. My eyes are hazel. While I am slender, I am not tall enough to suit me.

I don't live by the Thames any more and that is what I miss the most about my old home – I loved the sight and sound of the river at all hours. I live now in a flat in Glebe Place. It is small and furnished within an inch of its life, and the owner won't be back from the United States until November, so I have the run of his house until then. I wish I had a dog, but the building management does not allow pets! Kensington Gardens aren't far, so if I begin to feel cooped up I can walk to the park, hire a deck chair for a shilling, loll about under the trees, watch the passers-by and children play, and I am soothed – somewhat.

81 Oakley Street was demolished by a random V-1 just over a year ago. Most of the damage was to the row of houses behind mine, but three floors of Number 81 were shorn off, and my flat is now a pile of rubble. I hope Mr Grant, the owner, will rebuild – for I want my flat, or a facsimile of it, back again just as it was – with Cheyne Walk and the river outside my windows.

Luckily, I was away in Bury when the V-1 hit. Sidney Stark, my friend and now publisher, met my train that evening and took me home, and we viewed the huge mountain of rubble and what was left of the building. With part of the wall gone, I could see my shredded curtains waving in the breeze and my desk, three-legged and slumped on the slanting floor that was left. My books were a muddy, sopping pile and although I could see my mother's portrait on the wall – half gouged out and sooty – there was no safe way to recover it. The only intact possession was my large crystal paper-weight – with *Carpe Diem* carved across the top. It had belonged to my father – and there it sat, whole and unchipped, on top of a pile of broken bricks and splintered wood. I could not do without it so Sidney clambered over the rubble and retrieved it for me.

I was a fairly nice child until my parents died when I was twelve. I left our farm in Suffolk and went to live with my great-uncle in London. I was a furious, bitter, morose little girl. I ran away twice, causing my uncle no end of trouble – and at the time I was very glad to do so. I am ashamed now when I think about how I treated him. He died when I was seventeen so I was never able to apologise.

When I was thirteen, my uncle decided I should go away to boarding school. I went, mulish as usual, and met the headmistress, who marched me into the dining room. She led me to a table with four other girls. I sat, arms crossed, hands under my armpits, glaring like a moulting eagle, looking for someone to hate. I hit upon

Sophie Stark, Sidney's younger sister. Perfect, she had golden curls, big blue eyes and a sweet, sweet smile. She made an effort to talk to me. I didn't answer until she said, 'I hope you will be happy here.' I told her I wouldn't be staying long enough to find out. 'As soon as I find out about the trains, I am gone!' said I.

That night I climbed out on to the dormitory roof, meaning to sit there and have a good brood in the dark. In a few minutes, Sophie crawled out – with a railway timetable for me.

Needless to say, I didn't run away. I stayed – with Sophie as my new friend. Her mother would often invite me to their house for the holidays, which was where I met Sidney. He was ten years older than me and was, of course, a god. He later changed into a bossy older brother, and later still, into one of my dearest friends.

Sophie and I left school and – wanting no more of academic life, but LIFE instead – we went to London and shared rooms Sidney had found for us. We worked together for a while in a bookshop, and at night I wrote – and threw away – stories.

Then the *Daily Mirror* sponsored an essay contest – five hundred words on 'What Women Fear Most'. I knew what the *Mirror* was after, but I'm far more afraid of chickens than I am of men, so I wrote about that. The judges, thrilled at not having to read another word about sex, awarded me first prize. Five pounds and I was, at last, in print. The *Daily Mirror* received so many fan letters, they commissioned me to write an article, then another one. I soon began to write feature stories for other newspapers and magazines. Then the war broke out, and I was invited to write a semi-weekly column for the *Spectator*, called 'Izzy Bickerstaff Goes to War'. Sophie met and fell in love with an airman, Alexander Strachan. They married and Sophie moved to his family's farm in Scotland. I am godmother to their son, Dominic, and though I haven't taught him any hymns, we did pull the hinges off the cellar door last time I saw him – it was a Pictish ambush.

I suppose I do have a suitor, but I'm not really used to him yet. He's terribly charming and he plies me with delicious meals, but I sometimes think I prefer suitors in books rather than right in front of me. How awful, backward, cowardly, and mentally warped that will be if it turns out to be true.

Sidney published a book of my Izzy Bickerstaff columns and I went on a book tour. And then – I began writing letters to strangers in Guernsey, now friends, whom I would indeed like to come and see.

Yours,

Juliet

From Eli to Juliet

21st April 1946

Dear Miss Ashton,

Thank you for the blocks of wood. They are beautiful. I could not believe what I saw when I opened your box – all those sizes and shades, from pale to dark.

How did you find all those different pieces of wood? You must have gone to so many places. I bet you did and I don't know how to thank you. They came at just the right time too. Kit's favourite animal was a snake she saw in a book, and he was easy to carve, being so long and thin. Now she's mad about ferrets. She says she won't ever touch my knife again if I'll carve her a ferret. I don't think it will be too hard to make one, for they are pointy, too. Because of your gift, I have wood to practise with.

Is there an animal you would like to have? I want to carve a present for you, but I'd like it to be something you'd favour. Would you like a mouse? I am good at mice.

Yours truly,

Eli

From Eben to Juliet

22nd April 1946

Dear Miss Ashton,

Your box for Eli came on Friday – how kind of you. He sits and studies the blocks of wood – as if he sees something hidden inside them, and he can make it come out with his knife.

You asked if all the Guernsey children were evacuated to England. No – some stayed, and when I missed Eli, I looked at the little ones around me and was glad he had gone. The children here had a bad time, for there wasn't enough food to grow on. I remember picking up Bill LePell's boy – he was twelve but weighed no more than a child of seven.

It was a terrible thing to decide – send your children away to live among strangers, or let them stay with you. Maybe the Germans wouldn't come, but if they did – how would they treat us? But, come to that, what if they invaded England, too – how would the children manage without their families beside them?

Do you know the state we were in when the Germans came? Shock is what I'd call it. The truth is, we didn't think they'd want us. It was England they were after, and we were of no use to them. We thought we'd be in the audience, like, not up on the stage itself.

Then in the spring of 1940 Hitler got himself through Europe like a hot knife through butter. Every place fell to him. It was so fast – windows all over Guernsey shook and rattled from the explosions in France, and once the coast of France was gone, it was plain as day that England could not use up her men and ships to defend us. They needed to save them for when their own invasion began in earnest. So we were left to ourselves.

In the middle of June, when it became pretty certain we were in for it, the States got on the telephone to London and asked if they would send ships for our children and take them to England. They couldn't fly, for fear of being shot down by the Luftwaffe. London said yes, but the children had to be ready at once. The ships would have to hurry here and back again while there was still time.

Jane had no more strength than a cat then, but she knew her mind. She wanted Eli to go. Other ladies were in a dither – go or stay? – and they were frantic to talk, but Jane told Elizabeth to keep them away. 'I don't want to hear them fuss,' she said. 'It's bad for the baby.' Jane had an idea that babies knew everything that happened around them, even before they were born.

The time for dithering was soon over. Families had one day to decide, and five years to abide by it. School-age children and babies with their mothers went first on the 19th and 20th of June. The States gave out pocket money to the children, if their parents had none to spare. The littlest ones were all excited about the sweets they could buy with it. Some thought it was like a Sunday School outing, and they'd be back before dark. They were lucky in that. The older children, like Eli, knew better.

Of all the sights I saw the day they left, there is one picture I can't get out of my mind. Two little girls, all dressed up in pink dresses, stiff petticoats, shiny shoes – as if they were going to a party. How cold they must have been crossing the Channel.

All the children were to be dropped off at the school by their parents. It was there we had to say our goodbyes. Buses came to take the children down to the pier. The boats, just back from Dunkirk, had to cross the Channel again for the children. There was no time to get a convoy together to escort them. There was no time to get enough lifeboats on board – or life jackets.

That morning we stopped first at the hospital for Eli to say goodbye to his mother. He couldn't do it. His jaw was clamped shut so tight, he could only nod. Jane held him for a bit, and then Elizabeth and I walked him down to the school. I hugged him hard and that was the last time I saw him for five years. Elizabeth stayed because she had volunteered to help get the children inside ready.

I was walking back to Jane in the hospital, when I remembered something Eli had once said to me. He was about five years old, and we were walking down to La Courbière to see the fishing boats come in. There was an old canvas bathing shoe lying in the middle of the path. Eli walked round it, staring. Finally, he said, 'That shoe is all alone, Grandpa.' I answered that yes it was. He looked at it again, and then we walked on. After a bit, he said, 'Grandpa, that's something I never am.' I asked him, 'What's that?' And he said, 'Lonesome in my spirits.'

There! I had something happy to tell Jane after all, and I prayed it would stay true for him.

Isola says she wants to write to you herself about what happened at the school. She says she was witness to a scene you will want to know about as an authoress: Elizabeth slapped Adelaide Addison in the face and made her leave. You do not know Miss Addison, and you are fortunate in that – she is a woman too good for daily wear.

Isola told me you that might come to Guernsey. I would be glad to offer you hospitality.

Yours,

Eben Ramsey

Telegram from Juliet to Isola

23rd April 1946

Did Elizabeth really slap Adelaide Addison STOP If only I had been there STOP Please send details STOP Love Juliet

24th April 1946

Dear Juliet,

Yes, she did – slapped her right across the face. It was lovely.

We were all at the St Brioc School to help the children get ready for the buses to take them down to the ships. The States didn't want the parents to come into the school itself – too crowded and too sad. Better to say their goodbyes outside. One child crying might set them all off.

So it was strangers who tied up shoelaces, wiped noses, put a nametag around each child's neck. We did up buttons and played games with them until the buses came. I had one bunch trying to touch their tongues to their noses, and Elizabeth had another lot playing that game that teaches them how to lie with a straight face – I forget what it's called – when Adelaide Addison came in with that doleful mug of hers, all piety and no sense.

She gathered a circle of children around her and started to sing 'For Those in Peril on the Sea' over their little heads. But no, 'safety from storms' *wasn't enough* for her. She set about ordering the poor things to pray for their parents every night – who knew what the German soldiers might do to them? Then she said to be especially good little boys and girls so that Mummy and Daddy could look down on them from Heaven and BE PROUD OF THEM.

Honestly, Juliet, she had those children crying and sobbing as though their hearts were breaking. I was too shocked to move, but not Elizabeth. No, quick as an adder's tongue, she grabbed Adelaide's arm and told her to SHUT UP.

Adelaide cried, 'Let me go! I am speaking the Word of God!'

Elizabeth, she got a look that would turn the devil to stone, and then she slapped Adelaide right across the face – nice and sharp, so her head wobbled on her shoulders – and dragged her over to the door, shoved her out, and locked it. Old Adelaide kept hammering on the door, but no one took any notice. I lie – silly Daphne Post did try to open it, but I got her round the neck and she stopped.

It is my belief that the sight of a good fight shocked the fear out of those babies, and they stopped crying, and the buses came and we loaded the children on. Elizabeth and me, we didn't go home, we stood in the road and waved till the buses was out of sight.

I hope I never live to see another such day, even with Adelaide getting slapped. All those little children bereft in the world – I was glad I did not have any.

Thank you for your life story. You have had such sadness with your mum and dad and your home by the river, for which I am sorry. But me, I am glad you have dear friends like Sophie and her mother and Sidney. As for Sidney, he sounds a very fine man – but bossy. It's a failing common in men.

Clovis Fossey has asked if you would send the Society a copy of your prize-winning essay on chickens. He thinks it would be nice to read aloud at a meeting. Then we could put it in our archives, if we ever have any. I'd like to read it too, chickens being the reason I fell off a hen-house roof – they'd chased me there. How they all came at me – with their razor lips and rolling eyeballs! People don't know how chickens can turn on you, but they can – just like mad dogs. I didn't keep hens until the war came – then I had to, but I am never easy in their company. I would rather have Ariel butt me on my bottom – that's open and honest and not like a sly chicken, sneaking up to jab you.

I would like it if you came to see us. So would Eben and Amelia and Dawsey – and Eli, too. Kit is not so sure, but you mustn't mind that. She might come round. Your newspaper article will be printed soon, so you could come here and have a rest. You might find a story here you'd like to tell about.

Your friend,

Isola

From Dawsey to Juliet

26th April 1946

Dear Miss Ashton,

My temporary job at the quarry is over, and Kit is staying with me for a while. She is sitting under the table I'm writing on, whispering. What's that you're whispering, I asked, and there was a long quiet. Then she commenced whispering again, and I can make out my own name amongst the other sounds. This is what generals call a war of nerves, and I know who is going to win.

Kit doesn't resemble Elizabeth very much, except for her grey eyes and a look she gets when she is concentrating hard. But she is like her mother inside – fierce in her feelings. Even when she was tiny, she howled until the glass shivered in the windows, and when she gripped my finger in her little fist, it turned white. I knew nothing about babies, but Elizabeth made me learn. She said I was fated to be a father and she had a responsibility to make sure I knew more than the usual run of them. She missed Christian, not just for herself, for Kit, too.

Kit knows her father is dead. Amelia and I told her that, but we didn't know how to speak of Elizabeth. In the end, we said that she'd been sent away and we hoped she'd return soon. Kit looked from me to Amelia and back, but she didn't ask any questions. She just went out and sat in the barn. I don't know if we did right.

Some days I wear myself out wishing for Elizabeth to come home. We have learnt that Sir Ambrose Ivers was killed in one of the last bombing raids in London, and, as Elizabeth inherited his estate, his solicitors have begun a search for her. They must have better ways to find her than we have, so I am hopeful that Mr Dilwyn will get some word from her – or about her – soon. Wouldn't it be a blessed thing for Kit and for all of us if Elizabeth could be found?

The Society is having an outing on Saturday. We are attending the Guernsey Repertory Company's performance of *Julius Caesar* – John Booker is to be Mark Antony and Clovis Fossey is going to play Caesar. Isola has been reading Clovis his lines, and she says we will all be astonished by his acting, especially when, after he's dead, he hisses, 'Thou shalt see me at Philippi!' Just thinking of the way Clovis hisses has kept her awake for three nights, she says. Isola exaggerates, but only enough to enjoy herself.

Kit's stopped whispering. I've just peered under the table, and she's asleep. It's later than I thought.

Yours,

Dawsey Adams

From Mark to Juliet

30th April 1946

Darling,

Just got in – the entire trip could have been avoided if Hendry had telephoned, but I smacked a few heads together and they've cleared the whole shipment through customs. I feel as though I've been away for years. Can I see you tonight? I need to talk to you.

Love,

M.

From Juliet to Mark

Of course. Do you want to come here? I've got a sausage.

  Juliet

From Mark to Juliet

A sausage – how appetising.
  Suzette, at eight?
  Love,

  M.

From Juliet to Mark

Say please.

  J.

From Mark to Juliet

Pleased to see you at Suzette at eight.
  Love,

  M.

1st May 1946

Dear Mark,

I didn't refuse, you know. I said I wanted to think about it. You were so busy ranting about Sidney and Guernsey that perhaps you didn't notice – I only said I wanted time. I've known you *two months*. It's not long enough for me to be certain that we should spend the rest of our lives together, even if you are. I once made a terrible mistake and almost married a man I hardly knew (perhaps you read about it in the papers) – and at least in that case the war was an extenuating circumstance. I won't be such a fool again.

Think about it: I've never seen your home – I don't even know where it is, really. New York, but which street? What does it look like? What colour are your walls? Your sofa? Do you arrange your books alphabetically? (I hope not.) Are your drawers tidy or messy? Do you ever hum, and if so, what? Do you prefer cats or dogs? Or fish? What on earth do you eat for breakfast – or do you have a cook?

You see? I don't know you well enough to marry you.

I have one other piece of news that may interest you: Sidney is not your rival. I am not now nor have I ever been in love with Sidney, nor he with me. Nor will I ever marry him. Is that decisive enough for you?

Are you absolutely certain you wouldn't rather be married to someone more tractable?

Juliet

1st May 1946

Dearest Sophie,

I wish you were here. I wish we still lived together in our lovely little studio and worked in dear Mr Hawke's shop and ate biscuits and cheese for supper every night. I want so much to talk to you. I want you to tell me whether I should marry Mark Reynolds.

He asked me last night – no bended knee, but a diamond as big as a pigeon's egg – at a romantic French restaurant. I'm not certain he still wants to marry me this morning – he's absolutely furious because I didn't give him an unequivocal yes. I tried to explain that I hadn't known him long enough and I needed time to think, but he wouldn't listen to me. He was certain that I was rejecting him because of a secret passion – for Sidney! They really are obsessed with each another, those two.

Thank God we were at his flat by then – he started shouting about Sidney and godforsaken islands and women who care more about strangers than men who are right in front of them (that's Guernsey and my new friends there). I kept trying to explain and he kept shouting until I began to cry from frustration. Then he felt remorseful, which was so unlike him and endearing that I almost changed my mind and said yes. But then I imagined a lifetime of having to cry to get him to be kind, and I went back to no again. We argued and he lectured and I wept a bit more because I was so exhausted, and eventually he called his chauffeur to take me home. As he shut me into the car, he leaned in to kiss me and said, 'You're an idiot, Juliet.'

And maybe he's right. Do you remember those awful, awful Cheslayne Fair novels we read the summer we were thirteen? My favourite was *The Master of Blackheath*. I must have read it twenty times (and so did you, don't pretend you didn't). Do you remember

Ransom – how he manfully hid his love for the girlish Eulalie so that she could choose freely, little knowing that she had been mad about him ever since she fell off her horse when she was twelve? The thing is, Sophie – Mark Reynolds is exactly like Ransom. He's tall and handsome, with a crooked smile and a chiselled jaw. He shoulders his way through the crowd, careless of the glances that follow him. He's impatient and magnetic, and when I go to powder my nose I overhear other women talking about him, just like Eulalie did in the museum. People notice him. He doesn't try to make them – they can't help it.

I used to get the shivers about Ransom. Sometimes I do about Mark, too – when I look at him – but I can't get over the nagging feeling that I'm no Eulalie. If I were ever to fall off a horse, it would be lovely to be picked up by Mark, but I don't think I'm likely to fall off a horse in the near future. I'm much more likely to go to Guernsey and write a book about the Occupation, and Mark can't abide the thought. He wants me to stay in London and go to restaurants and theatres and marry him like a reasonable person.

Write and tell me what to do.

Love to Dominic – and to you and Alexander.

Juliet

From Juliet to Sidney

3rd May 1946

Dear Sidney,

I may not be as distraught as Stephens & Stark is without you, but I do miss you and want you to advise me. Please drop everything you are doing and write to me at once.

I want to get out of London. I want to go to Guernsey. You know

I've grown very fond of my Guernsey friends, and I'm fascinated by their lives under the Germans – and since. I've visited the Channel Islands Refugee Committee and read their files. I have read the Red Cross reports. I've read all I can find on Todt slave workers – there hasn't, so far, been much. I've interviewed some of the soldiers who liberated Guernsey and talked to Royal Engineers who removed the thousands of mines from the beaches. I've read all the 'unclassified' government reports on the state of the Islanders' health, or lack of it; their happiness, or lack of it; their food supplies, or lack of them. But I want to know more. I want to know the stories of the people who were there, and I can never learn those by sitting in a library in London.

For example – yesterday I was reading an article on the liberation. A reporter asked a Guernsey Islander, 'What was the most difficult experience you had during the Germans' rule?' He made fun of the man's answer, but it made perfect sense to me. The Islander told him, 'You know they took away all our wirelesses? If you were caught with one, you'd get sent off to prison on the Continent. Well, those of us who had secret wirelesses, we heard about the Allies landing in Normandy. Trouble was, we weren't supposed to know it had happened! Hardest thing I ever did was walk around St Peter Port on the 7th of June, not grinning, not smiling, not doing anything to let those Germans know that I KNEW their end was coming. If they'd caught on, someone would be in for it – so we had to pretend. It was very hard to pretend not to know D-Day had happened.'

I want to talk to people like him (though he's probably off writers now) and hear about their war, because that's what I'd like to read, instead of statistics about grain. I'm not sure what form a book would take, or if I could even write one at all. But I would like to go to St Peter Port and find out.

Do I have your blessing?

Love to you and Piers,

Juliet

Cable from Sidney to Juliet

10th May 1946

Herewith my blessing! Guernsey is a wonderful idea, both for you and for a book. But will Reynolds allow it? Love, Sidney

Cable from Juliet to Sidney

11th May 1946

Blessing received. Mark Reynolds is not in a position to forbid or allow. Love, Juliet

From Amelia to Juliet

13th May 1946

My dear,

I was delighted to receive your telegram yesterday and learn that you are coming to visit us!

I followed your instructions and spread the news at once – you have sent the Society into a whirlwind of excitement. The members instantly offered to provide you with anything you might need: bed, board, introductions, a supply of electric clothes pegs. Isola is ecstatic that you are coming and is already at work on behalf of your book. Though I warned her that it was only an idea so far, she is determined to find material for you. She has asked (perhaps threatened) everyone she knows in the market to send you letters about the Occupation; she thinks you'll need them to persuade your publisher that the subject is book-worthy. Don't be surprised if you are inundated with letters in the next few weeks.

Isola also went to see Mr Dilwyn at the bank this afternoon and asked him to let you rent Elizabeth's cottage. It is a lovely site, in a meadow below the Big House, and it is small enough for you to manage easily. Elizabeth moved there when the German officers confiscated the larger house for their use. You would be very comfortable there, and Isola assured Mr Dilwyn that he need only stir himself to draw up a lease for you. She herself will see to everything else: airing the rooms, washing the windows, beating the rugs, and killing spiders.

Please don't feel as though these arrangements place you under any obligation. Mr Dilwyn was planning in any case to assess the property for its rental possibilities. Sir Ambrose's solicitors have begun an inquiry into Elizabeth's whereabouts. They have found that there is no record of her arrival in Germany, only that she was put on a transport in France, with Frankfurt as the intended destination of the train. There will be further investigations, and I pray that they will lead to Elizabeth, but in the meantime, Mr Dilwyn wants to rent the property left to Elizabeth by Sir Ambrose in order to provide income for Kit.

I sometimes think that we are morally obliged to begin a search for Kit's German relations, but I cannot bring myself to do it. Christian was a rare soul, and he detested what his country was doing, but the same cannot be true for many Germans, who believed in the dream of the Thousand-Year Reich. And how could we send our Kit away to a foreign – and destroyed – land, even if her relations could be found? We are the only family she's ever known.

When Kit was born, Elizabeth kept her paternity a secret from the authorities. Not out of shame, but because she was afraid that the baby would be taken from her and sent to Germany. There were dreadful rumours of such things. I wonder if Kit's heritage could have saved Elizabeth if she had made it known when she was arrested. But as she didn't, it is not my place to do so.

Excuse my unburdening myself. My worries travel round my head on their well-worn path, and it is a relief to put them on paper. I will turn to more cheerful subjects – such as last evening's meeting of the Society. After the uproar about your visit had subsided, the Society read your article about books in *The Times*. Everyone enjoyed it – not just because we were reading about ourselves, but because you brought us views we'd never thought to apply to our reading before. Dr Stubbins pronounced that you alone had transformed 'distraction' into an honourable word – instead of a character flaw. The article was delightful, and we were all so proud and pleased to be mentioned in it.

Will Thisbee wants to have a welcome party for you. He will bake a Potato-Peel Pie for the event and has devised a cocoa icing for it. He made a surprise pudding for our meeting last night – cherries flambé, which fortunately burnt to a crisp so we did not have to eat it. I wish Will would leave cookery alone and go back to ironmongery.

We all look forward to welcoming you. You mentioned that you have to finish several reviews before you can leave London – but we will be delighted to see you whenever you come. Just let us know the date and time of your arrival. Certainly, an aeroplane flight to Guernsey would be faster and more comfortable than the mail boat (Clovis Fossey said to tell you that air hostesses give gin to passengers – and the mail boat doesn't). But unless you are bedevilled by sea-sickness, I would catch the afternoon boat from Weymouth. There is no more beautiful approach to Guernsey than the one by sea – either with the sun going down, or with gold-tipped, black stormclouds, or the Island just emerging through the mist. This is the way I first saw Guernsey, as a new bride.

Fondly,

Amelia

14th May 1946

Dear Juliet,

I have been getting your house ready for you. I have asked several of my friends at the market to write to you about their experiences, so I hope they do. If Mr Tatum writes and asks for money for his recollections, don't pay him a penny. He is a big liar.

Would you like to know about my first sight of the Germans? I will use adjectives to make it more lively. I don't usually – I prefer stark facts.

Guernsey seemed quiet that Tuesday – but we knew they were there! Planes and ships carrying soldiers had come in the day before. Huge Junkers thumped down, and after unloading all their men, they flew off again. Being lighter now, and more frolicsome, they hedge-hopped, swooping up and swooping down all over Guernsey, scaring the cows in the fields.

Elizabeth was at my house, but we didn't have the heart to make hair tonic even though my yarrow was in. We just drifted around like a couple of ghouls. Then Elizabeth pulled herself together. 'Come on,' she says. 'I'm not going to sit inside waiting for them. I'm going into town to find the enemy.'

'And what are you going to do after you've found him?' I asks, sort of snappish.

'I'm going to look at him,' she says. 'We're not animals in a cage – they are. They're stuck on this island with us, same as we're stuck with them. Come on, let's go and stare.'

I liked that idea, so we put on our hats and went. But you would never believe the sights we saw in St Peter Port. Oh, there were hundreds of German soldiers – and they were SHOPPING! Arm in arm they went strolling along Fountain Street – smiling, laughing, peering into shop windows, going inside and coming out with their

122

arms full of parcels, calling out to one another. North Esplanade was filled with soldiers too. Some were just lolling about, others touched their caps to us and bowed, polite-like. One man said to me, 'Your island is beautiful. We will be fighting in London soon, but now we have this – a holiday in the sun.'

Another poor idiot actually thought he was in Brighton. They were buying ice lollies for the streams of children following them. Laughing and having a fine time, they were. If it weren't for those green uniforms, we'd have thought the tour boat from Weymouth was in!

We started to go along Candie Gardens, and there everything changed – carnival to nightmare. First, we heard noise – the loud steady rhythm of boots coming down heavy on hard stones. Then a troop of goose-stepping soldiers turned on to our street. Everything about them gleamed: buttons, boots, those metal coal-scuttle hats. Their eyes didn't see anyone or anything – just stared straight ahead. That was scarier than the rifles slung over their shoulders, or the knives and grenades stuck in their boot-tops.

Mr Ferre, who'd been behind us, grabbed my arm. He'd fought on the Somme. Tears were running down his face, and not knowing it, he was twisting my arm, wringing it, saying, 'How can they be doing this again? We beat them and here they are again. How did we let them do this again?'

Finally, Elizabeth said, 'I've seen enough. I need a drink.'

I keep a good supply of gin in my cupboard, so we came home.

I will close now, but I will be able to see you soon and that gives me joy. We all want to come and meet you – but a new fear has struck me. There could be twenty other passengers on the mail boat, and how will I know which one is you? That book photo is a blurry little thing and I don't want to go kissing the wrong woman. Could you wear a big red hat with a veil and carry lilies?

Your friend,

Isola

Wednesday evening

Dear Miss,

I too am a member of the Guernsey Literary and Potato Peel Pie Society – but I didn't write to you about my books, because I only read two – children's tales about dogs, loyal, brave and true. Isola says you are coming to maybe write about the Occupation, and I think you should know the truth of what our States did to animals! Our own government, mind, not the dirty Germans! They would be ashamed to tell of it, but I am not.

I don't much care for people – never have, never will. I got my reasons. I never met a man half so true as a dog. Treat a dog right and he'll treat you right – he'll keep you company, be your friend, never ask you no questions. Cats is different, but I never held that against them.

You should know what some Guernsey people did to their pets when they got scared the Germans was coming. Thousands of them left the island – sailed away to England, and left their dogs and cats behind. Deserted them, left them to roam the streets, hungry and thirsty – the swine!

I took in as many dogs as I could find, but it wasn't enough. Then the States stepped in to take care of the problem – and did worse, far worse. The States warned in the newspapers that, because of the war, there might not be enough food for humans, let alone animals. 'You may keep one family pet,' they said, 'but the States will have to put the rest to sleep. Feral cats and dogs, roaming the island, will be a danger to the children.' And that is what they did. The States gathered them animals into trucks, and took them to St Andrew's Animal Shelter, and those people put them all to sleep. As fast as they could kill one truckload of pets, another truckload would arrive.

I saw it all – the collecting, the unloading at the shelter, and the burying. I saw one woman come out of the shelter and stand in the fresh air, gulping it down. She looked sick enough to die herself. She had a cigarette and then she went back in to help with the killing. It took two days to kill all the animals.

That's all I want to say, but put it in your book.

An Animal Lover

From Sally Ann Frobisher to Juliet

15th May 1946

Dear Miss Ashton,

Miss Pribby told me you would be coming to Guernsey to hear about the war. I hope we will meet then, but I am writing now because I like to write letters. I like to write anything, really. I thought you'd like to know how I was personally humiliated during the war – in 1943, when I was twelve. I had scabies.

There wasn't enough soap in Guernsey to keep clean – not our clothes or ourselves. Everyone had skin diseases of one sort or another – scales or pustules or lice. I myself had scabies on my head – under my hair – and they wouldn't go away. Eventually, Dr Ormond said I must go to Town Hospital and have my head shaved and the tops of the scabs cut off to let the pus out. I hope you will never know the shame of a seeping scalp. I wanted to die.

That is where I met my friend Elizabeth McKenna. She helped the nurses on my ward. The nurses were always kind, but Miss McKenna was kind *and* funny. Her being funny helped me in my darkest hour. When my head had been shaved, she came into my room with a basin, a bottle of Dettol, and a sharp scalpel.

I said, 'This isn't going to hurt, is it? Dr Ormond said it wouldn't hurt.' I tried not to cry.

'He lied,' Miss McKenna said. 'It's going to hurt like hell. Don't tell your mother I said hell.'

I started to giggle, and she made the first slice before I had time to be afraid. It did hurt, but not like hell. We played a game while she cut the rest of the tops off – we shouted out the names of every woman who had ever suffered under the blade. 'Mary, Queen of Scots – snip-snap!' 'Anne Boleyn – thunk!' 'Marie Antoinette – whoosh!' And we'd finished.

It hurt, but it was fun too because Miss McKenna had turned it into a game.

She swabbed my bald head with Dettol and came in to visit me that evening – with a silk scarf of her own to wrap round my head as a turban. 'There,' she said, and handed me a mirror. I looked into it – the scarf was lovely, but my nose looked too big for my face, just as it always did. I wondered if I'd ever be pretty, and asked Miss McKenna.

When I asked my mother the same question, she said she had no patience with such nonsense and beauty was only skin-deep. But not Miss McKenna. She looked at me, considering, and then she said, 'In a little while, Sally, you're going to be stunning. Keep looking in the mirror and you'll see. It's bones that count, and you've got them in spades. With that elegant nose of yours, you'll be the new Nefertiti. You'd better practise looking imperious.'

Mrs Maugery came to visit me in hospital and I asked her who Nefertiti was, and if she was dead. It sounded like it. Mrs Maugery said she was indeed dead, but also immortal. Later on, she found a picture of Nefertiti for me. I wasn't exactly sure what imperious was, so I tried to look like her. As yet, I haven't grown into my nose, but I'm sure it will come – Miss McKenna said so.

Another sad story about the Occupation is my Aunt Letty. She used to have a big gloomy old house out on the cliffs near La Fontenelle. The Germans said it was in their big guns' line of fire, and interfered with their gun practice. So they blew it up. Aunt Letty lives with us now.

Yours sincerely

Sally Ann Frobisher

From Micah Daniels to Juliet

15th May 1946

Dear Miss Ashton,

Isola gave me your address because she is sure you would like to see my list for your book.

If you was to take me to Paris today, and sit me down in a fine French restaurant – the kind of place what has white-lace table-cloths, candles on the walls, and silver covers over all the plates – well, I tell you it would be nothing, nothing compared to my *Vega* box. In case you don't know, the *Vega* was a Red Cross ship that come first to Guernsey on 27th December 1944. They brought food to us then, and five more times – and it kept us alive until the end of the war. Yes, I do say it – kept us alive! Food had not been so plentiful for several years by then. Except for what the devils in the Black Market had, not a spoonful of sugar was left on the Island. All the flour for bread had run out by the beginning of December 1944. Them German soldiers was as hungry as we was – with bloated bellies and no body warmth from food. Well, I was sick to death of boiled potatoes and turnips, and I would have soon turned up my toes and died, when the *Vega* came into our port.

Mr Churchill, he wouldn't let the Red Cross ships bring us any food before then because he said the Germans would just take it and eat it themselves. Now that may sound like clever planning to you – to starve the villains out! But to me it said he just didn't care if we starved along with them. Well, something shoved his soul up a notch or two and he decided we could eat. He says to the Red Cross, 'Oh, all right, go ahead and feed them.'

Miss Ashton, there were TWO BOXES of food for every man, woman and child on Guernsey stored in the *Vega*'s hold. There was other stuff too: nails, seeds for planting, candles, cooking oil, matches, clothes and shoes. Even a few layettes for any new babies around. There was flour and tobacco – Moses can talk about manna all he wants, but he never seen anything like this! I am going to tell you what was in my box. I wrote it all down in my memory book.

Six ounces of chocolate	Twenty ounces of biscuits
Four ounces of tea	Twenty ounces of butter
Six ounces of sugar	Thirteen ounces of Spam
Two ounces of tinned milk	Eight ounces of raisins
Fifteen ounces of marmalade	Ten ounces of tinned salmon
Five ounces of tinned sardines	Four ounces of cheese
Six ounces of prunes	One ounce of pepper
One ounce of salt	A tablet of soap

I gave my prunes away – but wasn't that something? When I die I am going to leave all my money to the Red Cross. I have written to tell them.

There is something else I should say to you. It may be about those Germans, but honour due is honour due. They unloaded all those boxes of food for us from the *Vega*, and they didn't take none, not one box of it, for themselves. Of course, their Commandant had told them, 'That food is for the Islanders. It is not yours. Steal one bit and I'll have you shot.' Then he gave each man unloading the ship a teaspoon, so he could scrape up any spilt flour or grain. They could eat that.

In fact, those soldiers were a pitiful sight. Stealing from gardens, knocking on doors asking for scraps. One day I saw a soldier snatch up a cat and slam its head against a wall. Then he cut the head off, and hid the cat in his jacket. I followed him until he come to a field.

That German skinned that cat and boiled him up in his billy can, and ate it. That was truly, truly a sorrowful sight to see. It made me sick, but underneath my sick, I thought, There goes Hitler's Third Reich – dining out, and then I started laughing fit to burst. I am ashamed of that now, but that is what I did.

That is all I have to say. I wish you well with your book writing. Yours truly,

Micah Daniels

From John Booker to Juliet

16th May 1946

Dear Miss Ashton,

Amelia told us you are coming to Guernsey to find stories for your book. I will welcome you with all my heart, but I won't be able to tell you about what happened to me because I get the shakes when I talk about it. Maybe if I write it down, you won't need me to say it out loud. It isn't about Guernsey anyway – I wasn't here. I was in Neuengamme Concentration Camp in Germany.

You know how I pretended I was Lord Tobias for three years? Peter Jenkins's daughter, Lisa, was going out with German soldiers. Any German soldier, as long as he gave her stockings or lipstick. This was so until she took up with Sergeant Willy Gurtz. He was a mean little runt. The thought of them together benasties the mind. It was Lisa who betrayed me to the German Commandant.

It was March 1944. Lisa was at the hairdresser's, where she found an old, pre-war copy of *Tatler* magazine. There, on page 124, was a picture of Lord and Lady Tobias Penn-Piers. They were at a wedding in Sussex – drinking champagne and eating oysters. The words under the picture told all about her dress, her diamonds, her shoes, her face and his money. The magazine mentioned that they were owners of an estate, called La Fort, on the island of Guernsey.

Well, it was pretty plain – even to Lisa, who's thick as a post – that Lord Tobias Penn-Piers was not me. She did not wait for her hair to be combed out, but left at once to show the picture to Willy Gurtz, who took it straight to the Commandant. It made the Germans feel like fools, bowing and scraping all that time to a servant – so they were extra spiteful and sent me to the camp at Neuengamme.

I did not think I would live out the first week. With other prisoners, I was sent out to clear unexploded bombs during air raids. What a choice – to run into a square with the bombs raining down or to be killed by the guards for refusing. I scuttled like a rat and tried to cover myself when I heard bombs whistle past my head and somehow I was alive at the end of it. That's what I told myself – Well, you're still alive. I think all of us said the same each morning when we woke up – Well, I'm still alive. But the truth is, *we weren't*. What we were – it wasn't dead, but it wasn't alive either. I was a living soul only a few minutes a day, when I was in my bunk. Then, I tried to think of something happy, something I'd liked – but not something I loved, because that made it worse. Just a small thing, like a school picnic or bicycling downhill – that's all I could stand.

It felt like thirty years, but it was only one. In April 1945, the Commandant at Neuengamme picked out those of us who were still fit enough to work and sent us to Belsen. We spent several days in a big open truck – no food, no blankets, no water, but we were glad we weren't walking. The puddles in the road were red.

I imagine you already know about Belsen and what happened there. When we got off the truck, we were handed shovels. We were to dig great pits to bury the dead. They led us through the camp to the spot, and I feared I'd lost my mind because everyone I saw was dead. Even the living looked like corpses, and the corpses were lying where they'd dropped. I didn't know why they were bothering to bury them. The fact was, the Russians were coming from the east, and the Allies were coming from the west – and the Germans were terrified of what they'd see when they got there.

The crematorium could not burn the bodies fast enough – so after we'd dug long trenches, we pulled and dragged the bodies to the edges and threw them in. You won't believe it, but the SS forced the prisoners' orchestra to play music as we lugged the corpses – and for that, I hope they burn in hell with polkas blaring. When the trenches were full, the SS poured petrol over the bodies and set fire to them. Afterwards, we were supposed to cover them with soil, as if you could hide such a thing.

The British got there the next day, and dear God, were we glad to see them. I was strong enough to walk down the road, so I saw the tanks crash down the gates and I saw the British flag painted on their sides. I turned to a man sitting against a fence near by and called out, 'We're saved! It's the British!' Then I saw that he was dead. He had missed it by minutes. I sat down in the mud and sobbed as though he'd been my best friend. The Tommies were weeping too – even the officers. Those good men fed us, gave us blankets, took us to hospitals. And bless them, they burnt Belsen to the ground a month later.

I read in the newspaper that they've put up a war refugee camp in its place now. It gives me the shivers to think of new barracks being built there, even for a good purpose. To my mind, that land should be a blank for ever.

I'll write no more of this, and I hope you understand if I do not care to speak of it. As Seneca says, 'Light griefs are loquacious, but the great are dumb.'

I do have a memory you might like to know about for your book. It happened in Guernsey, when I was still pretending to be Lord Tobias. Sometimes of an evening Elizabeth and I would walk up to the headlands to watch the bombers flying over – hundreds of them, on their way to bomb London. It was terrible to watch, and know where they were headed and what they meant to do. The German radio had told us that London was levelled, flattened, with nothing left but rubble and ashes. We didn't quite believe them, German propaganda being what it is, but still.

We were walking through St Peter Port when we passed the McLaren House. That was a beautiful old house taken over by German officers. A window was open and from the wireless we heard music. We stopped to listen, thinking it might be a programme from Berlin. But when the music ended we heard Big Ben strike and a British voice said, 'This is the BBC – London.' You can never mistake the sound of Big Ben. London was still there! Still there. Elizabeth and I hugged, and started waltzing up the road. That was one of the times I could not think about while I was in Neuengamme.

Yours sincerely,

John Booker

From Dawsey to Juliet

16th May 1946

Dear Miss Ashton,

There's nothing left to do for your arrival except wait. Isola has washed, starched and ironed Elizabeth's curtains, looked up the chimney for bats, cleaned the windows, made up the beds, and aired all the rooms.

Eli has carved a present for you, Eben has filled your woodshed and Clovis has scythed your meadow – leaving, he says, the clumps of wild flowers for you to enjoy. Amelia is planning a supper party for you on your first evening.

My only job is to keep Isola alive until you get here. Heights make her giddy, but nevertheless she climbed up to the roof of Elizabeth's cottage to stomp for loose tiles. Fortunately, Kit saw her before she reached the eaves and ran for me to come and talk her down.

I wish I could do more for your welcome – I hope it will be soon. I am glad you are coming.

Yours,

Dawsey Adams

From Juliet to Dawsey

19th May 1946

Dear Mr Adams,

I'll be there the day after tomorrow! I am far too cowardly to fly, even with the inducement of gin, so I shall come by the evening mail boat.

Would you give Isola a message for me? Please tell her that I don't own a hat with a veil, and I can't carry lilies – they make me sneeze – but I do have a red wool cape and I'll wear that on the boat.

There isn't anything you could do to make me feel more welcome in Guernsey than you already have. I'm having trouble believing that I am going to meet you all at last.

Yours,

Juliet Ashton

From Mark to Juliet

20th May 1946

Dear Juliet,

You asked me to give you time, and I have. You asked me not to mention marriage, and I haven't. But now you tell me that you're off to bloody Guernsey for – what? A week? A month? For ever? Do you think I'm going to sit back and let you go?

You're being ridiculous, Juliet. Any halfwit can see that you're trying to run away, but what nobody can understand is why. We're right together – you make me happy, you never bore me, you're interested in the things I'm interested in, and I hope I'm not deluded when I say I think the same is true for you. We belong together. I know you loathe it when I tell you I know what's best for you, but in this case I do.

For God's sake, forget about that miserable island and marry me. I'll take you there on our honeymoon – if I must.

Love,

Mark

From Juliet to Mark

20th May 1946

Dear Mark,

You're probably right, but even so, I'm going to Guernsey tomorrow and *you can't stop me.*

I'm sorry I can't give you the answer you want. I would like to be able to.

Love,

Juliet

P.S. Thank you for the roses.

From Mark to Juliet

Oh for God's sake. Do you want me to drive you down to Weymouth?

Mark

From Juliet to Mark

Will you promise not to lecture me?

Juliet

From Mark to Juliet

No lectures. However, all other forms of persuasion will be employed.

Mark

From Juliet to Mark

Can't scare me. What can you possibly do while driving?

  Juliet

From Mark to Juliet

You'd be surprised. See you tomorrow.

  M.

PART TWO

From Juliet to Sidney

22nd May 1946

Dear Sidney,

There's so much to tell you. I've been in Guernsey only twenty hours, but each one has been so full of new faces and ideas that I've got reams to write. You see how conducive to writing island life is? Look at Victor Hugo – I may grow prolific if I stay here for any length of time.

The voyage from Weymouth was ghastly, with the mail boat groaning and creaking and threatening to break to pieces in the waves. I almost wished it would, to put me out of my misery, except that I wanted to see Guernsey before I died. And as soon as we came in sight of the island, I gave up the notion altogether because the sun broke beneath the clouds and set the cliffs shimmering into silver.

As the mail boat lurched into the harbour, I saw St Peter Port rising up from the sea, with a church at the top like a cake decoration, and I realised that my heart was galloping. However much I tried to persuade myself it was the thrill of the scenery, I knew better. All those people I've come to know and even love a little, waiting to see – me. And I, without any paper to hide behind. Sidney, in these past two or three years, I have become better at writing than living – and think what you do to my writing. On the page, I'm perfectly charming, but that's just a trick I've learnt. It has nothing to do with me. At least, that's what I was thinking as the boat approached the pier. I had a cowardly impulse to throw my red cape overboard and pretend I was someone else.

I could see the faces of the people waiting – and then there was no going back. I knew them by their letters. There was Isola in a mad hat and a purple shawl pinned with a glittering brooch. She was smiling fixedly in the wrong direction and I loved her instantly. Next to her stood a man with a lined face, and at his side, a boy, all height and angles. Eben and his grandson Eli. I waved to Eli and he smiled like a beam of light and nudged his grandfather – and then I went shy and lost myself in the crowd that was pushing down the gangplank.

Isola reached me first by leaping over a crate of lobsters and pulled me up in a fierce hug that swung me off my feet. 'Ah, lovey!' she cried while I dangled. Wasn't that sweet? All my nervousness was squeezed out of me along with my breath. The others came towards me more quietly, but with no less warmth. Eben shook my hand and smiled. You can tell he was broad and hardy once, but he is too thin now. He manages to look grave and friendly at the same time. How does he do that? I found myself wanting to impress him.

Eli swung Kit up on his shoulders, and they came forward together. Kit has chubby little legs and a stern face – dark curls, big grey eyes – and she didn't take to me one bit. Eli's jersey was speckled with wood shavings, and he had a present for me in his pocket – an adorable little mouse with crooked whiskers, carved from walnut. I gave him a kiss on the cheek and survived Kit's malevolent glare. She has a very forbidding way about her for a four-year-old.

Then Dawsey held out his hands. I had been expecting him to look like Charles Lamb, and he does, a little – he has the same steady gaze. He presented me with a bouquet of carnations from Booker, who couldn't be present; he had concussed himself during rehearsal and was in hospital overnight for observation. Dawsey is dark and wiry, and his face has a quiet, watchful look about it – until he smiles. Except for a certain sister of yours, he has the sweetest smile I've ever seen, and I remembered Amelia writing that he has a rare gift for persuasion – I can believe it. Like Eben – like everyone here – he is too thin. His hair is going grey, and he has deep-set brown eyes, so dark they look black. The lines around his eyes make him seem to be starting a smile even when he's not. I don't think he's more than forty. He is only a little taller than I am and limps slightly, but he's strong – he loaded all my luggage, me, Amelia and Kit into his cart with no trouble.

I shook hands with him (I can't remember if he said anything) and then he stepped aside for Amelia. She's one of those women who are more beautiful at sixty than they could possibly have been at twenty (oh, how I hope someone says that about me one day!). Small, thin-faced, lovely smile, grey hair in plaits wound round her head, she gripped my hand tightly and said, 'Juliet, I am glad you are here at last. Let's get your things and go home.' It sounded wonderful, as though it really was my home.

As we stood there on the pier, some glint of light kept flashing in my eyes, and then around the dock. Isola snorted and said it was Adelaide Addison, at her window with her opera glasses, watching every move we made. Isola waved vigorously at the gleam and it stopped. While we were laughing about that, Dawsey was gathering up my luggage and ensuring that Kit didn't fall off the pier and generally making himself useful. I began to see that this is what he does – and that everyone depends on him to do it.

Off we went out into the countryside. There are rolling fields, but they end suddenly in cliffs, and all around is the moist salt smell of the sea. As we drove, the sun set and the mist rose. You know how sounds become magnified by fog? Well, it was like that – every bird's cry was weighty and symbolic. Clouds boiled up over the cliffs, and the fields were swathed in grey by the time we reached the manor house, but I saw ghostly shapes that I think were the cement bunkers built by the Todt workers.

Kit sat beside me in the cart and sent me many sideways glances. I was not so foolish as to try to talk to her, but I played my severed-thumb trick – you know, the one that makes your thumb look as though it's been sliced in two. I did it over and over again, casually, not looking at her, while she watched me like a baby hawk. She was intent and fascinated but not gullible enough to break into giggles. She just said at last, 'Show me how you do that.'

She sat opposite me at supper and refused her spinach with a thrust-out arm, hand straight up like a policeman. 'Not for me,' she said, and I, for one, wouldn't care to disobey her. She pulled her chair close to Dawsey's and ate with one elbow planted firmly on his arm, pinning him in his place. He didn't seem to mind, even if it did make cutting his chicken difficult, and when supper was over, she climbed on to his lap. It is obviously her rightful throne, and though Dawsey seemed to be attending to the conversation, I spied him poking out a napkin-rabbit while we talked about food shortages during the Occupation. Did you know that the Islanders ground bird-seed for flour until they ran out of it?

I must have passed some test I didn't know I was being given, because Kit asked me to tuck her up in bed. She wanted to hear a story about a ferret. She liked vermin. Did I? Would I kiss a rat on the lips? I said, 'Never,' and that seemed to win her over – I was plainly a coward, but not a hypocrite. I told her the story and she presented her cheek an infinitesimal quarter of an inch to be kissed.

What a long letter – and it only contains the first four hours of the twenty. You'll have to wait for the other sixteen.

Love,

Juliet

From Juliet to Sophie

24th May 1946

Dearest Sophie,

Yes, I'm here. Mark did his best to stop me, but I resisted him mulishly, right up to the bitter end. I've always considered dogged-ness one of my least appealing characteristics, but it was valuable last week.

It was only as the boat pulled away, and I saw him standing on the pier, tall and scowling – and somehow wanting to marry *me* – that I began to think perhaps he was right. Maybe I am a complete idiot. I know of three women who are mad about him – he'll be snapped up in a trice, and I'll spend my declining years in a grimy bed-sit, with my teeth falling out one by one. Oh, I can see it all now: no one will buy my books, and I'll ply Sidney with tattered, illegible manuscripts, which he'll pretend to publish out of pity. Doddering and muttering, I'll wander the streets carrying my pathetic turnips in a string bag, with newspaper tucked into my shoes. You'll send me affectionate cards at Christmas (won't you?) and I'll boast to strangers that I was once nearly engaged to Markham Reynolds, the publishing tycoon. They'll shake their heads – the poor old thing's crazy as a coot, of course, but harmless.

Oh God. This way lies insanity.

Guernsey is beautiful and my new friends have welcomed me so generously, so warmly, that I hadn't doubted that I was right to come here – until just a moment ago, when I started thinking about my teeth. I'm going to stop thinking about them. I'm going to run through the wild-flower meadow outside my door and up to the cliff as fast as I can. Then I'm going to lie down and look at the sky, which is shimmering like a pearl this afternoon, and breathe in the warm scent of grass and pretend that Markham V. Reynolds doesn't exist.

I'm back indoors. It's hours later – the setting sun has rimmed the clouds in blazing gold and the sea is moaning below the cliffs. Mark Reynolds? Who's he?

Love always,

Juliet

27th May 1946

Dear Sidney,

Elizabeth's cottage was plainly built for an exalted guest, because it's quite spacious. There is a big sitting room, a bathroom, a larder and a huge kitchen downstairs. There are three bedrooms, and best of all, there are windows everywhere, so the sea air can sweep into every room.

I've shoved a writing table by the biggest window in my sitting room. The only flaw in this arrangement is the constant temptation to go outside and walk over to the cliff edge. The sea and the clouds don't stay the same for five minutes running and I'm frightened I'll miss something if I stay inside. When I got up this morning, the sea was full of sun pennies – and now it seems to be covered in lemon scrim. Writers ought to live far inland or next to the city dump if they are ever to get any work done. Or perhaps they need to be stronger-minded than I am.

If I needed any encouragement to be fascinated by Elizabeth, which I don't, her possessions would do it for me. The Germans arrived to take over Sir Ambrose's house and gave her only six hours to move her belongings to the cottage. Isola said Elizabeth brought only a few pots and pans, some cutlery and everyday china (the Germans kept the good china, silver, crystal and wine for themselves), her art supplies, an old wind-up gramophone, some records, and armloads of books. So many books, Sidney, that I haven't had time to investigate them – they fill the living-room shelves and overflow into the kitchen. She even stacked some at one end of the sofa to use for a table – wasn't that brilliant?

In every nook, I find little things that tell me about her. She was a noticer, Sidney, like me: all the shelves are lined with shells, feathers, dried sea grass, pebbles, eggshells, and the skeleton of something that might be a bat. They're just bits that were lying on the ground, that anyone else would step over or on, but she saw they were beautiful and brought them home. I wonder if she used them for still lifes? I wonder if her sketchbooks are here somewhere? There's prowling to be done. Work first, but the anticipation is like Christmas Eve seven days a week.

Elizabeth also carried down one of Sir Ambrose's paintings. It is a portrait of her, painted I imagine when she was about eight years old. She is sitting on a swing, all ready to fly up and away – but having to sit still for Sir Ambrose to paint. You can tell by her eyebrows that she doesn't like it. Glares must be inheritable, because she and Kit have identical ones.

The Big House (for want of a better name) is the one that Elizabeth came to close up for Ambrose. It is just up the drive from the cottage and is wonderful. Two-storeyed, L-shaped, and made of beautiful blue-grey stone. It's slate-roofed with dormer windows and a terrace stretching from the crook of the L down its length. The top of the crooked end has a windowed turret and faces the sea. Most of the huge old trees had to be cut down for firewood, but Mr Dilwyn has asked Eben and Eli to plant new trees – chestnuts and oaks. He is also going to have peach trees espaliered in the walled garden, as soon as that is rebuilt too. The lawn is growing green and lush again, covering up the wheel ruts of German cars and trucks.

Escorted at different times by Eben, Eli, Dawsey or Isola, I have been round the island's ten parishes in the past five days; Guernsey is very beautiful in all its variety – fields, woods, hedgerows, dells, manors, dolmens, wild cliffs, witches' corners, Tudor houses and Norman stone cottages. I have been told stories of her history (very lawless) with almost every new site and building. Guernsey pirates had superior taste – they built beautiful homes and impressive public buildings. These are sadly dilapidated and in need of repair, but their architectural splendour still shows through. Dawsey took me to a tiny church – every inch of which is a mosaic of broken china and smashed pottery. One priest did this all by himself – he must have made pastoral visits with a sledgehammer.

My guides are as various as the sights. Isola tells me about cursed pirate chests bound with bleached bones washing up on the beaches, and what Mr Hallette is hiding in his barn (he says it's a calf, but we know better). Eben describes how things used to look before the war, and Eli disappears suddenly and then returns with peach juice and an angelic smile on his face. Dawsey says the least, but he takes me to see wonders – like the tiny church. Then he stands back and lets me enjoy them for as long as I want. He's the most unhurrying person I've ever met. As we were walking along the road yesterday, I noticed that it cut very close to the cliffs and there was a path leading down to the beach below. 'Is this where you met Christian Hellman?' I asked. Dawsey seemed startled and said yes, this was the spot. 'What did he look like?' I asked, because I wanted to picture the scene. I thought it was a futile request, given that men can't describe each other, but Dawsey surprised me. 'He looked like the German you imagine – tall, blond hair, blue eyes – except he could feel pain.'

With Amelia and Kit, I have walked into town several times for tea. Cee Cee was right in his rapture at sailing into St Peter Port. The harbour, with the town traipsing up steeply to the sky, must be one of the most beautiful in the world. Shop windows on High Street and the Pollet are sparklingly clean and beginning to fill up with new goods. St Peter Port may be essentially drab at the moment – so many buildings need restoring – but it does not give off the dead-tired air poor London does. It must be because of the bright light that flows down on everything and the clean, clean air and the flowers growing everywhere – in fields, on verges, in crannies between paving stones.

You really have to be Kit's height to see this world properly. She's marvellous at pointing out things I would otherwise miss – butterflies, spiders, flowers growing tiny and low to the ground – they're hard to see when you're faced with a blazing wall of fuchsias and bougainvillea. Yesterday, I came across Kit and Dawsey crouched in the undergrowth beside the gate, quiet as thieves. They weren't stealing though, they were watching a blackbird tug a worm out of the ground. The worm put up a good fight, and the three of us sat there in silence until the blackbird finally got it down his gullet. I'd never really seen the whole process before. It's revolting.

Kit carries a little box with her sometimes when we go to town – a cardboard box, tied up tightly with string and with a red-yarn handle. Even when we have tea, she holds it on her lap and is very protective of it. There are no air-holes in the box, so it can't be a ferret. Or, oh Lord, perhaps it's a dead ferret. I'd love to know what's in it, but of course I can't ask.

I do like it here, and I've settled in well enough to start work now. I will, as soon as I come back from fishing with Eben and Eli this afternoon.

Love to you and Piers,

Juliet

From Juliet to Sidney

30th May 1946

Dear Sidney,

Do you remember when you sat me down for fifteen sessions of the Sidney Stark School of Perfect Mnemonics? You said that writers who sat scribbling notes during an interview were rude, lazy and incompetent and you were going to make sure I never disgraced you. You were unbearably arrogant and I loathed you, but I learnt your lessons well – and now you can see the fruits of your labour.

I went to my first meeting of the Guernsey Literary and Potato Peel Pie Society last night. It was held in Clovis and Nancy Fossey's living room (spilling over into the kitchen). The speaker of the evening was a new member, Jonas Skeeter, who was to talk about *The Meditations of Marcus Aurelius*.

Mr Skeeter strode to the front of the room, glared at us all, and announced that he didn't want to be there and had only read Marcus Aurelius' silly book because his oldest, his dearest, and his *former* friend, Woodrow Cutter, had shamed him into it. Everyone turned to look at Woodrow, and Woodrow sat there, obviously shocked, his mouth agape.

'Woodrow,' Jonas Skeeter went on, 'came across my field where I was busy with my compost. He was holding this little book in his hands and he said he'd just finished reading it. He'd like me to read it too, he said – it was very *profound*.

"Woodrow, I've got no time to be *profound*," I said.

'He said, "You should make time, Jonas. If you'd read it, we'd have better things to talk about at Mad Bella's. We'd have more fun over a pint."

'Now, that hurt my feelings, no good saying it didn't. My childhood friend had been thinking himself above me for some time – all because he read books for you people and I didn't. I'd let it pass before – each to his own, as my mum always said. But now he had gone too far. He had insulted me. *He put himself above me in conversation.*

'"Jonas," he said, "Marcus was a Roman emperor and a mighty warrior. This book is what he thought about, down there among the Quadi. They were barbarians who was waiting in the woods to kill all the Romans. And Marcus, hard-pressed as he was by those Quadi, took the time to write up this little book of his thoughts. He had long, long thoughts, and we could use some of those, Jonas."

'So I pushed down my hurt and took the damned book, but I came here tonight to say before all, Shame, Woodrow! Shame on you, to put a book above your boyhood friend! But I did read it and here is what I think. Marcus Aurelius was an *old woman* – forever taking his mind's temperature, forever wondering about what he had done, or what he had not done. Was he right – or was he wrong? Was the rest of the world in error? Could it be him instead? No, it was everybody else who was wrong, and he set matters straight for them. Broody hen that he was, he never had a tiny thought that he

148

couldn't turn into a sermon. Why, I bet the man couldn't even have a piss –'

Someone gasped. 'Piss! He said piss in front of the ladies!'

'Make him apologise!' cried another.

'He doesn't have to apologise. He's supposed to say what he thinks, and that's what he thinks. Like it or not!'

'Woodrow, how could you hurt your friend so?'

'For shame, Woodrow!'

The room fell quiet when Woodrow stood up. The two men met in the middle of the floor. Jonas held out his hand to Woodrow, and Woodrow clapped Jonas on the back, and the two of them left, arm in arm, for Mad Bella's. I hope that's a pub and not a woman.

Love,

Juliet

P.S. Dawsey was the only Society member who seemed to find last night's meeting at all funny. He's too polite to laugh out loud, but I saw his shoulders shaking. I gathered from the others that it had been a satisfying but by no means extraordinary evening.

Love again,

Juliet

From Juliet to Sidney

31st May 1946

Dear Sidney,

Please read the enclosed letter – I found it slipped under my door this morning.

Dear Miss Ashton,

Miss Pribby told me you wanted to know about our recent Occupation by the German Army – so here is my letter.

I am a small man, and though Mother says I never had a prime, I did. I just didn't tell her about it. I am a champion whistler. I have won contests and prizes for my whistling. During the Occupation, I used this talent to unman the enemy.

After Mother was asleep, I would creep out of the house. I'd make my silent way down to the Germans' brothel, if you'll pardon the expression, on Saumarez Street. I'd hide in the shadows until a soldier emerged from his tryst. I do not know if ladies are aware of this, but men are not at their peak of fitness after such an occasion. The soldier would start walking back to his quarters, often whistling. I'd start slowly walking, whistling the same tune (but much better). He'd stop whistling, but I *would not stop whistling*. He'd pause a second, thinking that what he had taken for an echo was *actually another person in the dark – following him. But who?* He would look back, I'd have slipped into a doorway. He'd see no one – he'd start on his way again, but not whistling. I'd start to walk again and to whistle again. He'd stop – I'd stop. He'd hurry on, but I'd still whistle, following him with firm footsteps. The soldier would hasten to his quarters, and I'd return to the brothel to wait for another German to stalk. I do believe I made many a soldier unfit to perform his duties well the next day. Do you see?

Now, if you'll forgive me, I will say more about brothels. I do not believe those young ladies were there because they wanted to be. They were sent from the Occupied territories of Europe, same as the Todt slave workers. It could not have been nice work. To the soldiers' credit, they demanded that the German authorities give the women an extra food allowance, same as given to the island's heavy workers. Furthermore, I saw some of these same ladies share their food with the Todt workers, who were sometimes let out of their camps at night to hunt for food.

My mother's sister lives in Jersey. Now that the war is over, she's able to visit us – more's the pity. Being the sort of woman she is, she told a nasty story. After D-Day the Germans decided to send their brothel ladies back to France, so they put them all on a boat to St Malo. Now those waters are very wayward, broiled up and ugly. Their boat was swept on to the rocks and all aboard were drowned. You could see the bodies of those poor women – their yellow hair (bleached hussies, my aunt called them) spread out in the water, washing against the rocks. 'Served them right, the whores,' my aunt said. She and my mother laughed.

It was not to be borne! I jumped up from my chair and knocked the tea table over on them deliberately. I called them dirty old bats.

My aunt says she will never set foot in our house again, and Mother hasn't spoken to me since. I find it all very peaceful.

Yours truly,

Henry A. Toussant

From Juliet to Sidney

Mr Sidney Stark
Stephens & Stark Ltd
21 St James's Place
London SW1

6th June 1946

Dear Sidney,

I could hardly believe it was you, telephoning from London last night! How wise of you not to tell me you were flying home. You know how planes terrify me – even when they aren't dropping bombs. Wonderful to know you are no longer five oceans away, but only across the Channel. Will you come to see us as soon as you can?

Isola is better than a stalking horse. She has brought seven people over to tell me their Occupation stories – and I have a growing pile of interview notes. But for now, notes are all they are. I don't know yet if a book is possible – or, if possible, what form it should take.

Kit has taken to spending some of her mornings here. She brings rocks or shells and sits quietly – well, fairly quietly – on the floor and plays with them while I work. When I've finished we take a picnic lunch down to the beach. If it's too foggy, we play indoors; either hairdressers – brushing each other's hair until it crackles – or Dead Bride.

Dead Bride is not a complicated game like Snakes and Ladders; it's quite simple. The bride veils herself in a lace curtain and stuffs herself into the laundry basket, where she lies as though dead while the anguished bridegroom hunts for her. When he finally discovers her entombed in the laundry basket, he breaks into loud wails. Then and only then does the bride jump up, shout 'Surprise!' and clutch him to her. Then it is all joy and smiles and kisses. Privately, I don't give that marriage much of a chance.

I know that all children are gruesome, but I don't know whether I am supposed to encourage them. I'm afraid to ask Sophie if Dead Bride is too morbid a game for a four-year-old. If she says yes, we'll have to stop playing, and I don't want to stop. I love Dead Bride.

So many questions arise when you are spending your days with a child. For instance, if one likes to cross one's eyes a lot, might they get stuck like that for ever – or is that a rumour? My mother said they would, and I believed her, but Kit is made of sterner stuff and doubts it.

I am trying hard to remember my parents' ideas about bringing up children but, as the child in question, I'm hardly one to judge. I know I was spanked for spitting my peas across the table at Mrs Morris, but that's all I can remember. Perhaps she deserved it. Kit seems to show no ill-effects from having been brought up piece-meal by Society members. It certainly hasn't made her fearful and retiring. I asked Amelia about it yesterday. She smiled and said there was no chance of a child of Elizabeth's being fearful and retiring. Then she told me a lovely story about her son, Ian, and Elizabeth when they were children.

He was to be sent to school in England, and he was not at all happy about it, so he decided to run away from home. He consulted Jane and Elizabeth, and Elizabeth persuaded him to buy her boat for his escape. The trouble was, she had no boat – but she didn't tell him that. Instead, she built one herself in three days. On the appointed afternoon, they carried it down to the beach, and Ian set off, with Elizabeth and Jane waving their hankies from the shore. About half a mile out, the boat began to sink – fast. Jane was all for running to get her father, but Elizabeth said there wasn't time and, as it was all her fault, she would have to save him. She took off her shoes, dived into the waves, and swam out to Ian.

Together, they pulled the wreckage to shore, and she brought the boy to Sir Ambrose's house to dry off. She returned his money, and as they sat steaming before the fire, she turned to him and said gloomily, 'We'll just have to steal a boat, that's all.' Ian told his mother that he'd decided it would be simpler to go to school after all.

I know it will take you a prodigious amount of time to catch up on your work. If you do have a moment to spare, could you find a book of paper dolls for me? One full of glamorous evening gowns, please.

I know Kit is growing fond of me – she pats my knee in passing.
Love,

Juliet

From Juliet to Sidney

10th June 1946

Dear Sidney,

I've just received a wonderful parcel from your new secretary. Is her name really Billee Bee Jones? Never mind, she's a genius anyway. She found Kit two books of paper dolls, and not just any old paper dolls, either – Greta Garbo and *Gone with the Wind* paper dolls, pages of lovely gowns, furs, hats, boas . . . oh they are wonderful. Billee Bee also sent a pair of blunt scissors, a piece of thoughtfulness that would never have occurred to me. Kit is using them now.

This is not a letter but a thank-you note. I'm writing one to Billee Bee too. How did you find such an efficient person? I hope she's plump and motherly, because that's how I imagine her. She enclosed a note saying that eyes do not stay crossed permanently – it's an old wives' tale. Kit is thrilled and intends to cross her eyes until supper.

Love to you,

Juliet

P.S. I would like to point out that contrary to certain insinuating remarks in your last, Dawsey Adams makes no appearance in this letter. I haven't seen Mr Dawsey Adams since Friday afternoon, when he came to pick up Kit. He found us decked out in our finest jewels and marching around the room to the stirring strains of *Pomp and Circumstance* on the gramophone. Kit made him a tea-towel cape, and he marched with us. I think he has an aristocrat lurking in his genealogy: he can gaze into the middle distance just like a duke.

To 'Eben' or 'Isola' or Any Member of a Book Society on Guernsey, Channel Islands

Delivered to Eben, 14th June 1946

Dear Guernsey Book Society

I greet you as those dear to my friend Elizabeth McKenna. I write to you now so that I may tell you of her death in Ravensbrück Concentration Camp. She was executed there in March 1945.

In those days before the Russian Army arrived to free the camp, the SS carried truckloads of papers to the crematorium and burnt them in the furnaces there. Thus I feared you might never learn of Elizabeth's imprisonment and death.

Elizabeth spoke often to me of Amelia, Isola, Dawsey, Eben and Booker. I recall no surnames, but believe the names Eben and Isola to be unusual Christian names and thus hope you may be found easily on Guernsey.

I know that she cherished you as her family, and she felt gratitude and peace that her daughter Kit was in your care. Therefore I write so you and the child will know of her and the strength she showed to us in the camp. Not strength only, but a métier she had for making us forget where we were for a small while. Elizabeth was my friend, and in that place friendship was all that aided one to remain human.

I reside now at the Hospice La Forêt in Louviers in Normandy. My English is yet poor, so Sister Touvier is improving my sentences as she writes them down. I am now twenty-four years old. In 1944, I was caught by the Gestapo at Plouha in Brittany, with a packet of forged ration cards. I was questioned and beaten only, and sent to Ravensbrück Concentration Camp. I was put in Block Eleven, and it was here that I met Elizabeth.

I will tell you how we met. One evening she came to me and said my name, Remy. I had a joy and surprise to hear my name spoken. She said, 'Come with me. I have a wonderful surprise for you.' I did not understand her meaning, but I ran with her to the back of the barracks. A broken window there was stuffed with papers and she pulled them out. We climbed out and ran towards the Lagerstrasse. Then I saw fully what she had meant by a wonderful surprise. The sky showing above the walls looked to be on fire – low-flying clouds of red and purple, lit from below with dark gold. They changed shapes and shades as they raced together across the sky. We stood there, hand in hand, until the darkness came. I do not think that anyone outside such a place could know how much that meant to me, to spend such a quiet moment together.

Our home, Block Eleven, held almost four hundred women. In front of each barracks was a cinder path where roll call was held twice a day, at 5.30 a.m. and in the evening after work. The women from each barracks stood in squares of one hundred women each – ten women in ten rows. The squares would stretch so far to the right and left of ours we could often not see the end of them in the fog.

Our beds were on wooden shelves, built in platforms of three. There were pallets of straw to sleep on, sour-smelling and alive with fleas and lice. There were large yellow rats that ran over our feet at night. This was a good thing, for the overseers hated the rats and stench, so we would have freedom from them in the late nights. Then Elizabeth told me about your island of Guernsey and your book society. These things seemed like Heaven to me. In the bunks, the air we breathed was weighted with sickness and filth, but when Elizabeth spoke, I could imagine the good fresh sea air and the smell of fruit in the hot sun. Though it cannot be true, I don't remember the sun shining one day on Ravensbrück. I loved to hear, too, about how your book society came to be. I almost laughed when she told of the roasted pig, but I didn't. Laughter made trouble in the barracks.

There were several standpipes with cold water to wash in. Once a week we were taken for showers and given a piece of soap. This was necessary for us, for the thing we feared most was to be dirty, to fester.

We dared not become ill, for then we could not work. We would be of no further use to the Germans and they would have us put to death.

Elizabeth and I walked out with our group each morning at six to the Siemens factory, where we worked. It was outside the walls of the prison. Once there, we pushed handcarts to the railway siding and unloaded heavy metal sheets on to the carts. We were given wheat paste and peas at noon, and returned to camp for roll call at 6 p.m. and a supper of turnip soup.

Our duties changed according to need, and one day we were ordered to dig a trench to store potatoes for the winter. Our friend Alina stole a potato but dropped it on the ground. All digging stopped until the overseer could discover the thief. Alina had ulcerated corneas, and it was necessary that the overseers not notice this, for they might think her to be going blind. Elizabeth said quickly she had taken the potato, and was sent to the punishment bunker for one week.

The cells in the bunker were very small. One day, while Elizabeth was there, a guard opened the door to each cell and turned high-pressure water hoses on the prisoners. The force of the water pushed Elizabeth to the floor, but she was fortunate that the water never reached her blanket. She was eventually able to rise and lie under her blanket until the shivering stopped. But a young pregnant girl in the next cell was not so fortunate or so strong as to get up. She died that night, frozen to the floor.

I am perhaps saying too much, things you do not wish to hear. But I must do this to tell you how Elizabeth lived – and how she held on hard to her kindness and her courage. I would like her daughter to know this also.

Now I must tell you the cause of her death. Often, within months of being in the camp, most women stopped menstruation, but some did not. The camp doctors made no provision for the prisoners' hygiene during this time – no rags, no sanitary towels. The women who were menstruating just had to let the blood run down their legs. The overseers liked this, this oh so unsightly blood; it gave them an excuse to scream, to hit. A woman named Binta was the overseer for our evening roll call and she began to rage at a bleeding girl. Rage at her, and threaten her with her upraised rod. Then she began to beat the girl.

Elizabeth broke out of our line fast – so fast. She grabbed the rod from Binta's hand and turned it on her, hitting her over and over again. Guards came running and two of them struck Elizabeth to the ground with their rifles. They threw her into a truck and took her again to the punishment bunker.

One of the guards told me that the next morning soldiers formed a guard around Elizabeth and took her from the cell. Outside the camp walls there was a grove of poplar trees. The branches of the trees formed an allée and Elizabeth walked down this by herself, unaided. She knelt on the ground and they shot her in the back of her head.

I will stop now. I know that I often felt my friend beside me when I was ill after the camp. I had fevers, and I imagined Elizabeth and I were sailing to Guernsey in a little boat. We had planned this in Ravensbrück – how we would live together in her cottage with her baby Kit. It helped me to sleep. I hope you will come to feel Elizabeth by your side as I do. Her strength did not fail her, nor her mind – not ever – she just saw one cruelty too many.

Please accept my best wishes,

Remy Giraud

Note from Sister Cécile Touvier, in the envelope with Remy's letter

Sister Cécile Touvier, Nurse, writing to you. I have made Remy go to rest now. I do not approve of this long letter, but she insisted on writing it.

She will not tell you how ill she has been, but I will. In the few days before the Russians arrived at Ravensbrück, those filthy Nazis ordered anyone who could walk to leave. Opened the gates and turned them loose upon the devastated countryside. 'Go,' they ordered. 'Go – find any Allied troops that you can.'

They left those exhausted, starving women to walk miles and miles without any food or water. There were not even any gleanings left in the fields they walked past. Was it any wonder their walk became a death march? Hundreds of the women died on the road.

After several days, Remy's legs and body were so swollen with famine oedema she could not continue to walk. So she just lay down in the road to die. Fortunately, a company of American soldiers found her. They tried to give her something to eat, but her body would not receive it. They carried her to a field hospital, where she was given a bed, and quarts of water were drained from her body. After many months in hospital, she was well enough to be sent to this hospice in Louviers. I will tell you she weighed less than sixty pounds when she arrived here. Otherwise, she would have written to you sooner.

It is my belief that she will get her strength back once she has written this letter and she can set about laying her friend to rest. You may, of course, write to her, but please do not ask her questions about Ravensbrück. It will be best for her to forget.

Yours truly,

Sister Cécile Touvier

From Amelia to Remy Giraud

Mademoiselle Remy Giraud
Hospice La Forêt
Louviers
France

16th June 1946

Dear Mademoiselle Giraud,

How good you were to write to us – how good and how kind. It could not have been an easy task to call up your own terrible memories in order to tell us of Elizabeth's death. We had been praying that she would return to us, but it is better to know the truth than to live in uncertainty. We were grateful to learn of your friendship with Elizabeth and to think of the comfort you gave to one another.

May Dawsey Adams and I come and visit you in Louviers? We would like to, very much, but not if you would find our visit too disturbing. We want to know you and we have an idea to put to you. But again, if you'd prefer it that we didn't, we won't come.

Always, our blessings for your kindness and courage,

Sincerely,

Amelia Maugery

From Juliet to Sidney

16th June 1946

Dear Sidney,

How comforting it was to hear you say, 'God damn, oh God damn.' That's the only honest thing to say, isn't it? Elizabeth's death is an abomination and it will never be anything else.

It's odd, I suppose, to mourn someone you've never met. But I do. I have felt Elizabeth's presence all along; she lingers in every room I enter, not just in the cottage but in Amelia's library, which she stocked with books, and Isola's kitchen, where she stirred up potions. Everyone always speaks of her – even now – in the present tense, and I had convinced myself that she would return. I wanted so much to know her. It's worse for everyone else. When I saw Eben yesterday, he seemed older than ever. I'm glad he has Eli. Isola has disappeared. Amelia says not to worry: she does that when she's sick at heart.

Dawsey and Amelia have decided to go to Louviers to try to persuade Mademoiselle Giraud to come to Guernsey. There was a heart-rending moment in her letter – Elizabeth used to help her go to sleep in the camp by planning their future in Guernsey. She said it sounded like heaven. The poor girl is due for some heaven: she has already been through hell.

I am to look after Kit while they're away. I am so sad for her – she will never know her mother – except by hearsay. I wonder about her future, too, as she is now – officially – an orphan. Mr Dilwyn said there was plenty of time to decide. 'Let us leave well alone at the moment.' He's not like any other banker or trustee I've ever heard of, bless his heart.

All my love,

Juliet

From Juliet to Mark

17th June 1946

Dear Mark,

I'm sorry that our conversation ended badly last night. It's very difficult to convey shades of meaning while roaring into the telephone. It's true – I don't want you to come this weekend. But it has nothing whatsoever to do with you. My friends have just been dealt a terrible blow. Elizabeth was the centre of the circle here, and the news of her death has shaken us all. How strange – when I picture you reading that sentence. I see you wondering why this woman's death has anything to do with me or you or your plans for the weekend. It does. I feel as though I've lost someone very close to me. I am in mourning.

Do you understand a little better now?

Yours,

Juliet

Miss Juliet Ashton
Grand Manoir, Cottage
La Bouvée
St Martin's, Guernsey

21st June 1946

Dear Juliet,

We are here in Louviers, though we have not been to see Remy yet. The trip has tired Amelia very much and she wants to rest for a night before we go to the hospice.

It was a dreadful journey across Normandy. Piles of blasted stone walls and twisted metal line the roads in the towns. There are big gaps between buildings, and the ones left look like black, broken-off teeth. Whole fronts of houses are gone and you can see in, to the flowered wallpaper and the tilted bedsteads clinging somehow to the floors. I know now how fortunate Guernsey really was in the war.

Many people are still in the streets, removing bricks and stone in wheelbarrows and carts. They've made roads of heavy wire netting placed over rubble, and tractors are moving along them. Outside the towns are ruined fields with huge craters and broken hedges. It is grievous to see the trees. No big poplars, elms or chestnuts. What's left is pitiful, charred black and stunted – sticks without shade. Monsieur Piaget, who owns this pension, told us that the German engineers ordered the soldiers to fell whole woods and coppices. Then they stripped off the branches, smeared the tree trunks with creosote and stuck them upright in holes dug in the fields. The trees were called Rommel's Asparagus and were meant to keep Allied gliders from landing and soldiers from parachuting.

Amelia went to bed straight after supper, so I walked round

Louviers. The town is pretty in places, though much of it was bombed and the Germans set fire to it when they retreated. I cannot see how it will become a living town again.

I came back and sat on the terrace until dark, thinking about tomorrow.

Give Kit a hug from me.

Yours ever,

Dawsey

From Amelia to Juliet

23rd June 1946

Dear Juliet,

We met Remy yesterday. I felt unequal somehow to meeting her. But not, thank heavens, Dawsey. He calmly pulled up garden chairs, sat us down under a shady tree, and asked a nurse if we could have some tea.

I wanted Remy to like us, to feel safe with us. I wanted to learn more about Elizabeth, but I was frightened of Remy's fragility and Sister Touvier's admonitions. Remy is very small and far too thin. Her dark curly hair is cut close to her head and her eyes are enormous and haunted. You can see that she was a beauty in better times, but now – she is like glass. Her hands tremble a good deal, and she is careful to hold them in her lap. She welcomed us as much as she was able, but she was very reserved until she asked about Kit – had she gone to Sir Ambrose in London?

Dawsey told her that Sir Ambrose had died and that we are bringing up Kit. He showed her the photograph of you and Kit that he carries. She smiled then and said, 'She is Elizabeth's child. Is she strong?' I couldn't speak, thinking of our lost Elizabeth, but Dawsey said yes, very strong, and told her about Kit's passion for ferrets. That made her smile again.

Remy is alone in the world. Her father died long before the war; in 1943, her mother was sent to Drancy for harbouring enemies of the government and later died in Auschwitz. Remy's two brothers are missing; she thought she saw one of them at a German station on her way to Ravensbrück, but he did not turn when she screamed his name. The other she has not seen since 1941. She believes that they, too, must be dead. I was glad Dawsey had the courage to ask her questions – Remy seemed to find relief in speaking of her family.

Eventually I broached the subject of Remy coming to Guernsey. She went quiet, and then explained that she was leaving the hospice very soon. The French government is offering allowances to concentration-camp survivors: for time lost, for permanent injuries, and for recognition of suffering. There are also stipends for those wishing to resume their education. The government will help Remy pay the rent of a room or share a flat with other survivors, so she has decided to go to Paris and seek an apprenticeship in a bakery.

She was adamant about her plans, so I left the matter there, but I don't believe Dawsey is willing to do so. He thinks that looking after Remy is a moral debt we owe to Elizabeth. Perhaps he is right, or perhaps it is simply a way to relieve our sense of helplessness. In any case, he has arranged to go back tomorrow and take Remy for a walk along the canal and visit a certain patisserie he saw in Louviers. Sometimes I wonder where our shy Dawsey has gone.

I feel well, though I am unusually tired – perhaps it is seeing my beloved Normandy so devastated. I will be glad to be home, my dear.

A kiss for you and Kit,

Amelia

From Juliet to Sidney

28th June 1946

Dear Sidney

What an inspired present you sent Kit – red satin tap shoes covered with sequins. Wherever did you find them? Where are mine?

Amelia has been tired since her return from France, so it seems best for Kit to stay with me, especially if Remy decides to come to Amelia's when she leaves the hospice. Kit seems to like the idea too – heaven be thanked! Kit knows now that her mother is dead. Dawsey told her. I'm not sure what she feels. She hasn't said anything, and I wouldn't dream of pressing her. I try not to hover unduly or give her special treats. After Mother and Father died, Reverend Simpless's cook brought me huge slices of cake, and then stood there, watching me mournfully while I tried to swallow. I hated her for thinking that cake would somehow make up for losing my parents. Of course, I was a wretched twelve-year-old, and Kit is only four – she would probably like some extra cake, but you understand what I mean.

Sidney, I am in trouble with my book. I have much of the data from the States' records and masses of personal interviews – but I can't make them come together in a structure that pleases me. Straight chronology is too tedious. Shall I send my pages to you? They need a finer and more impersonal eye than mine. Would you have time to look them over now, or is the backlog from the Australian trip still so heavy? If it is, don't worry – I'm working anyway and something brilliant may yet come to me.

Love,

Juliet

P.S. Thank you for the lovely cutting of Mark dancing with Ursula Fent. If you were hoping to send me into a jealous rage, you have failed. Especially as Mark had already telephoned to tell me that Ursula follows him about like a lovesick bloodhound. You see? The two of you *do* have something in common: you both want me to be miserable. Perhaps you could start a club.

From Sidney to Juliet

1st July 1946

Dear Juliet,

Don't bundle them up. I want to come to Guernsey myself. Does this weekend suit you? I want to see you, Kit and Guernsey – in that order. I have no intention of reading your work while you pace up and down in front of me – I'll bring the manuscript back to London.

I can arrive Friday afternoon on the five o'clock plane and stay until Monday evening. Will you book me a hotel room? Can you also manage a small dinner party? I want to meet Eben, Isola, Dawsey and Amelia. I'll bring the wine.

Love,

Sidney

From Juliet to Sidney

Wednesday

Dear Sidney,

Wonderful! Isola won't hear of you staying at the inn (she hints of bedbugs). She wants to put you up herself and needs to know if noises at dawn are likely to bother you. That is when Ariel, her goat, arises. Zenobia, the parrot, is a late sleeper.

Dawsey and I and his cart will meet you at the airfield. May Friday hurry up and get here.

Love,

Juliet

From Isola to Juliet (left under Juliet's door)

Friday – close to dawn

Lovey, I can't stop, I must hurry to my market stall. I am glad your friend will be staying with me. I've put lavender sprigs in his sheets. Is there one of my elixirs you'd like me to slip in his coffee? Just nod to me at the market and I'll know which one you mean. XXX Isola

From Sidney to Sophie

3rd July 1946

Dear Sophie,

I am, at last, in Guernsey with Juliet and am ready to tell you three or four of the dozen things you asked me to find out.

First and foremost, Kit seems as fond of Juliet as you and I are. She is a spirited little thing, affectionate in a reserved way (which is not as contradictory as it sounds) and quick to smile when she is with one of her adoptive parents from the Literary Society. She is adorable, too, with round cheeks, round curls and round eyes. The temptation to cuddle her is nearly overwhelming, but it would be a slight on her dignity, and I am not brave enough to try it. When she sees someone she doesn't like, she has a stare that would shrivel Medea. Isola says she keeps it for cruel Mr Smythe, who beats his dog, and evil Mrs Gilbert, who called Juliet a nosy parker and told her she should go back to London where she belonged.

I'll tell you one story about Kit and Juliet together. Dawsey (more about him later) dropped in to take Kit to watch Eben's fishing boat coming in. Kit said goodbye, flew out, then flew back in, ran up to Juliet, lifted her skirt a quarter of an inch, kissed her knee-cap, and flew out again. Juliet looked dumbfounded – and then as happy as you or I have ever seen her.

I know you think Juliet seemed tired, worn, frazzled and pale when you saw her last winter. I don't think you realise how harrowing those teas and interviews can be; she looks as healthy as a horse now and is full of her old zest. So full, Sophie, I think she may never want to live in London again – though she doesn't know it yet. Sea air, sunshine, green fields, flowers, the ever-changing sky and sea, and most of all the people, seem to have seduced her away from city life. I can easily see why. It's such a welcoming place. Isola is the kind of hostess you always wish you'd come across on a visit to the country but never do. She roused me out of bed the first morning to help her dry rose petals, churn butter, stir something (God knows what) in a big pot, feed her goat Ariel and go to the fish market to buy an eel. All this with Zenobia the parrot on my shoulder.

Now, about Dawsey Adams. I have inspected him, as per instructions. I liked what I saw. He's quiet, capable, trustworthy – oh God, I've made him sound like a dog – and he has a sense of humour. In short, he is utterly unlike any of Juliet's other swains – praise indeed. He didn't say much at our first meeting – nor at any of our meetings since, come to think of it – but let him into a room, and everyone in it seems to breathe a sigh of relief. I have never in my life had that effect on anyone; I can't imagine why not. Juliet seems a bit nervous of him – his silence *is* slightly daunting – and she made a dreadful mess of the tea things when he came round to pick up Kit yesterday. But Juliet has always shattered teacups – remember what she did to Mother's Spode? – so that may not signify. As for him, he watches her with dark steady eyes – until she looks at him and he glances away (I do hope you're appreciating my observational skills).

One thing I can say unequivocally: he's worth a dozen Mark Reynoldses. I know you think I'm unreasonable about Reynolds, but you haven't met him. He's all charm and oil, and he gets what he wants. It's one of his few principles. He wants Juliet because she's pretty and 'intellectual' at the same time, and he thinks they'll make an impressive couple. If she marries him, she'll spend the rest of her life on display at theatres and restaurants and she'll never write another book. As her editor, I'm dismayed by that prospect, but as her friend, I'm horrified. It will be the end of our Juliet.

It's hard to say what Juliet is thinking about Reynolds, if anything. I asked her if she missed him, and she said, 'Mark? I suppose so,' as if he were a distant uncle, and not even a favourite one at that. I'd be delighted if she forgot all about him, but I don't think he'll allow it.

To return to minor topics like the Occupation and Juliet's book, I was invited to accompany her on visits to several Islanders this afternoon. Her interviews were about Guernsey's Day of Liberation on 9 May last year. What a morning that must have been! The crowds were lined up along St Peter Port's harbour. Silent, absolutely silent: masses of people looking at the Royal Navy ships sitting just outside the harbour. Then when the Tommies landed and marched ashore, all hell broke loose. Hugs, kisses, crying, shouting. So many of the soldiers landing were Guernsey men. Men who hadn't seen or heard a word from their families for five years. You can imagine their eyes searching the crowds for family members as they marched – and the joy of their reunions.

Mr LeBrun, a retired postman, told us the most unusual story of all. Some British ships took leave of the fleet in St Peter Port and sailed a few miles north to St Sampson's Harbour. Crowds had gathered there, waiting to see the landing craft crash through the German anti-tank barriers and come up on to the beach. When the doors opened, out came not a platoon of uniformed soldiers but one lone man, got up as a caricature of an English gent in striped trousers, a morning coat, top hat, furled umbrella, and a copy of yesterday's *Times* in his hand. There was a split-second of silence before the joke sank in, and then the crowd roared. He was mobbed, clapped on the back, kissed, and put on the shoulders of four men to be paraded down the street. Someone shouted, 'News – news from London itself,' and snatched the *Times* out of his hand! Whoever that soldier was, he deserves a medal.

When the rest of the soldiers emerged, they were carrying chocolates, oranges, cigarettes to toss to the crowd. Brigadier Snow announced that the cable to England was being repaired, and soon they'd be able to talk to their evacuated children and families in England. The ships also brought in food, tons of it, and medicine, paraffin, animal feed, clothes, cloth, seeds and shoes!

There must be enough stories to fill three books – it may be a matter of culling. But don't worry if Juliet sounds nervous from time to time – she should. It's a daunting task.

I must stop now and get changed for Juliet's dinner party. Isola is swathed in three shawls and a lace tablecloth – and I want to do her proud.

Love to you all,

Sidney

From Juliet to Sophie

7th July 1946

Dear Sophie,

Just a note to tell you that Sidney is here and we can stop worrying about him – and his leg. He looks wonderful: tanned, fit, and without a noticeable limp. In fact, we threw his cane in the sea – I'm sure it's halfway to France by now.

I had a small dinner party for him – cooked by me, and edible, too. Will Thisbee gave me *The Beginner's Cook Book for Girl Guides.* It was just the thing; the writer assumes you know nothing about cookery and gives useful hints: 'When adding eggs, break the shells first.'

Sidney is having a lovely time as Isola's guest. Apparently they sat up late talking last night. Isola doesn't approve of small talk and believes in breaking the ice by stamping on it.

She asked him if he and I were engaged to be married. If not, why not? It was plain to everyone that we doted on each other. Sidney told her that indeed he did dote on me; always had and always would, but that we both knew that we could never marry – because he was a homosexual. Isola neither gasped, fainted, nor blinked. She fixed him with her fish eye and asked, 'And Juliet knows?' When he told her yes, I had always known, Isola jumped up, swooped down, kissed his forehead, and said, 'How nice – just like dear Booker. I'll not tell a soul; you can rely on me.'

Then she sat back down and began to talk about Oscar Wilde's plays. Weren't they a laugh? Sophie, wouldn't you have loved to have been a fly on the wall? I would.

Sidney and I are going shopping now for a present for Isola. I said she would love a warm, colourful shawl, but he wants to get her a cuckoo clock. Why???

Love,

Juliet

P.S. Mark doesn't write, he telephones. He rang me up only last week. It was one of those terrible connections that force you constantly to interrupt one another and bellow 'WHAT?' However, I managed to get the gist of the conversation – I should come home and marry him. I politely disagreed. It upset me much less than it would have done a month ago.

From Isola to Sidney

8th July 1946

Dear Sidney,

You are a very nice guest. I like you. So does Zenobia, or she would not have flown on to your shoulder and perched there so long.

I'm glad you like to sit up late and talk. I like that myself of an evening. I am going to the manor now to find the book you told me about. How is it that Juliet and Amelia never made mention of Miss Jane Austen to me?

I hope you will come and visit Guernsey again. Did you like Juliet's soup? Wasn't it tasty? She will be ready for pastry and gravy soon – you must go at cooking slowly, or you'll just make slops.

I was lonely after you left, so I invited Dawsey and Amelia to tea yesterday. You should have seen how I didn't utter a word when Amelia said she thought you and Juliet would get married. I even nodded and slitted my eyes, like I knew something they didn't, to throw them off the scent.

I do like my cuckoo clock. How cheering it is! I run into the kitchen to watch it. I am sorry Zenobia bit the little bird's head off – she has a jealous nature – but Eli said he'd carve me another one, as good as new. His little perch still pops out on the hour.

With fondness, your hostess,

Isola Pribby

From Juliet to Sidney

9th July 1946

Dear Sidney,

I knew it! I knew you'd love Guernsey. The next best thing to being here myself was having you here – even for such a short visit. I'm happy that you know all my friends now, and they you. I'm particularly happy you enjoyed Kit's company so much. I regret to tell you that some of her fondness for you is due to your present, *Elspeth the Lisping Bunny.* Her admiration for Elspeth has caused her to take up lisping, and I am sorry to say she is very good at it.

Dawsey has just brought Kit home – they have been visiting his new piglet. Kit asked if I was writing to Thidney. When I said yes, she said, 'Thay I want him to come back thoon.' Do you thee what I mean about Elspeth? That made Dawsey smile, which pleased me. I'm afraid you didn't see the best of Dawsey this weekend; he was extra-quiet at my dinner party. Perhaps it was my soup, but I think it more likely that he is preoccupied with Remy. He seems to think that she won't get better until she comes to Guernsey.

I am glad you took my pages home to read. God knows, I am at a loss to divine just *what exactly* is wrong with them. I only know something is.

What on earth did you say to Isola? She dropped in on her way to pick up *Pride and Prejudice* and to berate me for never telling her about Elizabeth Bennet and Mr Darcy. Why hadn't she known that there were love stories not riddled with ill-adjusted men, anguish, death and graveyards! What else had we been keeping from her?

I apologised for such a lapse and said you were absolutely right: *Pride and Prejudice* was one of the greatest love stories ever written – and she might actually die of suspense before she finished it.

Isola said that Zenobia is pining for you – she's off her feed. So am I, but I'm so grateful you could come at all.

Love,

Juliet

From Sidney to Juliet

12th July 1946

Dear Juliet,

I've read your chapters several times, and you're right – they won't do. Strings of anecdotes don't make a book.

Juliet, your book needs a centre. I don't mean more interviews. I mean one person's voice to tell what was happening all around her. As written now, the facts, as interesting as they are, seem like random scattered shots.

It would hurt like hell to write this letter to you, if it wasn't for one thing: you already have the core – you just don't know it yet.

I'm talking about Elizabeth McKenna. Have you noticed that

174

everyone you've interviewed sooner or later mentions Elizabeth? Lord, Juliet: who painted Booker's portrait and saved his life and danced down the street with him? Who thought up the lie about the Literary Society – and then made it true? Guernsey wasn't her home, but she adapted to it and to the loss of her freedom. How? She must have missed Ambrose and London, but she never, I gather, whined about it. She went to Ravensbrück for sheltering a slave worker. Look at how she died, and why.

Juliet, how did a girl, an art student, who had never had a job in her life, turn herself into a nurse, working six days a week in the hospital? She did have dear friends, but she had no one to call her own. She fell in love with an enemy officer and lost him; she had a baby alone during wartime. It must have been terrifying, despite all her good friends. You can only share responsibilities up to a point.

I'm returning the manuscript and your letters to me – read them again and see how often Elizabeth's name crops up. Ask yourself why. Talk to Dawsey and Eben. Talk to Isola and Amelia. Talk to Mr Dilwyn and to anyone else who knew her well. You live in her house. Look around you at her books, her belongings.

I think you should focus your book on Elizabeth. I think Kit would greatly value a story about her mother – it would give her something to hang on to, later. So, either give up altogether – or get to know Elizabeth well.

Think long and hard and let me know if you think Elizabeth could be the heart of your book.

Love to you and Kit,

Sidney

15th July 1946

Dear Sidney,

I don't need more time to think about it – the minute I read your letter, I knew you were right. So slow-witted! Here I've been, wishing that I had known Elizabeth, missing her as if I had – why did I never think of writing about her?

I'll begin tomorrow. I want to talk to Dawsey, Amelia, Eben, and Isola first. I feel that she belongs to them more than the others, and I want their blessing.

Remy wants to come to Guernsey, after all. Dawsey has been writing to her, and I knew he'd be able to persuade her to come. He could talk an angel out of heaven if he chose to speak, which is not often enough for my liking. Remy will stay with Amelia, so I'll keep Kit with me.

Undying love and gratitude,

Juliet

P.S. You don't suppose Elizabeth kept a diary, do you?

17th July 1946

Dear Sidney

No diary, but the good news is that she did draw while her paper and pencils lasted. I found some sketches stuffed into a large art folio on the bottom shelf of the sitting-room bookcase. Quick line drawings that seem marvellous portraits to me: Isola caught unawares, beating something with a wooden spoon; Dawsey digging the garden; Eben and Amelia with their heads together, talking.

As I sat on the floor, turning them over, Amelia dropped in. Together we pulled out several large sheets of paper, covered with sketch after sketch of Kit. Kit asleep, Kit on the move, on a lap, being rocked by Amelia, hypnotised by her toes, delighted with her spit bubbles. Perhaps every mother looks at her baby like that, with that intense focus, but Elizabeth put it on paper. There was one shaky drawing of a wizened little Kit, done the day after she was born, according to Amelia.

Then I found a sketch of a man with a good, strong, rather broad face; he's relaxed and appears to be looking over his shoulder, smiling at the artist. I knew at once that it was Christian – he and Kit have a double crown in exactly the same place. Amelia picked up the drawing; I had never heard her talk about him before and asked her if she'd liked him.

'Poor boy,' she said. 'I was so against him. I thought Elizabeth was mad to have chosen him – an enemy, a German – and I was afraid for her. For the rest of us, too. I thought that she was too trusting, and he would betray her and us – so I told her that I thought she should break it off with him. I was very stern with her.

'Elizabeth just stuck out her chin and said nothing. But the next day he came to visit me. Oh, I was appalled. I opened the door and there was an enormous, uniformed German standing before me. I was sure my house was about to be requisitioned and I began to protest, when he thrust forward a bunch of flowers – limp from being clutched. I noticed he was very nervous, so I stopped scolding and demanded to know his name. "Captain Christian Hellman," he said, and blushed like a boy. I was still suspicious – what was he up to? – and asked him the purpose of his visit. He blushed more and said softly, "I've come to tell you my intentions."

'"For my house?" I snapped.

'"No, for Elizabeth," he said. And that's what he did – just as if I were the Victorian father and he the suitor. He perched on the edge of a chair in my drawing room and told me that he planned to come back to the Island the moment the war was over, marry Elizabeth, grow freesias, read, and forget about war. By the time he'd finished, I was a little bit in love with him myself.'

Amelia was half in tears, so we put the sketches away and I made her some tea. Then Kit came in with a shattered gull's egg she wanted to glue together, and we were thankfully distracted.

Yesterday, Will Thisbee appeared at my door with a plate of little cakes, iced with prune whip, so I invited him to tea. He wanted to consult me about two different women; which one of the two I'd marry if I were a man, which I wasn't. (Do you have that straight?)

Miss X has always been a ditherer – she was a ten-month baby and has not improved in any material way since then. When she heard the Germans were coming, she buried her mother's silver teapot under an elm tree and now can't remember which tree. She is digging holes all over the island, vowing she won't stop until she finds it. 'Such determination,' said Will. 'Quite unlike her.' (Will was trying to be subtle, but Miss X is Daphne Post. She has round vacant eyes like a cow's and is famous for her trembling soprano in the church choir.

And then there is a Miss Y, a local seamstress. When the Germans arrived, they had only packed one Nazi flag. This they needed to hang over their headquarters, but that left them with nothing to run up a flag pole to remind the Islanders they'd been conquered. They visited Miss Y and ordered her to make a Nazi flag for them. She did – a black nasty swastika, stitched on to a circle of dingy puce. The surrounding field was not scarlet silk, but baby-bottom pink flannel. 'So inventive in her spite,' said Will. 'So forceful!' (Miss Y is Miss Le Roy, thin as one of her needles, with a lantern jaw and tight-folded lips.)

Which did I think would make the best companion for a man's nether years? I told him that if one had to ask which, it generally meant neither. He said, 'That's exactly what Dawsey said – those very words. Isola said Miss X would bore me to tears, and Miss Y would nag me to death. Thank you, thank you – I shall keep up my search. *She* is out there somewhere.'

He put on his cap, bowed and left. Sidney, he may have been polling the entire island, but I was so flattered to have been included – it made me feel like an Islander instead of an Outlander.

Love,

Juliet

P.S. I was interested to learn that Dawsey has opinions on marriage. I wish I knew more about them.

19th July 1946

Dear Sidney,

Stories about Elizabeth are everywhere – not just among the Society members. Listen to this: Kit and I walked to the churchyard this afternoon. Kit was playing among the graves, and I was stretched out on Mr Edwin Mulliss's tombstone – it's a table-top one with four stout legs – when Sam Withers, the ancient gravedigger, stopped beside me. He said I reminded him of Miss McKenna when she was a young girl. She used to take the sun right there on that very slab – brown as a walnut, she'd get. I sat up straight as an arrow and asked Sam if he'd known Elizabeth well.

Sam said, 'Well – not as to say real well, but I liked her. She and Eben's girl Jane used to come up here together to that very tombstone. They'd spread a cloth and eat their picnic – right on top of Mr Mulliss's dead bones.' He told me that the girls were always up to mischief – they tried to raise a ghost once and scared the living daylights out of the Vicar's wife. Then he looked over at Kit at the church gate and said, 'That's surely a sweet little girl of hers and Captain Hellman's.'

I pounced on that. Had he known Captain Hellman? Had he liked him? He glared at me and said, 'Yes, I did. He was a fine fellow, for all he was a German. You're not going to take that out on Miss McKenna's little girl, are you?'

'I wouldn't dream of it!' I said.

He wagged a finger at me. 'You'd better not, Miss! You'd best learn the truth of certain matters before you go trying to write a book about the Occupation. I hated the Occupation, too. Makes me angry to think of it. Some of those blighters was purely mean – they'd come into your house without knocking and push you to the ground. They was the sort to like having the upper hand, never

180

having had it before. But not all of them was like that – not all, not by a long shot.'

Christian, according to Sam, was not. Sam liked Christian. He and Elizabeth had come across Sam in the churchyard once, trying to dig a grave when the ground was ice-hard and as cold as Sam himself. Christian picked up the shovel and threw his back into it. 'He was a strong fellow, and he'd finished as soon as he'd started,' Sam said. 'Told him he could have a job with me any time, and he laughed.' The next day Elizabeth turned up with a Thermos jug full of hot coffee. Real coffee from real beans Christian had brought to her house. She gave Sam a warm sweater, too, that had belonged to Christian.

'To tell the truth,' Sam said, 'as long as the Occupation was to last, I met more than one nice German soldier. You would, you know, seeing some of them as much as every day for five years. You couldn't help but feel sorry for some of them – stuck here knowing their families at home were being bombed to pieces. Didn't matter then who started it in the first place. Not to me, anyway.

'Why, there'd be soldiers on guard in the back of potato lorries going to the army's mess hall – children would follow them, hoping potatoes would fall off into the street. Soldiers would look straight ahead, grim-like, and then flick potatoes off the pile – on purpose. They did the same thing with lumps of coal – my, those were precious when we didn't have enough fuel left.

'There was many such incidents: just ask Mrs Godfray about her boy. He had the pneumonia and she was worried half to death because she couldn't keep him warm nor give him good food to eat. One day there's a knock on her door, and when she opens it she sees an orderly from the German hospital. Without a word, he hands her a phial of that sulphonamide, tips his cap, and walks away. He had stolen it from their dispensary for her. They caught him later, trying to steal some again, and they sent him off to prison in Germany – maybe hanged him. We'd not be knowing.'

He glared at me again suddenly. 'And I say that if some toffee-nosed Englishwoman wants to call being human Collaboration, they'll need to talk to me and Mrs Godfray first!'

I tried to protest, but Sam turned his back and walked away. I gathered Kit up and we went home. Between the wilted flowers for Amelia and the gravedigging for Sam Withers, I felt I was beginning to know Kit's father – and why Elizabeth must have loved him.

Next week will bring Remy to Guernsey. Dawsey leaves for France on Tuesday to fetch her.

Love,

Juliet

From Juliet to Sophie

21st July 1946

Dear Sophie,

Burn this letter: I wouldn't want it to appear among your collected papers.

I've told you about Dawsey, of course. You know that he was the first here to write to me; that he is fond of Charles Lamb; that he is helping to bring up Kit; that she adores him. What I haven't told you is that on the very first evening I arrived on the Island, the moment Dawsey held out both his hands to me at the bottom of the gangplank, I felt an unaccountable jolt of excitement. Dawsey is so quiet and composed that I had no idea if it was only me, so I've struggled to be reasonable and casual and *usual* for the last two months. And I was doing very nicely – until tonight.

Dawsey came over to borrow a suitcase for his trip to Louviers – he is going to collect Remy. What kind of man doesn't even own a suitcase? Kit was sound asleep, so we put my case in his cart and walked up to the cliffs. The moon was rising and the sky was coloured in mother-of-pearl, like the inside of a shell. The sea for once was quiet, with only silvery ripples, barely moving. No wind. I have never known the world to be so silent, and it dawned on me that Dawsey himself was exactly that silent too, walking beside me. I was as close to him as I've ever been, so I began to take particular note of his wrists and hands. I wanted to touch them, and the thought made me light-headed. There was a knife-edgy feeling – you know the one – in the pit of my stomach.

All at once, Dawsey turned. His face was shadowed, but I could see his eyes, very dark, watching me, waiting. Who knows what might have happened – a kiss? A pat on the head? Nothing? – because in the next second we heard Wally Beall's horsedrawn carriage (our local taxi) outside my cottage, and Wally's passenger called out, 'Surprise, darling!' It was Mark – Markham V. Reynolds, Junior, resplendent in his exquisitely tailored suit, with a swathe of red roses over his arm.

I truly wished him dead, Sophie.

But what could I do? I went to greet him – and when he kissed me all I could think was, *Don't! Not in front of Dawsey!* He deposited the roses on my arm and turned to Dawsey with his steely smile. So I introduced them, wishing I could crawl into a hole – I don't know why, exactly – and watched stupidly as Dawsey shook Mark's hand, turned to me, shook my hand, and said, 'Thank you for the suitcase, Juliet. Goodnight.' He climbed into his cart and left. Left, without another word, without a backward glance.

I could have cried. Instead I invited Mark in and tried to seem like a woman who had just received a delightful surprise. The cart and the introductions had awakened Kit, who looked suspiciously at Mark and wanted to know where Dawsey had gone – he hadn't kissed her goodnight. Me neither, I thought to myself. I put Kit back to bed and persuaded Mark that my reputation would be in tatters if he didn't go to the Royal Hotel at once. Which he did, but with a very bad grace and many threats to appear on my doorstep the next morning at six.

Then I sat down and chewed my fingernails for three hours. Should I take myself over to Dawsey's house and try to pick up from where we had left off? But where *did* we leave off? I'm not sure. I don't want to make a fool of myself. What if he looks at me with polite incomprehension – or worse still, with pity?

And anyway, what am I thinking? Mark is here. Mark, who is rich and debonair and wants to marry me. Mark, whom I was doing very well without. Why can't I stop thinking about Dawsey, who probably doesn't give a fig about me? But maybe he does. Maybe I was about to find out what was on the other side of that silence.

Damn, damn and damn.

It's two in the morning, I haven't a fingernail to my name and I look at least a hundred years old. Maybe Mark will be repulsed by my haggard appearance when he sees me. Maybe he will spurn me. I don't know that I will be disappointed if he does.

Love,

Juliet

From Amelia to Juliet (left under Juliet's door)

23rd July 1946

Dear Juliet,

My raspberries have come in with a vengeance. I am picking this morning and making pies this afternoon. Would you and Kit like to come for tea (pie) this afternoon?

Love,

Amelia

From Juliet to Amelia

3rd July 1946

Dear Amelia,

I'm terribly sorry, I can't come. I have got a guest.
Love,

Juliet

P.S. Kit is delivering this in the hope of getting some pie. Can you keep her for the afternoon?

From Juliet to Sophie

24th July 1946

Dear Sophie,

You should probably burn this letter as well as the last one. I've refused Mark finally and irrevocably, and my elation is indecent. If I were a properly brought-up young lady, I'd draw the curtains and brood, but I can't. I'm *free*! Today I bounced out of bed feeling frisky as a lamb, and Kit and I spent the morning running races in the field. She won, but that's because she cheats.

Yesterday was horrible. You know how I felt when Mark appeared, but the next morning was even worse. He turned up at my door at seven, radiating confidence and certain that we'd have a wedding date set by noon. He wasn't the slightest bit interested in the Island, or the Occupation, or Elizabeth, or what I'd been doing since I arrived – he didn't ask a single question about any of it. Then

Kit came down to breakfast. That surprised him – he hadn't really registered her the night before. He had a nice way with her – they talked about dogs – but after a few minutes, it was obvious that he was waiting for her to clear off. I suppose, in his experience, nannies whisk the children away before they can annoy their parents. Of course, I tried to ignore his irritation and made Kit her breakfast as usual, but I could feel his displeasure billowing across the room.

At last Kit went outside to play, and the minute the door closed behind her, Mark said, 'Your new friends must be damned smart – they've managed to saddle you with their responsibilities in less than two months.' He shook his head – pitying me for being so gullible.

I just stared at him.

'She's a cute kid, but she's got no claim on you, Juliet, and you're going to have to be firm about it. Get her a nice dolly or something and say goodbye, before she starts thinking you're going to take care of her for the rest of her life.'

Now I was so angry I couldn't speak. I stood there, gripping Kit's porridge bowl with white knuckles. I didn't throw it at him, but I was close. When I could speak again, I whispered, 'Get out.'

'Sorry?'

'I never want to see you again.'

'Juliet?' He had no idea what I was talking about.

So I explained. Feeling better by the minute, I told him that I would never marry him or anyone else who didn't love Kit and Guernsey and Charles Lamb.

'What the hell does Charles Lamb have to do with anything?' he shouted (as well he might).

I declined to elucidate. He tried to argue with me, then to coax me, then to kiss me, then to argue with me again, but it was over and he knew it. For the first time for ages – since February, when I met him – I was absolutely sure that I had done the right thing. How could I ever have considered marrying him? One year as his wife, and I'd have become one of those abject, quaking women who look at their husbands when someone asks them a question. I've always despised that type, but I see how it happens now.

Two hours later, Mark was on his way to the airfield, never (I hope) to return. And I, disgracefully un-heartbroken, was gobbling raspberry pie at Amelia's. Last night, I slept the sleep of the innocent for ten blissful hours, and this morning I feel thirty-two again, instead of a hundred.

Kit and I are going to spend the afternoon at the beach, hunting for agates. What a beautiful, beautiful day.

Love,

Juliet

P.S. None of this means anything with regard to Dawsey. Charles Lamb just popped out of my mouth by coincidence. Dawsey didn't even come to say goodbye before he left. The more I think about it, the more convinced I am that he turned to me on the cliff to ask if he could borrow my umbrella.

From Juliet to Sidney

27th July 1946

Dear Sidney,

I knew that Elizabeth had been arrested for sheltering a Todt worker, but I hadn't known she had an accomplice until a few days ago, when by chance Eben mentioned Peter Sawyer, 'who was arrested with Elizabeth.' 'WHAT?' I screeched, and Eben said he'd let Peter tell me about it.

Peter lives in a nursing home near Le Grand Havre in Vale, so I telephoned him, and he said he'd be very glad to see me — especially if I had a tot of brandy about me.

'Always,' I said.

'Lovely. Come tomorrow,' he replied, and rang off.

Peter is in a wheelchair, but what a driver he is! He races it around like a madman, cuts corners and can turn on a sixpence. We went outside, sat under an arbour, and he tippled while he talked. This time, Sidney, I took notes – I couldn't bear to lose a word.

Peter was still living in his home in St Sampson's when he found the Todt worker, Lud Jaruzki, a sixteen-year-old Polish boy. Many of the Todt workers were permitted to leave their pens after dark to scrounge for food – as long as they came back. They were to return for work the next morning – and if they didn't, a hunt went up for them. This 'parole' was one way the Germans had to see the workers didn't starve – without wasting too much of their own foodstuffs on them.

Almost every Islander had a vegetable garden – some had hen houses and rabbit pens – a rich harvest for foragers. And that is what the Todt slave workers were – foragers. Most Islanders kept watch over their gardens at night – armed with sticks or poles to defend their vegetables. Peter stayed outside at night too, in the shadows of his hen house. No pole for him, but a big iron skillet and metal spoon to bang it with and sound the alarm for the neighbours.

One night he heard – then saw – Lud crawling through a gap in his hedgerow. Peter waited; the boy tried to stand but fell down; he tried to get up again, but couldn't – he just lay there. Peter wheeled over and stared down at the boy.

'He was a child, Juliet. Just a child – face-up in the dirt. Thin, my God he was thin, wasted and filthy, in rags. He was covered with vermin; they came out from his hair, crawled across his face, crawled over his eyelids. That poor boy didn't even feel them – no flicker, no nothing. All he wanted was a goddamned potato – and he didn't even have the strength to dig it up. To do this to boys!

'I tell you, I hated those Germans with all my heart. I couldn't bend down to see if he was breathing, but I got my feet off my chair pedals and managed to prod and poke him until his shoulders were turned to me. Now, my arms are strong, and I pulled the boy on to my lap. Somehow, I got us both up my ramp and into the kitchen –

there, I let the boy fall to the floor. I built up my fire, got a blanket, heated water; I wiped his poor face and hands and drowned every louse and maggot I picked off him.'

Peter couldn't ask his neighbours for help – they might report him to the Germans. The German Commandant had said that anyone who sheltered a Todt worker would be sent to a concentration camp or shot where they stood. Elizabeth was coming to Peter's house the next day – she was his nurse and visited once a week, sometimes more. He knew Elizabeth well enough to be pretty certain that she'd help him keep the boy alive, and that she'd keep quiet about it.

'She arrived around mid-morning the next day. I met her by the door and said I had trouble waiting inside, and if she didn't want trouble she shouldn't come in. She knew what I was trying to say, and she nodded and stepped inside. Her jaw clenched when she knelt by Lud on the floor – he smelt something awful – but she got down to business. She cut off his clothes and burnt them. She bathed him, washed his hair with tar soap – that made a mess, we did laugh, if you can believe it. Either that or the cold water woke him up a bit. He was startled – frightened until he saw who we were. Elizabeth kept speaking softly, not that he could understand a word she said, but he was soothed. She dragged him into my bedroom – we couldn't keep him in my kitchen, the neighbours might come in and see him.

'Well, Elizabeth nursed him. There wasn't any medicine but she got bones for broth and real bread on the Black Market. I had eggs, and little by little, day by day, he got his strength back. He slept a lot. Sometimes Elizabeth had to come after dark, before curfew. It wouldn't do for anyone to see her coming to my house too often. People told on their neighbours, you know – trying to curry favour, or food, from the Germans.

'But someone did notice, and someone did tell – I don't know who it was. They told the *Feldpolizei* and they came out on that Tuesday night. Elizabeth had brought some chicken and was feeding Lud. I sat by his bedstead.

'They surrounded the house, all quiet until they burst in. Well –

we was caught, fair and square. Taken that night, all of us, and God knows what they did to that boy.

'There wasn't any trial, and we was put on a boat to St Malo the next day. That's the last I saw of Elizabeth, led into the boat by one of the guards from the prison. She looked so cold. I don't know where they took her. They sent me to the prison in Coutances, but they didn't know what to do with a prisoner in a wheelchair, so they sent me home again after a week. They told me to be grateful for their lenience.'

Peter said that Elizabeth always left Kit with Amelia when she came to his house. Nobody knew Elizabeth was helping the Todt worker. He believes she let everyone think she was at the hospital.

Those are the bare bones, Sidney, but Peter asked if I'd come back again. I said yes, I'd love to – and he told me not to bring brandy, just myself. He would like to see some picture magazines, if I have any to hand. He wants to know who Rita Hayworth is.

Love,

Juliet

From Dawsey to Juliet

27th July 1946

Dear Juliet,

It will soon be time for me to collect Remy from the hospice, but as I have a few minutes, I will use them to write to you.

Remy seems stronger now than she was last month, but she is very frail yet. Sister Touvier took me aside to caution me – I must see to it that she gets enough to eat, that she stays warm, that she's not upset. She must be with people – cheerful people, if possible.

I've no doubt Remy will get nourishing food, and Amelia will see to it that she's warm enough, but how am I to serve up good cheer? Joking and suchlike is not natural to me. I didn't know what to say to the Sister, so I just nodded and tried to look jolly. I don't think it was very successful, because Sister glanced at me sharply.

Well, I will do my best, but you, blessed as you are with a sunny nature and a light heart, would make a better companion for Remy than I. I don't doubt she will take to you as we all have, these last months, and you will do her good.

Give Kit a hug and kiss for me. I will see you both on Tuesday.

Dawsey

From Juliet to Sophie

29th July 1946

Dear Sophie,

Please ignore everything I have ever said about Dawsey Adams. I am an idiot.

I have just received a letter from Dawsey praising the medicinal qualities of my 'sunny nature and light heart.' A sunny nature? A light heart? I have never been so insulted. Light-hearted is a short step from witless in my book. A cackling buffoon – that's what I am to Dawsey.

I am also humiliated – while I was feeling the knife-edge of attraction as we strolled through the moonlight, he was thinking about Remy and how my light-minded prattle would amuse her. No, it's clear that I was deluded and Dawsey doesn't give a fig for me.

I am too irritated to write more now.

Love always,

Juliet

1st August 1946

Dear Sidney,

Remy is here at last. She is petite and terribly thin, with short black hair and eyes that are nearly black too. I had imagined that she would look wounded, but she doesn't, except for a little limp, which shows itself as a mere hesitancy in her walk, and a rather stiff way of moving her neck.

Now I've made her sound waiflike, and she isn't really. You might think so from a distance, but never up close. There is a grave intensity in her that is almost unnerving. She is not cold and certainly not unfriendly, but she seems to be wary of spontaneity. I suppose if I had been through her experience, I would be the same – somewhat removed from everyday life.

You can cross out all the above when Remy is with Kit. At first, she seemed inclined to follow Kit with her eyes instead of talking to her, but that changed when Kit offered to teach her how to lisp. Remy looked startled, but she agreed to take lessons and they went off to Amelia's greenhouse together. Her lisp is hampered by her accent, but Kit doesn't hold that against her and has generously given her extra instructions.

Amelia had a small dinner party the evening Remy arrived. Everyone was on their best behaviour – Isola arrived with a big bottle of tonic under her arm, but she thought better of it once she saw Remy. 'Might kill her,' she muttered to me in the kitchen, and stuffed it in her coat pocket. Eli shook her hand nervously and then retreated – I think he was afraid he'd hurt her accidentally. I was pleased to see that Remy gets on well with Amelia – they will enjoy each other's company – but Dawsey is her favourite. When he came into the sitting room – a little later than the rest – she relaxed visibly and even smiled at him.

Yesterday was cold and foggy, but Remy and Kit and I built a sandcastle on Elizabeth's tiny beach. We spent a long time on its construction, and it was a splendid, towering specimen. I had made a Thermos of cocoa, and we sat drinking and waiting impatiently for the tide to come in and knock the castle down.

Kit ran up and down the shore, inciting the sea to rush in further and faster. Remy touched my shoulder and smiled. 'Elizabeth must have been like that once,' she said, 'the Empress of the seas.' I felt as if she had given me a gift – even a touch takes trust – and I was glad that she felt safe with me.

While Kit danced in the waves, Remy talked about Elizabeth. She had meant to keep her head down, conserve the strength she had left, and come home as quickly as she could after the war. 'We thought it would be possible. We knew of the invasion, we saw all the Allied bombers flying over the camp. We knew what was happening in Berlin. The guards could not keep their fear from us. Each night we lay sleepless, waiting to hear the Allied tanks at the gates. We whispered that we could be free the next day. We did not believe we would die.'

There didn't seem to be anything else to say after that – though I thought, If only Elizabeth could have held on for a few more weeks, she could have come home to Kit. Why, why, so close to the end, did she attack the overseer?

Remy watched the sea breathe in and out. Then she said, 'It would have been better for her not to have such a heart.'

Yes, but worse for the rest of us.

The tide came in then: cheers, screams and no more castle.

Love,

Juliet

From Isola to Sidney

1st August 1946

Dear Sidney,

I am the new Secretary of the Guernsey Literary and Potato Peel Pie Society. I thought you might like to see a sample of my first minutes, being as how you are interested in anything Juliet is interested in. Here they are:

30th July 1946, 7.30 p.m.
Night cold. Ocean noisy. Will Thisbee was host. House dusted, but curtains need washing.

Mrs Winslow Daubbs read a chapter from her auto-biography, *The Life and Loves of Delilah Daubbs*. Audience attentive – but silent afterwards. Except for Winslow, who wants a divorce. All were embarrassed, so Juliet and Amelia served the pudding, a lovely ribbon cake, on real china plates – which we don't usually run to.

Miss Minor then rose to ask if we were going to start being our own authors, could she read from a book of her very own thoughts? Her text is called *The Common Place Book of Mary Margaret Minor*. Everybody already knows what Mary Margaret thinks about everything, but we said 'Aye' because we all like Mary Margaret. Will Thisbee ventured to say that perhaps Mary Margaret will edit herself in writing, as she has never done in talking, so it might not be so bad.

I moved we have a specially called meeting next week so I don't have to wait to talk about Jane Austen. Dawsey seconded! All said 'Aye'. Meeting adjourned.
Miss Isola Pribby, Official Secretary to the Guernsey Literary and Potato Peel Pie Society.

Now that I'm Official Secretary, I could swear you in for a member if you'd like to be one. It's against the rules, because you're not an Islander, but I could do it in secret.

Your friend,

Isola

From Juliet to Sidney

3rd August 1946

Dear Sidney,

Someone – and I can't imagine who – has sent Isola a present from Stephens & Stark. It was published in the mid-1800s and is called *The New Illustrated Self-Instructor in Phrenology and Psychiatry: with Size and Shape Tables and Over One Hundred Illustrations*. If that is not enough, there's a subtitle: *Phrenology: the Science of Interpreting Bumps on the Head.*

Eben had Kit and me, Dawsey, Isola, Will, Amelia and Remy over for supper last night. Isola arrived with tables, sketches, graph paper, a measuring tape, calipers, and a new notebook. Then she cleared her throat and read the advertisement on the first page: 'You too can learn to read Head Bumps! Stun Your Friends, Confound Your Enemies with Indisputable Knowledge of Their Human Faculties or Lack of Them.'

She thumped the book on to the table. 'I'm going to become an adept,' she announced, 'in time for Harvest Festival.'

She has told Reverend Elstone that she will no longer dress up in shawls and pretend to read palms. No, from now on she will see the future in a scientific way, by reading head bumps! The church will make far more money from head bumps than Miss Sybil Beddoes does with her stall, WIN A KISS FROM SYBIL BEDDOES.

Will said she was absolutely right: Miss Beddoes wasn't a good kisser and he for one was tired of kissing her, even for sweet charity's sake.

Sidney, do you realise what you have unleashed on Guernsey? Isola's already read the lumps on Mr Singleton's head (his stall is next to hers at the market) and told him his Love of Fellow Creatures Bump had a shallow trench right down the middle – which was probably why he didn't feed his dog enough. Do you see where this could lead? One day she'll find someone with a Latent Killer Knot, and he'll shoot her – if Miss Beddoes doesn't get her first.

One wonderful, unexpected thing did come from your present. After pudding Isola began to read the bumps on Eben's head – dictating the measurements for me to write down. I glanced over at Remy, wondering what she would make of Eben's hair standing on end and Isola rummaging through it. Remy was trying to stifle a smile, but she couldn't manage it and burst out laughing. Dawsey and I stopped dead and stared at her! She's so quiet, not one of us could have imagined such a laugh. It was like water. I hope I'll hear it again.

Dawsey and I have not been as easy with each other as we once were, though he still comes often to visit Kit, or to bring Remy over. When we heard Remy laugh our eyes met for the first time for a fortnight. But perhaps he was only admiring how my sunny nature had rubbed off on her. I do, according to some people, have a sunny nature, Sidney. Did you know that?

Billee Bee sent a copy of *Screen Gems* magazine to Peter. There were photographs of Rita Hayworth – Peter was delighted, though surprised to see Miss Hayworth posing in her nightdress! Kneeling on a bed! What was the world coming to?

Sidney, isn't Billee Bee tired of being sent on errands for me? Love,

Juliet

From Susan Scott to Juliet

5th August 1946

Dear Juliet,

You know Sidney doesn't keep your letters clasped to his heart; he leaves them open on his desk for anyone to see, so of course I read them.

I am writing to reassure you about Billee Bee's errand-running. Sidney doesn't ask her. She begs to perform any little service she can for him, or you, or 'that dear child'. She all but coos at him and I all but gag at her. She wears a little angora cap with a chin-bow – the kind that Sonja Henie skates in. Need I say more?

Also, contrary to what Sidney thinks, she isn't an angel straight from heaven, she's from an *employment agency*. Meant to be *temporary*, she has dug herself in – and is now indispensable and *permanent*. Can't you think of some living creature Kit would like to have from the Galapagos? Billee Bee would sail on the next tide for it – and be gone for months. Possibly for ever, if some animal there would just eat her.

All my best to you and Kit.

Susan

From Isola to Sidney

5th August 1946

Dear Sidney,

I know it was you who sent *The New Illustrated Self-Instructor in Phrenology and Psychiatry: with Size and Shape Tables and Over One*

Hundred Illustrations. It is a very useful book and I thank you for it. I've been studying hard, so now I can finger through a whole headful of bumps without peeking into the book more than three or four times. I hope to make a mint for the church at Harvest Festival, as who would not desire to have their innermost workings – good and rotten – revealed by the Science of Phrenology? No one, that's who.

It's a real lightning bolt, this Science of Phrenology. I've found out more in the last three days than I knew in my whole life before. Mrs Gilbert has always been a nasty one, but now I know that she can't help it – she's got a big pit in her Benevolence spot. She fell into the quarry when she was a girl, and my guess is she cracked her Benevolence and was never the same since.

Even my own friends are full of surprises. Eben is garrulous! I never would have thought it of him, but he's got bags under his eyes and there's no two ways about it. I broke it to him gently. Juliet didn't want to have her bumps read at first, but she agreed when I told her that she was standing in the way of Science. She's awash in Amativeness, is Juliet. Also Conjugal Love. I told her it was a wonder she wasn't married, with such great mounds.

Will cackled, 'Your Mr Stark will be a lucky man, Juliet!' Juliet blushed red as a tomato, and I was tempted to say he didn't know much because Mr Stark is a homosexual, but I pulled myself together and kept your secret like I promised.

Dawsey up and left then, so I never got to his lumps but I'll pin him down soon. I think I don't understand Dawsey sometimes. For a while there he was downright chatty, but these days he doesn't have two words to rub together.

Thank you again for the fine book.

Your friend,

Isola

6th August 1946

Bought a small bagpipe for Dominic at Gunther's yesterday STOP Would Kit like one STOP Let me know soonest as they have only one left STOP How's the writing STOP Love to you and Kit STOP Sidney

From Juliet to Sidney

7th August 1946

Dear Sidney,

Kit would love a bagpipe. I would not.

I think the work is going splendidly, but I'd like to send you the first two chapters — I won't feel *settled* until you've read them. Do you have time?

Every biography should be written within a generation of its subject's life, while he or she is still in living memory. Think what I could have done for Anne Brontë if I'd been able to speak to her neighbours. Perhaps she wasn't really meek and melancholy — perhaps she had a screaming temper and dashed crockery to the floor regularly once a week.

Every day I learn something new about Elizabeth. How I wish I had known her myself! As I write, I catch myself thinking of her as a friend, remembering things she did as though I'd been there — she's so full of life that I have to remind myself that she's dead, and then I feel the wrench of losing her again.

I heard a story about her today that made me want to lie down and weep. We had supper with Eben this evening, and afterwards Eli and Kit went out to dig for worms (a task best done by the light of the moon). Eben and I took our coffee outside, and for the first time he chose to talk about Elizabeth to me.

It happened at the school where Eli and the other children were waiting for the Evacuation ships. Eben wasn't there, because the families were not allowed, but Isola saw it happen, and she told him about it that night.

She said that the room was full of children, and Elizabeth was buttoning up Eli's coat when he told her he was scared of getting on the boat – leaving his mother and his home. If their ship *was* bombed, he asked, who would he say goodbye to? Isola said that Elizabeth took her time, as if she was studying his question. Then she pulled up her jumper and unpinned samething from her blouse. It was her father's medal from the first war and she always wore it.

She held it in her hand and explained to him that it was a magic badge, that nothing bad could happen to him while he wore it. Then she got Eli to spit on it twice to call up the charm. Isola saw Eli's face over Elizabeth's shoulder and told Eben that it had that beautiful light children have before the Age of Reason gets at them.

Of all the things that happened during the war, sending children away to try to keep them safe was surely the most terrible. I don't know how the parents endured it. It defies the animal instinct to protect your young. I see myself becoming bearlike around Kit. Even when I'm not actually watching her, I'm watching her. If she's in any sort of danger (which she often is, given her taste in climbing), my hackles rise – I didn't even know I *had* hackles before – and I run to rescue her. When her enemy, the Vicar's nephew, threw plums at her, I roared at him. And through some queer sort of intuition I always know where she is, just as I know where my hands are – and if I didn't, I'd be ill with worry. This is how the species survives, I suppose, but the war put a spanner in all that. How did the mothers of Guernsey live, not knowing where their children were? I can't imagine.

Love,

Juliet

P.S. What about a flute?

9th August 1946

Darling Sophie,

What marvellous news – a new baby! Wonderful! I do hope you won't have to eat dry biscuits and suck lemons this time. I know you two don't care which/what/who you have, but I would love a girl. To that end, I am knitting a tiny matinee jacket and hat in pink wool. Of course Alexander is delighted, but what about Dominic?

I told Isola your news, and I'm afraid she may send you a bottle of her Pre-Birthing Tonic. Sophie – please don't drink it, and don't dispose of it where the dogs might find it. There may not be anything actually poisonous in tonics, but I don't think you should take any chances.

Your enquiries about Dawsey are misdirected. Send them to Kit – or Remy. I hardly see the man any more, and when I do, he's silent. Not silent in a romantic, brooding way, like Mr Rochester, but in a grave and sober way that indicates disapproval. I don't know what the matter is, I really don't. When I arrived in Guernsey, Dawsey was my friend. We talked about Charles Lamb and we walked all over the Island together. I enjoyed his company as much as that of anyone I've ever known. Then, after that appalling night on the cliffs, he stopped talking – to me, anyway. It's been a terrible disappointment. I miss the sense that we understood each other, but I'm beginning to think that was only my delusion all along.

Not being silent myself, I am wildly curious about people who are. As Dawsey doesn't talk about himself – doesn't talk at all to me – I was reduced to questioning Isola about his head bumps in order to find out about his past. But Isola is beginning to fear that the bumps may lie after all, and she offered as proof the fact that Dawsey's violence-prone node isn't as big as it should be, given that he nearly beat Eddie Meares to death!!! Those exclamation marks are mine. Isola seemed to think nothing of it.

It seems that Eddie Meares was big and nasty and gave/traded/sold information to the German authorities in exchange for favours. Everyone knew, which didn't seem to bother him, since he'd go to a bar to show off his new wealth: a loaf of white bread, cigarettes, silk stockings – which, he said, any girl on the Island would be grateful for.

A week after Elizabeth and Peter were arrested, he was showing off a silver cigarette case, hinting that it was a reward for reporting some goings-on he'd seen at Peter Sawyer's house. Dawsey heard about it and went to Mad Bella's the next night. Apparently, he walked up to Eddie Meares, grabbed him by the shirt collar, lifted him up off his stool and began banging his head on the bar. He called Eddie a lousy little shit, pounding his head down between each word. Then they set to it on the floor.

According to Isola, Dawsey was a mess: nose, mouth bleeding, one eye swollen shut, one rib cracked – but Eddie Meares was a bigger mess: two black eyes, two ribs broken, and stitches. The Court sentenced Dawsey to three months in the Guernsey jail, though they let him out after one. The Germans needed the space for more serious criminals – like Black Marketeers and the thieves who stole petrol from army lorries. 'And to this day, when Eddie Meares spies Dawsey coming through the door of Mad Bella's, his eyes go shifty, he spills his beer and not five minutes later, he's darting out the back door,' Isola concluded.

Naturally I was agog and begged for more. As she's disillusioned with bumps, Isola moved on to actual facts. Dawsey didn't have a very happy childhood. His father died when he was eleven, and Mrs Adams, who'd always been sickly, grew odd. She became fearful, first of going into town, then of going into her own garden, and finally she wouldn't leave the house at all. She would just sit in the kitchen, rocking and staring out at nothing Dawsey could ever see. She died shortly after the war began. Isola said that what with all this – his mother, farming, and stuttering so badly – he'd always been shy, and never, except for Eben, had any ready-made friends. Isola and Amelia were acquainted with him, but that was about all.

That was how it was until Elizabeth came – and made him be friends. Forced him, really, into the Literary Society. And then, Isola said, how he blossomed! Now he had books to talk about instead of swine fever – and friends to talk to. The more he talked, the less he stuttered.

He's a mysterious creature, isn't he? Perhaps he *is* like Mr Rochester, and has a secret sorrow. Or a mad wife down in his cellar. Anything is possible, I suppose, but it would have been difficult to feed a mad wife on one set of ration coupons during the war. Oh dear, I wish we were friends again. (Dawsey and I, not the mad wife.)

I meant to have done with Dawsey in a terse sentence or two, but I see that he's taken several sheets. Now I must rush to make myself presentable for tonight's meeting of the Society. I have one decent skirt to my name, and I have been feeling dowdy. Remy, for all she's so frail and thin, manages to look stylish at every turn. What is it about French women?

More anon.

Love,

Juliet

11th August 1946

Dear Sidney,

I am happy that you are happy with my progress on Elizabeth's biography. But more about that later – because I have something to tell you that simply cannot wait. I hardly dare believe it myself, but it's true. I saw it with my own eyes! If, and mind you only if, I am correct, Stephens & Stark will have the publishing coup of the century. Papers will be written, degrees granted, and Isola will be pursued by every scholar, university, library, and filthy-rich private collector in the Western hemisphere.

Here are the facts – Isola was to speak at last night's Society meeting on *Pride and Prejudice*, but Ariel ate her notes just before supper. So, in lieu of Jane, and in a desperate hurry, she grabbed some letters written to her dear Granny Pheen (short for Josephine). They, the letters, made up a kind of story.

She pulled them out of her pocket, and Will Thisbee, seeing them swathed in pink silk and tied with a satin bow, cried out, 'Love letters, I'll be bound! Will there be secrets? Intimacies? Should gentlemen leave the room?'

Isola told him to be quiet and sit down. She said they were letters to her Granny Pheen from a very kind man – a stranger – received when she was but a little girl. Granny had kept them in a biscuit tin and had often read them to Isola as a bedtime story. Sidney, there were eight letters, and I'm not going to attempt to describe their contents to you – I'd fail miserably.

Isola told us that when Granny Pheen was nine years old, her father drowned her cat. Muffin had apparently climbed on to the table and licked the butter dish. That was enough for Pheen's beastly father – he thrust Muffin into a sack, added some rocks, tied up the sack, and flung Muffin into the sea. Then, meeting Pheen walking home from school, he told her what he'd done – and good riddance, too. He then toddled off to the tavern and left Granny sitting in the middle of the road, sobbing her heart out.

A carriage, driving far too fast, came within a whisker of running her down. The coachman rose from his seat and began to curse her, but his passenger, a very big man in a dark coat with a fur collar, jumped out. He told the driver to be quiet, leaned over Pheen, and asked if he could help her. Granny Pheen said no, no – she was beyond help. Her cat was gone! Her dad had drowned Muffin, and now Muffin was dead – dead and gone for ever.

The man said, 'Of course Muffin's not dead. You do know cats have nine lives, don't you?' When Pheen said yes, she had heard of that before, the man said, 'Well, I happen to know your Muffin was only on her third life, so she has six lives left.' Pheen asked how he knew. He said he just did, He Always Knew – it was a gift he'd been born with. He didn't know how or why it happened, but cats would often appear in his mind and chat with him. Well, not in words, of course, but in pictures.

He sat down in the road beside her and told her to keep still – very still. He would see if Muffin wanted to visit him. They sat in silence for several minutes, when suddenly the man grabbed Pheen's hand!

'Ah – yes! There she is! She's being born this minute! In a mansion – no, a castle. I think she's in France – yes, she's in France. There's a little boy petting her, stroking her fur. He loves her already, and he's going to call her – how strange, he's going to call her Solange. That's a strange name for a cat, but still. She is going to have a long, venturesome life. This Solange has great spirit, great verve – I can tell already!'

Granny Pheen told Isola that she was so rapt by Muffin's new fate that she stopped crying. But she told the man she would still miss Muffin very much. The man lifted her to her feet and said of course she would – she *should* mourn such a fine cat as Muffin had been, and she would grieve for some time yet. However, he said, he would visit Solange every so often and find out how she was faring and what she was up to. He asked for Granny Pheen's name and the name of the farm where she lived. He wrote the answers down in a small notebook with a silver pencil, told her she'd be hearing from him, kissed her hand, got back into the carriage, and left.

Absurd as all this sounds, Sidney, Granny Pheen did receive letters. Eight long letters over a year – all about Muffin's life as the French cat Solange. She was, apparently, something of a feline musketeer. She was no idle cat, lolling about on cushions, lapping up cream – she lived through one wild adventure after another – the only cat ever to be awarded the red rosette of the Legion of Honour.

What a story this man made up for Pheen – lively, witty, full of drama and suspense. I can only tell you the effect it had on me – on all of us. We sat enchanted – even Will was left speechless. But here, at last, is why I need your sane head and sober counsel. When the reading was over (and much applauded), I asked Isola if I could see the letters, and she handed them to me.

Sidney, the writer had signed his letters with a grand flourish:

VERY TRULY YOURS,
O. F. O'F. W. W.

Sidney, do you suppose . . . could it possibly be that Isola has inherited eight letters written by Oscar Wilde? Oh God, I am beside myself. I believe it because I *want* to believe it, but is it recorded anywhere that Oscar Wilde ever set foot on Guernsey? Oh, bless Speranza, for giving her son such a preposterous name as Oscar Fingal O'Flahertie Wills Wilde.

In haste and love and please advise at once – I'm having difficulty breathing.

Juliet

13th August 1946

Let's believe it! Billee did some research and discovered that Oscar Wilde visited Jersey for a week in 1893, so it's possible he went to Guernsey then. The noted graphologist Sir William Otis will arrive on Friday, armed with some borrowed letters of Oscar Wilde's from his university's collection. I've booked rooms for him at the Royal Hotel. He's a very dignified sort, and I doubt that he'd want Zenobia on his shoulder.

If Will Thisbee finds the Holy Grail in his junk yard, don't tell me. My heart can't take much more.

Love to you and Kit and Isola,

Sidney

From Isola to Sidney

14th August 1946

Dear Sidney,

Juliet says you're sending a handwriting fellow to look at Granny Pheen's letters and decide if Mr Oscar Wilde wrote them. I bet he did, and even if he didn't, I think you will admire Solange's story. I did, Kit did, and I know Granny Pheen did. She would twirl, happy in her grave, to have so many others know about that nice man and his funny ideas.

Juliet told me that if Mr Wilde did write the letters, many teachers and schools and libraries would want to own them and would offer me sums of money for them. They would be sure to keep them in a safe, dry, properly cooled place. I say no to that! They are safe and dry and chilly now. Granny kept them in her biscuit tin, and in her biscuit tin they'll stay. Of course anyone who wants to come to see them can visit me here, and I'll let them have a look. Juliet said lots of scholars would probably come, which would be nice for me and Zenobia as we like company.

If you'd like the letters for a book, you can have them, though I hope you will let me write what Juliet calls the preface. I'd like to tell about Granny Pheen, and I have a picture of her and Muffin by the pump. Juliet told me about royalties: I could buy me a motorcycle with a sidecar – there is a red one, second-hand, down at Lenoux's Garage.

Your friend,

Isola Pribby

From Juliet to Sidney

18th August 1946

Dear Sidney,

Sir William has come and gone. Isola invited me to be present for the inspection, and of course I jumped at the chance. Promptly at nine, Sir William appeared on the kitchen steps; I panicked at the sight of him in his sober black suit – what if Granny Pheen's letters were merely the work of some fanciful farmer? What would Sir William do to us – and you – for wasting his time?

He settled solemnly among Isola's hemlock and hyssop, dusted his fingers with a snowy handkerchief, fitted a little glass into one eye, and slowly removed the first letter from the biscuit tin. A long silence followed. Isola and I looked at one another. Sir William took another letter from the biscuit tin. Isola and I held our breath. Sir William sighed. We twitched. 'Hmmmm,' he murmured. We nodded at him encouragingly, but it was no good – there was another silence. This one lasted several weeks.

Then he looked at us and nodded.

'Yes?' I said, hardly daring to breathe.

'I'm pleased to confirm that you are in possession of eight letters written by Oscar Wilde, madam,' he said to Isola with a little bow.

'GLORY BE!' Isola bellowed, and she reached over the table and clutched Sir William into a hug. He looked somewhat startled at first, but then he smiled and patted her cautiously on the back.

He took one page back with him to get the corroboration of another Wilde scholar, but he told me that was purely for 'show'. He was certain he was correct.

He may not tell you that Isola took him for a test drive of Mr Lenoux's motorcycle – Isola at the wheel, he in the sidecar, Zenobia on his shoulder. They received a fine for reckless driving, which Sir William assured Isola he would be 'privileged to pay'. As Isola says, for a noted graphologist, he's a good sport.

But he's no substitute for you. When are you going to come and see the letters – and, incidentally, me – for yourself. Kit will do a tap dance in your honour and I will stand on my head. I still can, you know.

Just to torment you, I won't tell you any news. You'll have to come and find out for yourself.

Love,

Juliet

Telegram from Billee Bee to Juliet

20th August 1946

Dear Mr Stark called suddenly to Rome STOP Asked me to come and collect letters this Thursday STOP Please send a telegram if this suits STOP Longing for *petite vacance* on darling island STOP Billee Bee Jones

Telegram from Juliet to Billee Bee

20th August 1946

I'd be delighted STOP Please let me know arrival time and I'll meet you STOP Juliet

From Juliet to Sophie

22nd August 1946

Dear Sophie,

Your brother is becoming altogether too august for my taste – he has sent an emissary to retrieve Oscar Wilde's letters for him! Billee Bee arrived on the morning mail boat. It was a very rough voyage so she was shaky-legged and green-faced – but game! She couldn't manage lunch, but she rallied for dinner and made a lively guest at tonight's Literary Society meeting.

One awkward moment – Kit doesn't seem to like her. She backed away and said, 'I don't kiss,' when Billee attempted one. What do you do when Dominic is rude – chastise him on the spot, which seems embarrassing for everyone, or wait until later for privacy? Billee Bee covered it up beautifully, but that shows her good manners, not Kit's. I waited, but I'd like your opinion.

Ever since I discovered that Elizabeth was dead and Kit was an orphan, I've been worried about her future – and about my own future without her. I think it would be unbearable. I'm going to make an appointment with Mr Dilwyn when he and Mrs Dilwyn return from their holiday. He is her legal guardian, and I want to discuss my possible guardianship/adoption/foster-parenting of Kit. Of course, I want to adopt her, but I'm not sure Mr Dilwyn would consider a spinster of flexible income and no fixed abode a desirable parent.

I haven't said a word about this to anyone here, or to Sidney. There is so much to worry about. What would Amelia say? Would Kit like the idea? Is she old enough to decide? Where would we live? Can I take her away from the place she loves to London? A restricted city life instead of going about in boats and playing tag in churchyards? Kit would have you, me, and Sidney in England, but what about Dawsey and Amelia and all the family she has here? It would be impossible to replace them. Can you imagine a London schoolteacher with Isola's flair? Of course not.

I argue myself all the way to one end of the question and back again several times a day. One thing I am sure of, though, is that I want to look after Kit for ever.

Love,

Juliet

P.S. If Mr Dilwyn says no, not possible, I might just whisk Kit away and come and hide in your barn.

23rd August 1946

Dear Sidney,

Called suddenly to Rome, were you? Have you been elected Pope? It had better be something at least as pressing, to excuse your sending Billee Bee to collect the letters in your place. And I don't know why copies won't do; Billee says that you insist on seeing the originals. Isola would not countenance such a request from any other person on earth, but for you, she'll do it. Please do be awfully careful with them, Sidney – they are the pride of her heart. And see that you return them *in person*.

Not that we don't like Billee Bee. She's a very enthusiastic guest – she's outside sketching wild flowers as I write. I can see her little cap among the grasses. She thoroughly enjoyed her introduction to the Literary Society last night. She made a little speech at the end of the meeting and even asked Will Thisbee for the recipe for his delicious Rhubarb Puff. This may have been carrying good manners too far – all we could see was a blob of pastry that wasn't cooked, covering a reddish substance in the middle.

I'm sorry you weren't in attendance, for the evening's speaker was Augustus Sarre, and he spoke on your favourite book, *The Canterbury Tales*. He chose to read 'The Parson's Tale' first because he knew what a parson did for a living – unlike those other fellows in the book: a Reeve, a Franklin, or a Summoner. 'The Parson's Tale' disgusted him so much he could read no more.

Fortunately for you, I made careful mental notes, so I can give you the gist of his remarks. To wit: Augustus would never let a child of his read Chaucer; it would turn him against Life in general and God in particular. To hear the Parson tell it, life was a *cesspool*, where a man must wade through the muck as best he could; evil ever seeking him out, and evil ever finding him. (Don't you think Augustus has a touch of the poet about him? I do.) Poor old man must forever be doing penance or atoning or fasting or lashing himself with knotted ropes. All because he was Born in Sin – and there he'd stay until the last minute of his life, when he would receive God's Mercy.

'Think of it, friends,' Augustus said, 'a lifetime of misery with God not letting you draw one easy breath. Then in your last few minutes – POOF! you'd get Mercy. Thanks for nothing, I say.

That's not all, friends: man must never think well of himself – that is called the sin of Pride. Friends, show me a man who hates himself, and I'll show you a man who hates his neighbours more! He'd have to – you wouldn't grant anyone else something you can't have for yourself – no love, no kindness, no respect! So I say, shame on the Parson! Shame on Chaucer!' Augustus sat down with a thump.

Two hours of lively discussion on Original Sin and Predestination followed. At last, Remy stood up to speak – she'd never done so before, and the room fell silent. She said softly, 'If there is Predestination, then God is the devil.' No one could argue with that – what kind of God would create Ravensbrück?

Isola is having several of us to supper tonight. Billee Bee will be guest of honour. Isola said that though she doesn't like rifling through a stranger's hair, she will read Billee Bee's bumps, as a favour to her dear friend Sidney.

Love,

Juliet

24th August 1946

Dear Juliet am appalled Billee Bee in Guernsey to collect letters STOP Do not I repeat DO NOT trust her STOP DO NOT give her anything STOP Ivor our new sub-editor saw Billee Bee and Gilly Gilbert (he of the *London Hue and Cry* and late victim of your teapot-throwing) exchanging long loose-lipped kisses in the park STOP The two of them together bodes ill STOP Send her packing without the Wilde letters STOP Love, Susan

From Juliet to Susan

25th August 1946
2 a.m.

Dear Susan,

You are a heroine! Isola herewith grants you honorary member-ship of the Guernsey Literary and Potato Peel Pie Society, and Kit is making you a special present that involves sand and paste (you'll want to open that parcel outside).

The telegram came in the nick of time. Isola and Kit had gone out early to collect herbs, and Billy Bee and I were alone in the house – I thought – when I read your telegram. I bolted upstairs and into her room – she was gone, her suitcase was gone, her handbag was gone, and the letters were gone!

I was terrified. I ran downstairs and telephoned Dawsey to come quickly and help look for her. He did, but first he called Booker and asked him to check the harbour. He was to stop Billee Bee from leaving Guernsey – at any cost!

Dawsey arrived quickly and we hurried down the road to the airfield. I was half-trotting along behind him, looking in hedgerows and behind bushes. We'd reached Isola's farm when Dawsey suddenly stopped short and began to laugh.

There, sitting on the ground in front of Isola's smokehouse, were Kit and Isola. Kit was holding her new ferret (a gift from Billy Bee) and a big brown envelope. Isola was sitting on Billee Bee's suitcase – a picture of innocence, both of them – while an awful squawking was coming from inside the smokehouse.

I rushed to hug Kit *and* the envelope to me, while Dawsey undid the wooden peg from the smokehouse hasp. There, crouched in a corner, cursing and flailing, was Billee Bee – Isola's parrot Zenobia flapping round her. She had already snatched off Billee Bee's little cap, and pieces of angora wool were floating through the air.

Dawsey lifted her up and carried her outside while she screamed. She'd been set upon by a mad witch! Assaulted by her Familiar, a child – clearly one of the Devil's Own! We'd regret it! There'd be legal action, arrests, prison for the lot of us! We wouldn't see daylight again!

'It's you who won't see daylight, you liar! Robber! Ingrate!' shouted Isola.

'You stole those letters,' I screamed. 'You stole them from Isola's biscuit tin and tried to sneak off with them! What were you and Gilly Gilbert going to do with them?'

Billee Bee shrieked, 'None of your business! Wait till I tell him what you've done to me!'

'You do that!' I snapped. 'Tell the world about you and Gilly. I can see the headlines now. "Gilly Gilbert Lures Girl into Life of Crime! From Love-Nest to Lock-up! See Page Three!"'

That shushed her for a moment and then, with the exquisite timing and presence of a great actor, Booker arrived, looking huge and vaguely official in an old army coat. Remy was with him, carrying a hoe! Booker viewed the scene and glared so fiercely at Billee Bee that I was almost sorry for her.

He took her arm and said, 'Now, you'll collect your rightful belongings and take your leave. I won't arrest you – not this time! I will escort you to the harbour and personally put you on to the next boat to England.'

Billee Bee stumbled forward and picked up her suitcase and handbag. Then she made a lunge for Kit and tore the quilted ferret from her arms. 'I'm sorry I ever gave it to you, you little brat.'

How I wanted to slap her! So I did – and I feel sure it jarred her back teeth loose. Island living must be going to my head.

My eyelids are drooping, but I must tell you the reason for Kit and Isola's early-morning herb collecting. Isola felt Billee Bee's head bumps last night and didn't like her reading at all. B.B.'s Duplicitous Bump was big as a goose egg. Kit told her she'd seen Billee Bee in her kitchen, prowling round the shelves. That was enough for Isola, and they put their surveillance plan in motion. They would shadow Billee Bee the next day and *see what they would see*!

They rose early, skulked behind bushes and saw Billee Bee tip-toeing out of my back door with a big envelope. They followed her until she reached Isola's farm. Isola pounced and pushed her into the smokehouse. Kit picked up all Billy Bee's possessions, and Isola went to get her claustrophobic parrot Zenobia, and threw her into the smokehouse with Billee Bee.

But, Susan, what on earth were she and Gilly Gilbert going to do with the letters? Weren't they worried about being arrested for theft?

I am so grateful to you and Ivor. Please thank him for everything: his keen eyesight, his suspicious mind and his good sense. Better still, kiss him for me. He's wonderful! Shouldn't Sidney promote him from sub-editor to Editor in Chief?

Love,

Juliet

26th August 1946

Dear Juliet,

Yes, Ivor is wonderful and I have told him so. I kissed him for you, and then once more for myself! Sidney did promote him – not to Editor in Chief, but I imagine he's well on his way.

What did Billee Bee and Gilly plan to do? You and I weren't in London when the 'teapot incident' broke – we missed the uproar. Every journalist and publisher who loathes Gilly Gilbert and *The London Hue and Cry* – and there are plenty – was delighted. They thought it was hilarious and Sidney's statement to the press didn't do much to soothe matters – just whipped them into fresh fits of laughter. Well, neither Gilly nor the *LH&C* believes in forgiveness. Their motto is get even – be quiet, be patient, and wait for the day of vengeance to come, as it surely will!

Billee Bee, poor besotted booby and Gilly's mistress, felt the shame even more keenly. Can't you see them huddled together, plotting? Billee Bee was to insinuate herself into Stephens & Stark, and find anything, anything at all, that would hurt you and Sidney, or better still, turn you into laughing stocks.

You know how rumours spread like wildfire round the publishing world. Everyone knows you're in Guernsey writing a book about the Occupation, and in the last two weeks, people have begun to whisper that you've discovered a new Oscar Wilde work there (Sir William may be distinguished, but he's not discreet).

It was too good for Gilly to resist. Billee Bee would steal the letters. *The London Hue and Cry* would publish them, and you and Sidney would be scuppered. What fun they'd have! They'd worry about legal action later. And of course, never mind what it would do to Isola.

It makes me feel sick to think how close they came to succeeding. Thank God for Ivor and Isola – and Billee Bee's Duplicitous Bump.

Ivor will fly over to copy the letters on Tuesday. He has found a yellow velvet ferret, with emerald-green feral eyes and ivory fangs for Kit. I think she'll want to kiss him for it. You can too – but keep it brief. I make no threats, Juliet – *but Ivor is mine!*

Love,

Susan

Telegram from Sidney to Juliet

26th August 1946

I'll never leave London again STOP Isola and Kit deserve a medal and so do you STOP Love Sidney

From Juliet to Sophie

29th August 1946

Dear Sophie,

Ivor has come and gone, and Oscar Wilde's letters are safely back in Isola's biscuit tin. I've settled down as much as I can until Sidney reads them – I'm dying to know what he thinks. I was very calm on the day of our adventure. It was only later, once Kit was in bed, that I began to feel skittish, and started pacing the floor.

Then there was a knock at the door. I was amazed – and a little flustered – to see Dawsey through the window. I threw open the door to greet him, only to be greeted by Remy, too. They had come to see how I was. How kind. How disappointing.

Surely Remy's homesick by now? I have been reading an article by a woman called Giselle Pelletier, a political prisoner held at Ravensbrück for five years. She writes about how difficult it is for you to get on with your life as a camp survivor. No one in France – neither friends nor family – wants to know anything about your life in the camps, and they think that the sooner you put it out of your mind – and out of their hearing – the happier you'll be.

According to Miss Pelletier, it is not that you want to belabour anyone with details, but it *did happen to you* and you can't pretend it didn't. 'Let's put everything behind us,' seems to be France's cry. 'Everything – the war, the Vichy, the Milice, Drancy, the Jews – it's all over now. After all, everyone suffered, not just you.' In the face of this institutional amnesia, she writes, the only thing that helps is to talk to fellow survivors. They know what life in the camps was. You speak, and they can speak back. They talk, they rail, they cry, they tell one story after another – some tragic, some absurd. Sometimes they can even laugh together. The relief is enormous, she says. Perhaps communication with other survivors would be a better cure for Remy's distress than bucolic Island life. She is physically stronger now – she's not as shockingly thin as she was – but she still seems haunted.

Mr Dilwyn is back from his holiday, and I must make an appointment to talk to him about Kit soon. I keep putting it off – I'm so dreadfully afraid that he'll refuse to consider it. I wish I looked more motherly – perhaps I could buy a fichu. If he asks for character references, will you give me one? Does Dominic know his alphabet yet? If so, he can write out this:

Dear Mr Dilwyn
    Juliet Dryhurst Ashton is a very nice lady – sober, clean and responsible. You should let her be Kit McKenna's mother.
    Yours sincerely,
    James Dominic Strachan

I didn't tell you, did I, about Mr Dilwyn's plans for Kit's inheritance in Guernsey? He's engaged Dawsey, and a crew Dawsey is to select, to restore the Big House: banisters replaced; graffiti removed from the walls and paintings; windows put in; torn-out plumbing replaced with new; chimneys cleaned; wiring checked and terrace paving stones repointed – or whatever it is you do to old stones. Mr Dilwyn is not yet certain what can be done with the wooden panelling in the library – it had a beautiful carved frieze of fruit and ribbons, which the Germans used for target practice.

As no one will want to holiday on the Continent for the next few years, Mr Dilwyn is hoping that the Channel Islands will become a tourist haven again – and Kit's house would make a wonderful holiday home.

But on to stranger events: the Benoit sisters asked me and Kit to tea this afternoon. I had never met them, and it was quite an odd invitation. They asked if Kit had 'a steady eye and a good aim'. Did she like rituals? Bewildered, I asked Eben if he knew the Benoit sisters. Were they sane? Was it safe to take Kit there? Eben roared with laughter and said yes, the sisters were safe and sane. He said Jane and Elizabeth had visited them every summer for five years. They always wore starched pinafores, polished court shoes and little lace gloves. We would have a lovely time, he said, and he was glad to know the old traditions were coming back. We would have a lavish tea, with entertainments afterwards, and we should go.

None of which told me what to expect. They are identical twins, in their eighties. Very prim and ladylike, dressed in ankle-length gowns of black georgette, larded with jet beads at bosom and hem, their white hair piled like swirls of whipped cream on top of their heads. So charming, Sophie. We did have a sinful tea, and I'd barely put my cup down when Yvonne (older by ten minutes) said, 'Sister, I do believe Elizabeth's child is too small yet.' Yvette said, 'I believe you're right, Sister. Perhaps Miss Ashton would help us?'

I think it was very brave of me to say, 'I'd be delighted,' when I had no idea what they were proposing.

'So kind, Miss Ashton. We denied ourselves during the war – so disloyal to the Crown, somehow. Our arthritis has grown very much worse; we cannot even join you in the rites. It will be our pleasure to watch!'

Yvette went to a drawer in the sideboard, while Yvonne opened one of the double doors between the drawing room and the dining room. Taped to the previously hidden panel was a full-page, full-length newspaper portrait in sepia of the Duchess of Windsor, *Mrs Wallis Simpson as was* (cut out, I gather, from the Society pages of the *Baltimore Sun* in the late '30s).

Yvette handed me four silver-tipped, finely balanced, evil-looking darts. 'Go for the eyes, dear,' she said. So I did.

'Splendid! Three-for-four, Sister. Almost as good as dear Jane! Elizabeth always fumbled at the last moment! Shall you want to try again next year?'

It's a simple story, but sad. Yvette and Yvonne adored the Prince of Wales. 'So darling in his little plus fours.' 'How the man could waltz!' 'How debonair in evening dress!' So admirable, so royal – until that hussy got hold of him. 'Snatched him from the throne! His crown – gone!' It broke their hearts. Kit was enthralled – as well she might be. I am going to practise my aim – four-for-four being my new goal in life.

Don't you wish we had known the Benoit sisters while we were growing up?

Love and kisses,

Juliet

From Juliet to Sidney

2nd September 1946

Dear Sidney,

Something happened this afternoon; while it ended well, it was disturbing, and I can't get to sleep. I am writing to you instead of

Sophie, because she's pregnant and you're not. You don't have a delicate condition to be upset in, and Sophie does – I am losing my grip on grammar.

Kit was with Isola, making gingerbread men. Remy and I needed some ink and Dawsey needed some sort of putty for the Big House, so we all walked together into St Peter Port. We took the cliff walk by Fermain Bay. It's beautiful – a rugged path that wanders up and around the headlands. I was a little in front of Remy and Dawsey because the path had narrowed. A tall, red-haired woman walked around the large boulder at the path's turning and came towards us. She had a dog with her, a huge Alsatian. He wasn't on a lead and seemed overjoyed to see me. I laughed, and the woman called out, 'Don't worry. He never bites.' He put his paws on my shoulders, attempting a big, slobbering kiss.

Then, behind me, I heard an awful gulping gasp: a deep gagging that went on and on. I can't describe it. I turned and saw that it was Remy; she was bent over almost double and vomiting. Dawsey had caught her and was holding her as she went on vomiting, deep spasms of it, over both of them. It was terrible to see and hear. Dawsey shouted, 'Get that dog away, Juliet! Now!'

I frantically pushed the dog away. The woman was crying and apologising, almost hysterical herself. I held on to the dog's collar and kept saying,' It's all right! It's all right! It's not your fault. Please go. Go!' At last she did, hauling her poor confused pet along by his collar. Remy was quiet then, only gasping for breath. Dawsey looked over her head and said, 'Let's get her to your house, Juliet. It's the nearest.' He picked her up and carried her, I trailing behind, helpless and frightened.

Remy was cold and shaking, so I ran her a bath, and once she was warm again, put her to bed. She was already half-asleep, so I gathered her clothes into a bundle, and went downstairs.

Dawsey was standing by the window, looking out. Without turning he said, 'She told me once that those guards used big dogs. Riled them up and deliberately let them loose on the lines of women standing for roll call – just to watch the fun. *Christ!* I've been

222

ignorant, Juliet. I thought being here with us would help her forget. Goodwill isn't enough, is it, Juliet? Not nearly enough.'

'No,' I said, 'it isn't.' He didn't say anything else, just nodded to me and left. I telephoned Amelia to tell her where Remy was and why and then started the washing. Isola brought Kit back; we had supper and played Snap until bedtime.

But I can't sleep. I'm so ashamed of myself. Had I really thought Remy well enough to go home – or did I just want her to go? Did I think it was well time for her to go back to France – to just get on with It, whatever It might be? I did – and it's sickening.

Love,

Juliet

P.S. As long as I'm confessing, I might as well tell you something else. Bad as it was to stand there holding Remy's awful clothes and smelling Dawsey's ruined ones, all I could think of was what he said: *Goodwill isn't enough, is it?* Does that mean that is all he feels for her? I've chewed over that errant thought all evening.

Night Letter from Sidney to Juliet

4th September 1946

Dear Juliet,

All that errant thought means is that you're in love with Dawsey yourself. Surprised? I'm not. Don't know what took you so long to realise it – sea air is supposed to clear your head. I want to come and see you and Oscar's letters for myself, but I can't get away till the 13th. All right?

Love,

Sidney

5th September 1946

You're insufferable especially when you're right STOP Lovely to see you anyhow on the 13th STOP Love Juliet

From Isola to Sidney

6th September 1946

Dear Sidney,

Juliet says you're coming to see Granny Pheen's letters with your own eyes, and I say it's about time. Not that I minded Ivor; he was a nice fellow, though he should stop wearing those little hairbow ties. I told him they didn't do much for him, but he was more interested in hearing about my suspicions of Billy Bee Jones, how I shadowed her and locked her up in the smokehouse. He said it was a fine piece of detective work and Miss Marple couldn't have done better herself! Miss Marple is not a friend of his, she is a lady detective in fiction books, who uses all she knows about HUMAN NATURE to work out mysteries and solve crimes that the police can't.

He set me thinking about how wonderful it would be to solve mysteries myself. If only I knew of any. Ivor said skulduggery is everywhere, and with my fine instincts, I could train myself to become another Miss Marple. 'You clearly have excellent observational skills. All you need now is practice. Note everything and write it down.'

I went to Amelia's and borrowed a few books with Miss Marple in them. She's a caution, isn't she? Just sitting there quietly, knitting away; seeing things everybody else misses. I could keep my ears open for what doesn't sound right, see things from the sides of my eyes. Mind you, we don't have any unsolved mysteries in Guernsey, but that's not to say we won't one day – and when we do, I'll be ready.

I still cherish the head-bump book you sent me and I hope your feelings are not hurt that I want to pursue another calling. I still trust the truth of lumps; it's just that I've read the head bumps of everyone I care for, except yours, and it can get tedious.

Juliet says you're coming next Friday. I could meet your plane and take you to Juliet's. Eben is having a party on the beach the next evening, and he says you are most welcome. Eben hardly ever gives parties, but he said this one is to make a happy announcement to us all. A celebration! But of What? Does he mean to announce nuptials? But whose? I hope he is not getting married hisself; wives don't generally let husbands out by themselves of an evening and I would miss Eben's company.

Your friend,

Isola

From Juliet to Sophie

7th September 1946

Dear Sophie,

At last, I mustered my courage and told Amelia that I wanted to adopt Kit. Her opinion means a great deal to me – she loved Elizabeth so dearly; she knows Kit so well – and me, almost well enough. I was anxious for her approval – and terrified that I wouldn't get it. I choked on my tea but in the end managed to get the words out. Her relief was so visible I was shocked. I hadn't realised how worried she'd been about Kit's future.

She started to say, 'If I could have one –' then stopped and started again. 'I think it would be a wonderful thing for both of you. It would be the best possible thing –' She broke off and pulled out a handkerchief. And then, of course, I pulled out my handkerchief. After we'd finished crying, we plotted. Amelia will come with me to see Mr Dilwyn. 'I have known him since he was in short trousers,' she said. 'He won't dare refuse me.' Having Amelia on your side is like having the Third Army at your back.

But something wonderful – even more wonderful than having Amelia's approval – has happened. My last doubt has shrunk to less than pinpoint-size. Do you remember my telling you about the little box Kit carried, tied up with string? The one I thought might hold a dead ferret? She came into my room this morning and patted my face until I woke up. She was carrying her box.

Without a word, she began to undo the string. She took the lid off, parted the tissue paper and gave the box to me. Sophie – she stood back and watched my face as I turned over the things in the box and then lifted them all out on to the bedcover. The articles were a tiny, eyelet-covered baby pillow; a small photograph of Elizabeth digging in her garden and laughing up at Dawsey; a woman's linen handkerchief, smelling faintly of jasmine; a man's signet ring; and a small leather book of Rilke's poetry with the inscription, *For Elizabeth, who turns darkness into light, Christian.* Tucked into the book was a much-folded scrap of paper. Kit nodded, so I carefully opened it and read, 'Amelia – kiss her for me when she wakes up. I'll be back by six. Elizabeth. P.S. Doesn't she have the most beautiful feet?'

She was showing me her treasures, Sophie – her eyes didn't once leave my face. We were both so solemn, and I, for once, didn't start crying, I just held out my arms. She climbed into them, and under the covers with me – and went straight to sleep. Not me! I couldn't. I was too happy planning the rest of our lives.

I don't care about living in London – I love Guernsey and I want to stay here, even after I've finished Elizabeth's book. I can't imagine Kit living in London, having to wear shoes all the time, having to walk instead of run, having no pigs to visit. No fishing with Eben and Eli, no visits to Amelia, no potion-mixing with Isola, and most of all, no time spent with Dawsey.

I think, if I become Kit's guardian, we could continue to live in Elizabeth's cottage. I could take my vast profits from *Izzy* and buy a flat for Kit and me to stay in when we visit London. Her home is here, and mine can be. Writers can write on Guernsey – look at Victor Hugo. The only things I'd really miss about London are Sidney and Susan, the nearness to Scotland, new plays, and Harrods Food Hall.

Pray for Mr Dilwyn's good sense. I know he has it, I know he likes me, I know he knows Kit is happy living with me, and that I am solvent enough for two at the moment – and who can say better than that in these decadent times? Amelia thinks that if he does say no to adoption without a husband, he will gladly grant me guardianship.

Sidney is coming to Guernsey again next week. I wish you were coming, too – I miss you.

Love,

Juliet

From Juliet to Sidney

8th September 1946

Dear Sidney,

Kit and I took a picnic out to the meadow to watch Dawsey rebuilding Elizabeth's stone wall. It was a wonderful excuse to spy on Dawsey and his way of going at things. He studied each rock, felt the weight of it, brooded, and placed it on the wall. Smiled if it accorded with the picture in his head. Took it off if it didn't and searched for a different stone. He is very calming to the spirit.

He grew so accustomed to our admiring gazes that he issued an unprecedented invitation to supper. Kit had a prior engagement with Amelia, but I accepted with unbecoming haste and then fell into an absurd twitter about being alone with him. We were both a bit awkward when I arrived, but he at least had the cooking to occupy him and retired to the kitchen, refusing help. I took the opportunity to snoop through his books. He hasn't got very many, but his taste is superior – Dickens, Mark Twain, Balzac, Boswell, and dear old Leigh Hunt, *The Sir Roger de Coverley Papers*, Anne Brontë's novels (I wonder why he had those) and my biography of her. I didn't know he had that: he's never said a word – perhaps he loathed it.

Over supper, we discussed Jonathan Swift, pigs, and the trials in Nuremberg. Doesn't that reveal a breathtaking range of interests? I think it does. We talked easily enough, but neither of us ate much – even though he had made a delicious sorrel soup (much better than I could). After coffee, we strolled down to his farmyard for a pig-viewing. Grown pigs don't improve on acquaintance, but piglets are a different matter – Dawsey's are spotted and frisky and sly. Every day they dig a new hole under his fence, ostensibly to escape, but really just for the amusement of watching Dawsey fill in the gap. You should have seen them grin as he approached the fence.

Dawsey's barn is extraordinarily clean. He also stacks his hay beautifully.

I believe I am becoming pathetic.

I'll go further. I believe that I am in love with a flower-growing, wood-carving quarryman/carpenter/pig farmer. In fact, I know I am. Perhaps tomorrow I will become entirely miserable at the thought that he doesn't love me back – may, even, care for Remy – but at this precise moment I am succumbing to euphoria. My head and stomach feel quite odd.

See you on Friday. Feel free to give yourself airs for discovering that I love Dawsey. You may even preen in my presence – this one time, but never again.

Love and XXXX,

Juliet

Telegram from Juliet to Sidney

11th September 1946

Am entirely miserable STOP Saw Dawsey in St Peter Port this afternoon buying suitcase with Remy on his arm both wreathed in smiles STOP Is it for their honeymoon STOP What a fool I am STOP I blame you STOP Wretchedly Juliet

Detection Notes of Miss Isola Pribby
Private: Not to Be Read, Even after Death

Sunday

This book with lines in it is from my friend Sidney Stark. It came to me in the post yesterday. It had *PENSÉES* written in gold on the cover, but I scratched it off, because that's French for THOUGHTS and I am only going to write down FACTS. Facts gleaned from keen eyes and ears. I don't expect too much of myself at first – I must learn to be more observant.

Here are some of the observations I made today. Kit loves being in Juliet's company – she looks peaceful when Juliet comes into the room and she doesn't make faces behind people's backs any more. Also she can wiggle her ears now – which she couldn't before Juliet came.

My friend Sidney is coming to read Oscar's letters. He will stay with Juliet this time, because she's cleaned out Elizabeth's store room and put a bed in it for him.

Saw Daphne Post digging a big hole under Mr Ferre's elm tree. She always does it by the light of the moon. I think we should all go together and buy her a silver teapot so that she can stay at home at night.

Monday

Mrs Taylor has a rash on her arms. What, or who, from? Tomatoes or her husband? Look into further.

Tuesday

Nothing noteworthy today.

Wednesday

Nothing again.

Thursday

Remy came to see me today – she gives me the stamps from her letters from France – they are more colourful than English ones, so I stick them in my book. She had a letter in a brown envelope with a little open window in it, from the FRENCH GOVERNMENT. This is the fourth one she's got – what do they want from her? Find out.

I did start to observe something today – behind Mr Salles's market stall, but they stopped when they saw me. Never mind, Eben is having his beach picnic on Saturday – so I am sure to have something to observe there.

I have been looking at a book about artists and how they size up a picture they want to paint. Say they want to concentrate on an orange – do they study the shape direct? No, they don't. They fool their eyes and stare at the banana beside it, or look at it upside down, between their legs. They see the orange in a brand-new way. It's called getting perspective. So, I am going to try a new way of looking – not upside down between my legs, but by not staring at anything direct or straight ahead. I can move my eyes slyly if I keep my lids lowered a bit. Practise this!!!

Friday

It works – not staring headlong works. I went with Dawsey, Juliet, Remy and Kit in Dawsey's cart to the airfield to meet dear Sidney.

Here is what I observed: Juliet hugged him, and he swung her around like a brother would. He was pleased to meet Remy, and I could tell he was watching her sideways, like I was doing. Dawsey shook Sidney's hand, but he did not come in for apple cake when we got to Juliet's house. It was a little sunk in the middle, but it tasted good.

I had to put drops in my eyeballs before bed – it is a strain, always having to skitter them sideways. My eyelids ache from having to keep them halfway down, too.

Saturday

Remy, Kit, and Juliet came with me down to the beach to gather firewood for this evening's picnic. Amelia was out in the sun too. She looks more rested and I am happy to see her so. Dawsey, Sidney, and Eli carried Eben's big iron cauldron down. Dawsey is always nice and polite to Sidney, and Sidney is pleasant as can be to Dawsey, but he seems to stare at him in a wondering sort of way. Why is that?

Remy left the firewood and went over to talk to Eben, and he patted her on the shoulder. Why? Eben was never one to pat much. Then they talked for a while, but sadly out of my earshot.

When it was time to go home for lunch, Eli went off beach-combing. Juliet and Sidney each took hold of one of Kit's hands, and they walked her up the cliff path, playing that game of 'One Step. Two Step. Three Steps – LIFT UP!' Dawsey watched them go up the path, but he did not follow. No, he walked down to the shore and just stood there, looking out over the water. It suddenly struck me that Dawsey is a lonely person. I think it may be that he has always been lonely, but he didn't mind before, and now he minds. Why now?

Saturday Night

I did see something at the picnic, something important – and like dear Miss Marple, I must act upon it. It was a brisk night and the sky looked moody. But that was fine – we bundled up in jumpers and jackets, eating lobster, and laughing at Booker. He stood on a rock and gave an oration, pretending to be that Roman he's so wild about. I worry about Booker: he needs to read a new book. I think I will lend him Jane Austen.

I was sitting, senses alert, by the bonfire with Sidney, Kit, Juliet and Amelia. We were poking sticks in the fire, when Dawsey and Remy walked up to Eben and the lobster pot. Remy whispered to Eben, he smiled, and picked up his big spoon and banged on the pot. 'Attention all,' Eben shouted 'I have something to tell you.'

Everyone went quiet, except for Juliet, who drew in her breath so hard I heard her. She didn't let it out again, and went all over rigid – even her jaw. What could be the matter? I was so worried about her, having once been toppled by appendix myself, that I missed Eben's first few words.

'. . . and so tonight is a farewell party for Remy. She is leaving us next Tuesday for her new home in Paris. She will share rooms with friends and is apprenticed to the famous confectioner Raoul Guillemaux, in Paris. She has promised that she will come back to Guernsey and that her second home will be with me and Eli, so we may all rejoice in her good fortune.'

What an outpouring of cheers from the rest of us! Everyone ran to gather round Remy and congratulate her. Everyone except Juliet – she let out her breath in a whoosh and flopped backwards on to the sand, like a gaffed fish!

I peered round, thinking I should observe Dawsey. He wasn't hovering over Remy – but how sad he looked. All of a sudden, IT CAME TO ME! I HAD IT! Dawsey didn't want Remy to go, he was afraid she'd never return. He was in love with Remy, and too shy in his nature to tell her so.

Well, I'm not. I would tell her of his affections, and then she,

234

being *French*, would know what to do. She would let him know she'd find favour in his suit. Then they would marry, and she would not need to go off to Paris. What a blessing that I have no imagination and am able to see things clearly.

Sidney came up to Juliet and prodded her with his foot. 'Feel better?' he asked, and Juliet said yes, so I stopped worrying about her. Then he led her over to congratulate Remy. Kit was asleep in my lap, so I stayed where I was by the fire and thought carefully.

Remy, like most Frenchwomen, is practical. She would want evidence of Dawsey's feelings for her before she changed her plans willy-nilly. I would have to find the proof she needed.

A little bit later, when wine had been opened and toasts drunk, I walked up to Dawsey and said, 'Daws, I've noticed that your kitchen floor is dirty. I want to come and scrub it for you. Will Monday suit?'

He looked a little surprised, but he said yes. 'It's an early Christmas present,' I said. 'So you mustn't think of paying me. Leave the door open for me.'

And so it was settled, and I said goodnight to all.

Sunday

I have laid my plans for tomorrow. I am nervous. I will sweep and scrub Dawsey's house, keeping a lookout for evidence of his love for Remy. Maybe a poem, 'Ode to Remy', screwed up in his wastepaper basket? Or doodles of her name, scribbled all over his shopping list? Proof that Dawsey loves Remy must (or almost must) be in clear sight. Miss Marple never really snooped so I won't either – I will not force locks. But once I have proof of his devotion to Remy, she won't get on the aeroplane to Paris on Tuesday morning. She will know what to do, and then Dawsey will be happy.

All Day Monday: A Serious Error, A Joyous Night

I woke up too early and had to fiddle around with my hens until it was time for Dawsey to leave for work up at the Big House. Then, I cut along to his farm, checking every tree trunk for carved hearts. None.

With Dawsey gone, I went in with my mop, bucket and rags. For two hours I swept, scrubbed, dusted and waxed – and found nothing. I was beginning to despair, when I thought of the books on his shelves. I began to clap dust out of them, but no loose papers fell to the floor. Suddenly I saw his little red book on Charles Lamb's life. What was it doing here? I had seen him put it in the wooden treasure box Eli carved for his birthday present. But if the red book was here on the shelf, what was in his treasure box? And where was it? I tapped the walls. No hollow sounds anywhere. I thrust my arm into his flour bin – nothing but flour. Would he keep it in the barn? For rats to chew on? Never. What was left? His bed, under his bed!

I ran to his bedroom, fished under the bed and pulled out the treasure box. I lifted the lid and glanced inside. Nothing met my eye, so I was forced to dump everything out on the bed – still nothing: not a note from Remy, not a photograph of her, no cinema ticket stubs for *Gone With the Wind*, though I knew he'd taken her to see it. What had he done with them? No handkerchief with the initial *R* in the corner. There was one, but it was one of Juliet's scented ones and had a *J* embroidered on it. He must have forgotten to return it to her. Other things were in there, but *nothing of Remy's*.

I put everything back in the box and straightened the bed. My mission had failed! Remy would get on that aeroplane tomorrow, and Dawsey would stay lonely. I was heartsore. I gathered up my mops and bucket.

I was trudging home when I saw Amelia and Kit – they were going bird-watching. They asked me to come along, but I knew that not even birdsong could cheer me up. But I thought Juliet could cheer me – she usually does. I wouldn't stay long and bother her writing, but maybe she would ask me in for a cup of coffee. Sidney had left this morning, so maybe she'd be feeling bereft too. I hurried down the road to her house.

I found Juliet at home, papers awhirl on her desk, but she wasn't doing anything, just sitting there, staring out of the window. 'Isola!' she said. 'Just when I've been wanting company!' She started to get up when she saw my mops and pails. 'Have you come to clean my house? Forget that and come and have some coffee.' Then she had a good look at my face and said, 'Whatever is the matter? Are you ill? Come and sit down.'

The kindness was too much for my broken spirits, and I – I admit it – I started to howl. I said, 'No, no, I'm not ill. I have failed – failed in my mission. And now Dawsey will stay unhappy.'

Juliet took me over to her sofa. She patted my hand. I always get the hiccups when I cry, so she ran and got me a glass of water for her fail-safe cure – you pinch your nose shut with your two thumbs, and plug up both ears with your fingers, while a friend pours a glass of water down your throat without stopping. You stamp your foot when you are close to drowning, and your friend takes the glass away. It works every time – a miracle – no more hiccups.

'Now tell me, what was your mission? And why do you think you failed?'

So I told her all about it – my notion that Dawsey was in love with Remy, and how I'd cleaned his house, looking for proof. If I'd found any I'd have told Remy he loved her, and then she'd want to stay – perhaps even confess her love for him first, to soothe the way.

'He is so shy, Juliet. He always has been – I don't think anybody's ever been in love with him, or he with anybody before, so he wouldn't know what to do about it. It'd be just like him to hide away mementos and never say a word. I despair for him, I do.'

Juliet said, 'A lot of men don't keep mementos, Isola. Don't want keepsakes. That doesn't necessarily mean a thing. What on earth were you looking *for*?'

'Evidence, like Miss Marple does. But no, not even a picture of her. There's lots of pictures of you and Kit, and several of you by yourself. One of you wrapped up in that lace curtain, being a Dead

Bride. He's kept all your letters, tied up in that blue hair ribbon – the one you thought you'd lost. I know he wrote to Remy at the hospice, and she must have written back to him – but no, nary a letter from Remy. Not even her handkerchief – oh, he found one of yours. You might want it back – it's a pretty thing.'

She got up and went over to her desk. She stood there a while, then she picked up that crystal thing with Latin, *Carpe diem*, or some such, etched on the top. She studied it.

'"Seize the Day",' she said. 'That's an inspiring thought, isn't it, Isola?'

'I suppose so,' I said, 'if you like being goaded by a bit of rock.'

Juliet did surprise me then – she turned round to me and gave me that grin she has, the one that made me first like her so much. 'Where is Dawsey? Up at the Big House, isn't he?'

At my nodding, she bounded out the door, and raced up the drive to the Big House.

Oh wonderful Juliet! She was going to give Dawsey a piece of her mind for shirking his feelings for Remy.

Miss Marple never runs anywhere, she follows after slowly, like the old lady she is. So I did too. Juliet was inside the house by the time I got there.

I went on tippy-toes to the terrace and pressed myself into the wall by the library. The French windows were open. I heard Juliet open the door to the library. 'Good morning, gentlemen,' she said. I could hear Teddy Heckwith (he's a plasterer) and Chester (he's a joiner) say, 'Good morning, Miss Ashton.'

Dawsey said, 'Hello, Juliet.' He was on top of the big stepladder. I found that out later when he made so much noise coming down it.

Juliet said she would like a word with Dawsey, if the gentlemen could give her a minute. They said certainly, and left the room.

Dawsey said, 'Is something wrong, Juliet? Is Kit all right?'

'Kit's fine. It's me – I want to ask you something.'

Oh, I thought, she's going to tell him not to be a sissy. Tell him he must stir himself up and go and propose to Remy at once. But she didn't.

238

What she said was, 'Would you like to marry me?'

I liked to die where I stood.

There was quiet – complete quiet. Nothing! And on and on it went, not a word, not a sound.

But Juliet went on undisturbed, her voice steady – and me, I could not get so much as a breath of air into my chest. 'I'm in love with you, so I thought I'd ask.'

And then, Dawsey, dear Dawsey, swore. He took the Lord's name in vain. 'My God, yes,' he cried, and clattered down that stepladder, only his heels hit the rungs, which is how he sprained his ankle.

I kept to my scruples and did not look inside the room, tempted though I was. I waited. It was quiet in there, so I came on home to think. What good was training my eyes if I could not see things rightly? I had got everything wrong. Everything. It came out happy, so happy, in the end, but no thanks to me. I don't have Miss Marple's insight into the cavities of the human mind. That is sad, but best to admit it now.

Sir William told me there were motorcycle races in England – silver cups given for speed, rough riding, and not falling off. Perhaps I should train for that – I already have my bike. All I'd need would be a helmet – maybe goggles. For now, I will ask Kit over for supper and to spend the night with me so that Juliet and Dawsey can have the freedom of the shrubbery – just like Mr Darcy and Elizabeth Bennet.

From Juliet to Sidney

17th September 1946

Dear Sidney,

Terribly sorry to make you turn round and come right back across the Channel, but I require your presence – at my wedding. I have seized the day, and the night, too. Can you come and give me away in Amelia's back garden on Saturday? Eben to be best man, Isola to be bridesmaid (she is manufacturing a gown for the occasion), Kit to throw rose petals.

Dawsey to be groom.

Are you surprised? Probably not – but I am. I am in a constant state of surprise these days. Actually, now that I calculate, I've been betrothed only one full day, but it seems as though my whole life has come into existence in the last twenty-four hours. Think of it! We could have gone on longing for one another and pretending not to notice *for ever*. This obsession with dignity can ruin your life if you let it.

Is it unseemly to get married so quickly? I don't want to wait – I want to start at once. I've always thought that the story was over when the hero and heroine were safely engaged – after all, what's good enough for Jane Austen ought to be good enough for anyone. But it's a lie. The story is about to begin, and every day will be a new piece of the plot. Perhaps my next book will be about a fascinating married couple and all the things they learn about each other over time. Are you impressed by the beneficial effect of engagement on my writing?

Dawsey has just come down from the Big House and is demanding my immediate attention. His much-vaunted shyness has evaporated completely – I think it was a ploy to arouse my sympathies.

Love,

Juliet

P.S. I ran into Adelaide Addison in St Peter Port today. By way of congratulation, she said, 'I hear you and that pig-farmer are about to regularise your connection. Thank the Lord!'

Acknowledgements

The seed for this book was planted quite by accident. I had travelled to England to research another book and while there learned of the German Occupation of the Channel Islands. On a whim, I flew to Guernsey and was fascinated by my brief glimpse of the island's history and beauty. From that visit came this book, albeit many years later.

Unfortunately, books don't spring fully formed from their authors' foreheads. This one required years of research and writing, and above all, the patience and support of my husband, Dick Shaffer, and my daughters Liz and Morgan, who tell me that *they* never doubted I would finish this book, even if I did. Besides believing in my writing, they insisted that I actually sit down at the computer and type, and it was these twins forces at my back that propelled the book into being.

In addition to this small cluster of supporters at home, there was much larger group out in the world. First and in some ways most important were my friends and fellow writers Sara Loyster and Julia Poppy, who demanded and beguiled and cajoled – and read every word of the first dozen drafts. This book truly would not have been written without them. Pat Arrigoni's enthusiasm and editorial *savior-faire* were also instrumental in the early stages of writing. My sister Cynnie followed lifelong tradition in urging me to buckle down to work, and, in this case, I appreciate it.

I am grateful to Lisa Drew for directing my manuscript to my agent, Liza Dawson, who combines great editorial wisdom and pure publishing know-how to a degree I would not have believed possible. Her colleague Anna Olswanger was a source of a number of excellent ideas, for which I am in her debt. Thanks to them, my manuscript found its way to the desk of the amazing Susan Kamil, an editor both profoundly intelligent and deeply humane. I am also grateful to Chandler Crawford, who brought the book first to Bloomsbury Publishing in England and then turned it into a worldwide phenomenon, with editions in ten countries.

I must tender special thanks to my niece, Annie, who stepped in to finish this book after unexpected health issues interrupted my ability to work shortly after the manuscript was sold. Without blinking an eye, she put down the book she was writing, pushed up her sleeves, and set to work on my manuscript. It was my great good luck to have a writer like her in the family, and this book could not have been done without her.

If nothing else, I hope these characters and their story shed some light on the sufferings and strength of the people of the Channel Islands during the German Occupation. I hope, too, that my book will illuminate my belief that love of art – be it poetry, storytelling, painting, sculpture, or music – enables people to transcend any barrier man has yet devised.

Mary Ann Shaffer
December 2007

It was my good fortune to enter into this project armed with a lifetime of my aunt Mary Ann's stories and the editorial acumen of Susan Kamil. Susan's strength of vision was essential in making the book what it wanted to be, and I am truly privileged to have worked with her. I salute her invaluable Assistant Editor, Noah Eaker, as well.

I am grateful, too, to the team at Bloomsbury Publishing. There, Alexandra Pringle has been a paragon of patience and good humour, as well as a font of information about how to address a duke's offspring. I particularly appreciate Mary Morris, who dealt gracefully with a gorgon, and the marvellous Antonia Till, without whom British characters would be wearing pants, driving wagons, and eating candy. In Guernsey, Lynne Ashton at the Guernsey Museum and Art Gallery was most helpful, as was Clare Ogier.

Finally, I extend very special thanks to Liza Dawson, who made it all work.

Annie Barrows
December, 2007

A NOTE ON THE AUTHOR

Mary Ann Shaffer was born in 1934 in Martinsburg, West Virginia. She became interested in Guernsey while visiting London in 1976. On a whim, she decided to fly to Guernsey but became stranded there as a heavy fog descended and no boats or planes were permitted to leave the island. As she waited for the fog to clear, she came across a book called *Jersey Under the Jack-Boot*, and so her fascination with the Channel Isles began.

Many years later, when goaded by her own literary club to write a book, Mary Ann naturally thought of Guernsey. *The Guernsey Literary and Potato Peel Pie Society*, her only novel, would go on to be published in thirteen countries.

Mary Ann died in February 2008. She left a husband and two daughters.

A NOTE ON THE TYPE

The text of this book is set in Linotype Janson. The original types were cut in about 1690 by Nicholas Kis, a Hungarian working in Amsterdam. The face was misnamed after Anton Janson, a Dutchman who worked at the Ehrhardt Foundry in Leipzig, where the original Kis types were kept in the early eighteenth century. Monotype Ehrhardt is based on Janson. The original matrices survived in Germany and were acquired in 1919 by the Stempel Foundry. Hermann Zapf used these originals to redesign some of the weights and sizes for Stempel. This Linotype version was designed to follow the original types under the direction of C. H. Griffith.